ROBERT BLOCH

STRANGE EONS

I0633662

With a new introduction by
DAVID J. SCHOW

VALANCOURT BOOKS

This book is dedicated to HPL
who dedicated himself to other outsiders
and gave to them a silver key.

Strange Eons by Robert Bloch
Originally published by Whispers Press in 1978
First Valancourt Books edition 2025

Copyright © 1978 by Robert Bloch
Introduction © 2025 by David J. Schow

The Valancourt Books name and logo are federally registered trademarks of Valancourt Books, LLC.

Published by Valancourt Books, Richmond, Virginia
http://www.valancourtbooks.com

ISBN 978-1-960241-55-9 (trade paperback)
ISBN 978-1-960241-56-6 (trade hardcover)
Also available as an electronic book.

Set in Dante MT

STRANGE EONS

ROBERT BLOCH was born in 1917 in Chicago, the son of Raphael Bloch and Stella Loeb, both of German Jewish descent. When he was eight, he attended a screening of the Lon Chaney film *The Phantom of the Opera* (1925); the scene where Chaney removes his mask terrified the young Bloch and sparked an early interest in horror. A precocious child, he was already in the fourth grade at age eight and obtained a pass for the adult section of the library, where he was a voracious reader. At age ten, in 1927, Bloch discovered *Weird Tales* and became an avid fan, with H.P. Lovecraft, a frequent contributor to the magazine, becoming one of his favorite writers. In 1933 Bloch began a correspondence with Lovecraft, which would continue until the older writer's death in 1937. Bloch's early work would be heavily influenced by Lovecraft, and Lovecraft offered encouragement to the young writer.

Bloch's first short story was published in 1934 and would be followed by hundreds of others, many of them published in *Weird Tales*. His first collection of tales, *The Opener of the Way* (1945) was issued by August Derleth's Arkham House, joining an impressive list of horror writers that included Lovecraft, Derleth, Clark Ashton Smith, and Carl Jacobi. His first novel, *The Scarf*, would follow two years later, in 1947. He went on to publish numerous story collections and over thirty novels, of which the most famous is *Psycho* (1959), the basis for Alfred Hitchcock's classic film. He won the prestigious Hugo Award (for his story "The Hell-Bound Train") as well as the Bram Stoker Award and the World Fantasy Award. His work has been extensively adapted for film, television, radio, and comics. He died of cancer at age 77 in 1994.

DAVID J. SCHOW is a multiple-award-winning American writer. Ten novels, thirteen short story collections, comics (ten years with John Carpenter's *Storm King* imprint), movies (*The Crow, Leatherface: Texas Chainsaw Massacre III, The Hills Run Red*), television (*Masters of Horror, Mob City, Creepshow*), nonfiction (*The Outer Limits Companion, The Art of Drew Struzan*), and can be seen on various DVDs as expert witness or documentarian on over 40 films and television shows. Thanks to him, the word "splatterpunk" has been in the Oxford English Dictionary since 2002. Google him.

Also Available by Robert Bloch

The Opener of the Way
The Scarf
Pleasant Dreams
The Night of the Ripper
Midnight Pleasures

INTRODUCTION

Real Monsters in Our Midst
Revisiting Strange Eons

While receiving a Lifetime Achievement Award at the first World Fantasy Awards confab in 1977, Robert Bloch spoke fondly of his much-documented affinity for H.P. Lovecraft:

> *"Part of me died with him, I guess, not only because he was not a god, he was mortal, that is true, but because he had so little recognition in his own lifetime. There were no novels or collections published, no great realization, even here in Providence, of what was lost."*

That in essence is the driving fundament of *Strange Eons*.

Bloch sought to avoid the standardized mimetic pastiche as done previously by August Derleth and others. Filtering it through his own style, he produced a tripartite mashup of Cthulhu Mythos fiction, spy thriller and science fiction.

Since Bob spoke those words above over half a century ago, Lovecraft slingshot from his de facto cultural roost as second fiddle only to Edgar Allan Poe to denigration by fans who culturally cancelled him as racist, even demoting the World Fantasy trophy itself, formerly a bust of HPL sculpted by world-famous cartoonist Gahan Wilson . . . who himself has not been similarly proscribed.

Yet.

A 1971 adaptation of HPL's "Pickman's Model" (written by Alvin Sapinsley and directed by series producer Jack Laird) for *Rod Serling's Night Gallery* can also serve as an adequate visualization of the central inciting premise of *Strange Eons*, first published by Stuart David Schiff's Whispers Press in 1978, and as a paperback by Pinnacle Books in 1979.

In the TV episode, Richard Upton Pickman's painting is discovered within a bench cabinet inside a decrepit Boston garret where Pickman once lived. In the cellar waits a sealed-up well. (Hint: *Never* a good idea to pry such things open.)

It is more than believable that Bob Bloch might have gained his primary inspiration for *Strange Eons* from this very TV episode—Bob was a contributor to *Night Gallery* as well—and the exchange between Albert Keith and Simon Waverly in the beginning of *Strange Eons* definitely echoes that of Larry Rand (Jock Livingston) and Eliot Blackman (Joshua Bryant) in *Night Gallery* as they rhapsodize over the newly-unearthed canvas, which we learn is titled "Ghoul, Preparing to Dine":

> LARRY: *Well, I admit it does resemble a Pickman . . .*
>
> ELIOT: *Resemble, nothing! I'd be willing to bet on it!*
>
> LARRY: *But they all disappeared at the same time Pickman did, except for the four already hanging . . .*
>
> ELIOT: *And except for this one. Look at it, Larry—can you seriously doubt its authenticity?*
>
> LARRY (peering): *The signature looks real enough . . .* (laughs) *Eliot, do you realize what this is worth to you? The last Pickman brought close to a hundred thousand dollars at auction.*
>
> ELIOT: *But is it mine to sell?*
>
> LARRY: *The man vanished 75 years ago. He left no known relations. If it's in your possession, it's yours to sell. Now, I could make arrangements through my gallery . . . how did you come by it?*
>
> ELIOT (opens a cabinet in the garret): *I found it in here, yesterday, after I moved in.* (Jolt of realization) *Larry, at the time Pickman was living, where was his studio?*

Note that Larry's comment above puts Pickman's activities circa 1896. Today the distance between us and *Strange Eons* is over half a century.

Similarly to our guys above, in the present novel Albert Keith discovers a magnificent painting of a feasting, scaly, dog-like demon, from a warehouse auction back East . . . and buys it for five hundred dollars. His friend Waverly identifies it as "Pickman's Model" . . . and suggests, according to several Lovecraftian clues, that the painting inspired the story rather than the other way around.

Thus, we are off and running.

The epistemological touches in this book echo Bloch's own Lovecraft correspondence, like autobiographical seasoning. The novel itself allows Bloch to present as Lovecraft biographer, as well, first in the short section that follows Waverly's line, "Read these books, my friend . . ."

Quite clearly, Bloch is taking the reader by the hand and walking them through something dear to him. In the process, he also handily discredits as "superstitious nonsense" the modern-day protest of HPL racism . . . there, done! Another common complaint about Lovecraft's work is that it contains no credibly developed female characters at all, which moved Darrell Schweitzer to note:

> His most intriguing female character, Asenath Waite in "The Thing on the Doorstep," is really the father transferred into the daughter's body. Then there is Charles Dexter Ward's mom, an overly indulgent parent. She has something like a nervous breakdown and is sent to Atlantic City for a long rest. Lavinia Whateley is another much-put-upon mother (her father got her pregnant by Yog-Sothoth). Lovecraft had no interest in writing about romance, of course, except in "Sweet Ermengarde."

Bob Bloch, being much more commercially savvy in his work, may have proffered Kay Keith in *Strange Eons* as a remedy for all that.

Multi-tasking is at the center of this book's eldritch heart.

All the pulp shortcuts at Bob's disposal are on display here as well, the best of which is the hat-trick of a serial novel . . . three stories, basically novelette-length, united into book form, sparing the author the more mandarin labor of pounding a single premise overlong just to meet a word-count.

Homage? Absolutely. There are further allusions to HPL's "The Lurking Fear" and other core texts, but the *real* template for *Strange Eons* is Bob's "The Shadow from the Steeple" (*Weird Tales*, September 1950) which is, as my scholarly compatriot Stefan Dziemianowicz noted:

> . . . (a) *sort of the "closer of the way" for the trilogy that Bob*

> *inaugurated with "The Shambler from the Stars" and HPL*
> *extended through "The Haunter of the Dark." In "Shadow,"*
> *Bob has an avatar of Nyarlathotep chortling about humankind*
> *creating nuclear weapons as its avenue to self-destruction . . .*
> *all the better for the Great Old Ones. If Bob set "Shadow" in*
> *the dawning nuclear age, he updated* Strange Eons *further to*
> *the 1970s, when nuclear armaments/deterrence were part of the*
> *bedrock of global politics. And his emissary for all of the book's*
> *espionage subterfuges is yet another avatar of Nyarlathotep.*

"The Shadow from the Steeple" concludes the triptych begun by Bloch in 1935 with "The Shambler from the Stars," and continued by Lovecraft in 1936 with "The Haunter of the Dark."

Tribute? Also yes . . . except that where the avatars for Bloch ("Robert Blake") and Lovecraft kill each other off in "Steeple," in *Strange Eons*—another trifurcated narrative—Bloch is older, wiser, and completely prepared to wipe out everybody. (It is fairly well known that Bob had a signed document from HPL giving Bloch official permission to kill Lovecraft off in a weird tale.) In the same way the "Pickman's Model" painting actually becomes bona fide and causal in this book, so are the events of those three early stories recounted as factual. The whole story becomes a nesting-doll, a tapestry of Cthulhu Mythos in-jokes and easter eggs for the initiated.

But wait! Is Edmund Fiske in "Steeple" HPL in fictive disguise, or is he another iteration of "Robert Blake"? Wasn't Fiske similar to Wilbur Whateley (from "The Dunwich Horror") in that he had an unacknowledged, shunned, mysterious twin named Tarleton Fiske, a name baldly repurposed by Bloch/Blake as a pseudonym?!

About now you might be forgiven for hollering "balderdash!"— or something more pungent—and hurling this tome into the fireplace, as I admit upfront in the interest of full disclosure that never have I particularly been a fan of the writings of H.P. Lovecraft.

But Bob Bloch sure as hell was.

And I've already got the HPL completists cornered.

Since its debut, *Strange Eons* has suffered a disproportionate amount of abuse, mostly at the hands of embittered stylists who find Bloch too quaint or naive; reviewers on varying altitudes of diction eager to draw blood; ret-con obsessed revisionists who would pillory 1979 work for not hewing to populist 21st-century straw "norms"; or simple Lovecraft devotees—accent on the "simple"—who hunger to pull rank or demonstrate imaginary superiority to Bob's honest homage.

But few of them, if any, ever corresponded with HPL himself.

Fewer still—as in "none"—were feted in turn by Lovecraft creating a fictional avatar of them for a yarn, back when pulp wordmillers *had* to have some measure of fun with this stuff or suffer losing their marbles for a penny per word (or less) under the garrote of deadline.

Homage nearly always cues apologies, just as pastiche invites and tempts the mob howlers with their torches and pitchforks. The literary notion that select fictional stories were in fact truth is most often tarred as a conceit. Yet *all* stories are fiction, their lens tinted or tainted by the editorial viewpoint of the person telling you the tale, one reason you often see the title card "based on a true story" on the big screen—the Get Out of Jail Free card that excuses all liberties taken, no matter how monstrous.

(Bob Bloch had it both ways when he tackled the man once known as "America's Most Infamous Unknown Serial Killer"— Herman Webster Mudgett, aka H.H. Holmes, the scourge of the 1893 Columbian Exposition and subject vile of *The Devil in the White City*—in both fiction and nonfiction forms. First came the roman-à-clef novel *American Gothic* [1980] featuring "G. Gordon Gregg." Then followed the true-crime chronicle, "Dr. Holmes's Murder Castle" [*Tales of the Uncanny*, 1983].)

Consider the nature of much of the hue and cry over popular entertainment, and remember that when *Strange Eons* originally came out in paperback, some malcontents even pilloried David Hada's cover illustration. Now think about that for a moment: HPL fanatics got their noses unjointed by a drawing of something generally supposed as so horrible as to be indescribable.

Honesty in criticism? Sure thing: *Strange Eons* may not be Bloch at his best, but it is certainly Bloch in a comfy chair . . . and I know what I'm talking about, since I edited three entire volumes of Bob at "less than his best," rounding up obscurities in order to ensure *all* of his work had a better chance of remaining in print to modern eyes. Bob himself joked about this inevitable trend, that once an artist becomes worthy of perpetuation via reprint, there comes a commensurate caveat:

"I can only hope," Bob wrote, "that eventually I can offer a collection of mystery and suspense tales, even at the risk of seeing them appear as *The Worst of Robert Bloch*."*

After all, Bob could have just as easily written yet another novel about a psychopathic killer . . . which was probably the pressure-at-hand, and the reason *Strange Eons* saw its original printing as a Whispers Press hardcover, for a smaller, more eclectic readership than the majors.

All the gist you need to know is this: the posit that HPL's fiction was cautiously rendered prose code for what really lurks behind the veil.

Less a Mythos novel, and more an example of the storytelling style Bob Bloch developed *after* he broke free of HPL's mentorship.

It's also worth noting that "Pickman's Model"—the HPL story, not the painting here—was Bob's actual introduction to Lovecraft, as a ten-year-old reader new to *Weird Tales*. (This is cited in Bob's 1993 "unauthorized autobiography," *Once Around the Bloch*).

Now, if the recursive aspects of *Strange Eons* turn out to be true, as well . . . if Bob was writing a nonfiction account all along . . .

As Orin Sanderson tells Kay Keith:

"Never before has the world been as full of fear as it is now . . .
the Great Old Ones are strong again and their time has come.
The stars are right and the way is open at last."

DAVID J. SCHOW

(DJS would like to tender special thanks to Stefan Dziemianowicz and Darrell Schweitzer for their invaluable help with this account.)

---

* "Will the Real Robert Bloch Please Stand Up?" Afterword to *The Best of Robert Bloch*, edited by Lester Del Rey (Ballantine, 1977).

I

NOW

Albert Keith didn't believe in love at first sight until he saw the portrait.

It wasn't just another pretty face. In fact the features were rather canine; glaring reddish eyes, a flat snout of a nose, foam-flecked lips, and ears rising to a point. And the crouching body, caked with mold, was only vaguely humanoid—the upper limbs terminating in scale-covered bony claws, the feet below holding a hint of hooves.

The creature in the painting was gigantic, and the figure of the man clutched in its claws seemed small by comparison. Despite the layer of dust which covered the picture, Keith was able to note at once that the man's head had been nibbled at.

Standing there in the semi-darkness of the dingy back room of the little shop on South Alvarado Street, Keith began to tremble.

For a moment he tried to analyze the reason for his reaction. It wasn't fear—though the subject of the huge canvas resting against the wall was fearsome indeed. He'd succumbed to the collector's syndrome, trembling with eagerness and anticipation, for he realized he had to have this painting, whatever the cost.

Keith turned and glanced at the shop's proprietor standing beside him.

"How much?" he murmured.

The pudgy little man shrugged. "Make it five hundred."

"Five hundred dollars?"

The dealer's face was immobile. "Look at the size of it. If I was to clean it up a little and slap on a fancy frame, I wouldn't take less than a grand."

"For something like this?"

Keith frowned, but the dealer didn't waver; his was the professional poker-face of a man who had played this game with customers for years. "Sure, it's pretty wild, but you oughta see some of the weirdos who walk into this place. All I gotta do is stick this here picture in the front window and it'll be snapped up—pow!—just like that. Those gays from the fancy art-galleries over on La Cienega are always cruising around looking for freaky items. One look at this and they'd blow their minds."

Keith stared at the painting. It was mind-blowing, no doubt about that. The work had power, an authority of execution which transcended its sensational subject-matter.

"Who did it?" he asked.

The little man shook his head. "Search me. It's not signed." He gave Keith a sidelong glance. "I got a hunch maybe it was some big artist who didn't want his name on a far-out job like this. Could be worth a bundle."

"Where did it come from?"

"Blind lot. Warehouse auction back East. Tearing the place down, and they wanted to clear out all the unclaimed storage. Some stuff must of laid around maybe forty, fifty years. I got boxes of books and letters I ain't even gone through yet."

"Any more paintings?"

"No, this is the only one." The dealer shifted his glance to the canvas and nodded. "You know, come to think of it, maybe I'd be better off to do like I said. Clean it up, get a frame and shove it in the window—"

Keith stared at the painting: the huge dog-like figure crouched before him and for a moment he had the crazy notion that it was listening, waiting for him to speak. Its red eyes questioned, then commanded.

"I'll give you the five hundred," Keith said.

The dealer turned away, concealing his smile as Keith produced his checkbook and fumbled for a pen.

"Who do I make this out to?"

"Santiago. Felipe Santiago."

Keith nodded, wrote, tore the check from its stub and extended it. "Here you are. You need an ID?"

"No, that's okay." The little man lifted the canvas. "Where you parked?"

"Right in front."

Outside, where Keith's old Volvo stood at the curb, there were problems in logistics. The painting was too large to fit into the trunk. It took the combined efforts of the two men to angle the canvas through the door and onto the floor where it rested against the back seat. There it loomed and leered.

As Keith drove home in the gathering dusk, he could see the red eyes glaring at him in the rear-view mirror.

That night the dog-creature's eyes glared at Keith in the reflected flame of the fireplace. He'd propped the canvas up on the big table in his den, and it looked oddly appropriate in these surroundings. The firelight flickering across the gigantic figure played over the Ibo tribal masks hanging from the walls and danced along the rows of jade and ivory figurines lining the shelves of a Chinese cabinet. Stirred by the chimney updraft, the shrunken head dangling on a cord from the mantel made bobbing obeisance. Keith still wasn't sure the head was genuine, but the furtive gentleman from Ecuador had sworn it was an authentic Jibaro piece, and he'd paid a small fortune for it.

The painting, however, was genuine enough, and the dealer hadn't lied about its age. The layers of grime and dirt overlaying its surface must indeed have taken many decades to accumulate. And now, before considering the problems of framing and hanging his prize, Keith set about the task of cleaning it.

There were fluids and compounds for that purpose, but Keith had learned from experience that the best method was to use ordinary soap and water.

Slowly he began to work away, using a flannel cloth and rubbing carefully.

Gradually the nacreous surface cleared and brightened, so that the crouching creature emerged in bold relief against its background of shadow. The flesh-tones became livid blendings of pustulent ochre and myxa-like green, and the red eyes flared with renewed intensity. Hitherto-undisclosed details were revealed; the tiny black mites clinging to the furry forearms, the patches of *usnea humana* on the surface of the victim's skull, and the minute gobbets of flesh lodged between the feasting fangs.

"Good God!"

Keith turned, startled at the sound of the strident voice.

"Waverly," he said. "How did you get in here?"

The tall, bearded man moved toward him, smiling. At least Keith thought he was smiling, though the combination of beard and tinted glasses almost concealed his expression.

"The usual way." Simon Waverly shook his head. "You really ought to learn to lock the front door. And get those chimes repaired. I stood there knocking for a good five minutes."

"Sorry, didn't hear you." Keith indicated the basin of soapy water on the tabletop. "As I told you on the phone, I'm washing a ghoul." Me gestured toward the painting. "It *is* a ghoul, isn't it?"

His friend peered up at the canvas through the dark lenses, then uttered the low whistling sound that indicates astonishment.

"Not just *a* ghoul," he said. "It's *the* ghoul. Do you know what you've got here? *Pickman's Model.*"

"What?"

Simon Waverly nodded. "You remember—Pickman, the eccentric artist who did all the weird paintings of ghouls digging up graves in Boston cemeteries and climbing out of holes to attack people in subway tunnels? Finally he disappeared and his friend found a canvas in his cellar, a huge portrait of a thing like this. Tacked to the canvas was a picture of the model, showing the same creature. But it wasn't a drawing—it was a photograph from life."

"Where'd you come across such a crazy idea?"

"Lovecraft."

"Who?"

Waverly's dark glasses masked his surprise. "You mean to tell me you don't know H. P. Lovecraft?"

"Never heard of him."

"I'll be damned!" Waverly sighed. "I keep forgetting you're not much of a reader of fantasy. Always puzzled me, in view of your morbid tastes."

"I'm a collector, not a bibliophile," Keith said.

"Meaning you have the money to buy things we poor bastards

can only afford to read about." Waverly chuckled. "Still, with your interest in magic and the supernatural, you really should get acquainted with Howard Phillips Lovecraft. He happens to be one of the greatest modern writers in the horror field, and 'Pickman's Model' is one of his best stories. At least I always thought it was." Waverly's voice was soft. "But now that I see this, I'm not so sure."

"Sure of what?"

"That his story was fiction." Again Waverly stared at the canvas. "I swear to God this is the painting, exactly as he described it. Somebody really worked to reproduce what Lovecraft was writing about—a real labor of love, though that's hardly the *mot juste*, is it?" He chuckled once more. "Artists get their inspiration from the damndest places, but this tops anything I've ever run across. Who did it?"

"I don't know," Keith said. "There isn't any signature."

"Magnificent work." Waverly gestured. "The way those flesh-tones stand out—"

Keith picked up the flannel and began to rub the base of the canvas with a circular motion. "It'll look even better when I finish getting the dirt off," he said. "See how those hooves lighten? I never noticed the talons before. And the foreground comes up, too. It isn't all in shadow now, you can see the—"

"See the what?"

"Waverly, look at this! There *is* a signature, here in the corner, at the left."

Waverly squinted, shaking his head. "Can't make it out. Damn these glasses—ever since the cataract surgery I can't take bright light. What's it say?"

"Upton. And an initial. I think it's R." Keith nodded. "Yes, that's it. R. Upton."

Waverly made the whistling sound again, and Keith turned quickly. "What's wrong?" he said.

"'Pickman's Model,'" Waverly whispered. "The full name of the artist in the story is Richard Upton Pickman."

Later—much later—the two men sat over their coffee in Keith's kitchen. A Santa Ana rattled the shutters, but neither

Keith nor Waverly noticed the noise. The silence of thought can be more disturbing than any sound.

"Let's not jump to hasty conclusions," Keith said. "Consider the possibilities."

"Such as?"

"Coincidence, for one. Upton isn't all that uncommon a name. And we don't know that the initial stands for 'Richard'—it could be Roy, Roger, Raymond, Robert, Ralph, or any one of a dozen others. All we've got is 'R. Upton' and that in itself proves nothing."

"You're forgetting one thing," Waverly murmured. "The name alone may be inconclusive evidence, but it happens to be inscribed on a painting—the very painting Lovecraft wrote about. And that combination can't be coincidental."

"Then it's a hoax. Some artist read the story and decided to play a joke."

Waverly shook his head. "In that case, why didn't he follow the story and sign himself 'Richard Upton Pickman'?"

Keith frowned. "You've got a point there. And come to think of it, the painting is too skilfully executed to have been dashed off on impulse as a gag. If it weren't for the subject-matter, one could say it was the product of tender loving care."

"Subject-matter be damned," Waverly said. "It's a masterpiece."

"Then there's only one answer. The work was an artist's *homage*, a sincere tribute. The painting was inspired by Lovecraft's story."

"Suppose it was the other way around." Waverly spoke slowly, softly. "Suppose Lovecraft's story was inspired by the painting?"

Keith grimaced. "You're letting your imagination run away with you. Not that it matters, because we'll never know—"

"Don't be too sure," said Waverly. He tugged at his beard thoughtfully. "Didn't you mention something about that dealer having other things in this blind lot he bought up?"

"Yes, but there were no more paintings. Just some boxes of books and letters he hadn't examined yet."

"Well I'd like to examine them myself." Waverly's eyes glinted behind the dark glasses. "Suppose those things were the property of the artist. Maybe we'd find a clue, something that would tell us the answer. Look, why don't you call this fellow and ask if we can go through the material?"

"At this hour?" Keith set his coffee-cup down on the table. "It's past midnight."

"Tomorrow, then." Waverly rose. "I've got to run down to Acres Of Books in Long Beach, but I'll be back before dark. Let's plan on having dinner together and seeing him afterwards. Set up an appointment for sometime in the evening."

"I'll give it a try," Keith said. "But he may not want to stay open that long."

"You paid him five hundred dollars for a painting, remember?" There was a hint of a smile beneath Waverly's beard. "He'll have the welcome-mat ready and waiting when we arrive."

The satana was still strong, buffeting the windshield of the Volvo as Keith drove the freeway to the Alvarado off-ramp on the following evening.

Beside him, Waverly stared out of the window. When the car turned and headed south, he noted that the wind had blown the street-people away from their accustomed haunts. There were few figures on the sidewalks, and surprisingly little traffic for this time of night. The shops were shuttered and closed, leaving South Alvarado dark and deserted.

And when Keith's car pulled up at the curb before Santiago's place, it too was lightless. He frowned at his companion.

"I don't see any welcome-mat," he murmured.

Waverly shrugged. "When you called he said he'd be here at nine. Probably just saving on electricity."

But when the two men left the car and approached the door, they found it locked. Inside the store-window a large cardboard sign rested against the glass, its lettering plainly visible. Closed—Call Again.

Keith's frown indicated his irritation, but Waverly shook his head. "So he's a little late. Let's give him a few minutes."

Litter swirled in the street, dancing to the wail of the wind. "I don't like this," Keith said. "Been blowing for three days now."

"It's that time of the year." Waverly's soft voice was as expressionless as his face. "Relax."

"Gets on my nerves." Keith paced restlessly along the walk before the shop-front. "Kept me awake most of last night. Living up there in the hills makes you edgy. Every time a shutter banged, I jumped. And I couldn't put that painting out of my mind—the way the creature stares and crouches, as though it was ready to leap right out of the canvas and grab you by the throat."

"Isn't that why you bought it? I thought you liked that sort of thing."

"So did I. But this is different. There's something about it that makes it seem—real."

"But by God, Eliot, *it was a photograph from life.*"

"What?"

Waverly chuckled. "I was just quoting from the last line of 'Pickman's Model.' You'll have to read the story yourself. Matter of fact, you ought to read all of Lovecraft's stuff—and read *about* him, too. Remind me to bring you over some of the books."

"I'm not so sure I want you to."

"Come on, man—where's your intellectual curiosity? This is right up your alley."

"I don't like alleys," Keith said. "Not with a satana wind blowing up them, and a monster waiting for me at the far end." He smiled self-consciously. "Don't mind me, it's just nerves." Keith halted, glancing at his watch. "Where the devil is Santiago? It's almost nine-thirty."

As Keith turned to scan the deserted street, Waverly moved again to the front door of the shop.

"Wait a minute," he said.

Keith looked up.

"Maybe he's already here." Waverly was peering through the glass. "That door at the end of the aisle—it must lead to a back room. See the light shining underneath?"

"Right. He could have come in by a rear entrance."

Waverly rattled the doorknob, then pounded on the glass, but there was no response. "Doesn't hear us," he said. "Let's go around the back."

Keith gave him a wry glance. "I just told you I don't care for alleys."

Waverly's chuckle sounded again. "Well there's no monster

waiting for you in this one, that I'll guarantee. Come on."

He indicated a narrow passage along the side-wall of the building and started through it. Keith moved up behind, stumbling in
the shadows, then reluctantly followed Waverly into the deeper
darkness of the alleyway at the far end.

There was indeed a rear door here, and a stronger shimmer
of light streaming from beneath it. And in the alley itself stood a
battered, once-white pickup truck with the legend, F. SANTIAGO—
ANTIQUES plainly lettered on the door-panel.

"What did I tell you?" Waverly said. "Here's his car. And not a
monster in sight."

He walked over to the solid wooden shop-door and the echo
of his knock boomed along the alley, then faded into the moan of
the wind.

Lifting his hand to knock again, Waverly paused suddenly, his
fist uncurling as he reached down to grasp the doorknob.

"It's unlocked." The knob turned as he spoke and the door
swung open.

Keith moved up to the doorway. "Mr. Santiago—?"

He glanced forward into the light, then turned to Waverly
with a frown. "Look!"

The back room of the shop was empty. But under the glare
of the bare bulb overhead the two men stared at the evidence
of recent occupancy. The overturned chair—the desk-drawers
dumped on the floor, their contents cascading into white waves
of crumpled paper—the rifled file-cabinet leaning against the
wall—the jumble of empty boxes and cartons in the corner—all
were mute but unmistakable signs of search and seizure.

"Rip-off," Waverly muttered.

"But where's Santiago?"

As he spoke, Keith started across the room in the direction of
the closed door leading to the front of the shop. Just before reaching it he encountered another, smaller door to his right. It stood
slightly ajar, and Keith halted as he placed his hand on the knob.

"Wait." Waverly was at his side, gesturing caution. Keith noted
that he'd picked up a heavy old-fashioned metal letter-spindle
from the litter on the floor and was gripping it like a weapon.

"Let me go first," Waverly said.

He pushed the door inward and started forward through the opening.

Then he gasped.

Halting behind him, Keith gazed into the tiny bathroom beyond. There was no light, but the window on the far side was open.

And leaning silently over the sill he recognized the silhouette of Santiago.

Brushing past Waverly, he crossed the room and tapped Santiago's shoulder. The leaning figure turned, slumping sideways to the floor as Keith screamed.

For Felipe Santiago was dead. And on what remained of his chewed and gouged head there was no longer a face.

" 'The Lurking Fear,' " Waverly whispered. " 'The Lurking Fear.' "

"What are you talking about?" Keith blinked in the dawnlight stealing dimly across Waverly's study.

"Lovecraft's story. A man and his reporter friend investigate a deserted village where the inhabitants have been killed by something which apparently came out of burrows beneath the hills. A storm rises and they take shelter in a cabin. In the darkness the reporter leans out of the window, watching the tempest in the night. Finally his companion notices he hasn't moved. He touches him on the shoulder and—" Waverly broke off with a shrug. "You know the rest."

"I don't know anything," Keith said. "I still think we should have called the police, instead of running off."

Waverly sighed. "Let's not go over *that* again! If we had, you and I wouldn't be here now. We'd be sitting downtown in the slammer, booked on suspicion and waiting for questions from the D. A.'s staff. Questions neither of us can answer."

"But surely the police could see that we had nothing to do with Santiago's death!"

"The police tend to be very myopic in such matters. And even if they didn't file charges, we'd be bound over as material witnesses. You tell me you don't like alleys. Well, I'm allergic to jail-cells." Waverly shook his head. "When they find Santiago's body all hell is going to break loose. This sort of thing is bound to make a sensation, and neither of us need that kind of publicity. It's better that we don't get involved."

Keith glanced away towards the bookshelves lining the study walls. "But we are already," he said wearily. "The trouble is, I don't understand *what* we're involved in. You say this man Lovecraft wrote a story in which someone leaned out of a window and had his face chewed off. And now it happens in real life—"

Waverly interrupted him with an impatient gesture. "We needn't assume that. My guess is the coroner's report will show Santiago was beaten repeatedly about the head with some sharp instrument which gouged his features."

"But why? From the looks of things, the motive was robbery. Whoever perpetrated the crime didn't have to murder him. And even if he was killed accidentally, there was no reason to keep on slashing away at his face—or lean him across the window-sill the same way as in the story."

Waverly tugged at his beard. "Nature copies art," he said. "Or does art copy nature? Now we have two examples—Santiago's death and your painting. Both linked directly to the work of H. P. Lovecraft."

"But Lovecraft isn't linked to Santiago."

"I think he is." Waverly reached into his jacket pocket and pulled out a torn and crumpled scrap of yellowed paper. Smoothing its creases, he placed it on the table-top before him.

"What's that?" Keith said.

"Something I found on the floor of the back room when I picked up that letter-spindle," Waverly told him. "I didn't get a chance to look at it closely until we were on our way here. You were too busy driving and too shook up to notice—and when I saw what it was, I decided not to say anything. But now I think you ought to see for yourself."

He pushed the paper forward. Keith gazed down at the torn-away portion of a sheet of stationery covered with minute and distinctive lettering. The crabbed handwriting was difficult to read: Keith raised the paper to the light and deciphered the message slowly.

10 Barnes Street,
Providence, R.I.,
October 13, 1926

My dear Upton:

I write in some trepidation. In view of what you disclosed to me in Boston—verbally, and above all, visually—I feel it imperative that we meet again as quickly as possible. I must indeed see that other work you hinted about. Never in my wildest imaginings did I dream of the existence of such

The calligraphy ended abruptly at the jagged edge of the ripped fragment, and Keith glanced up to meet Waverly's stolid stare.

"*My dear Upton*," Waverly said slowly. "Now are you convinced?" He nodded. "There was such an artist, and Lovecraft knew him."

"But there's no signature. How do you know Lovecraft wrote this letter?"

"His address is on it. And anyone who has ever seen a specimen of his handwriting can recognize it instantly." Rising, Waverly moved to a bookshelf behind his chair and took down a small volume with a yellow dust-jacket. Keith caught a glimpse of the title—*Marginalia*—and of a cover-illustration of an ancient house set off by a frame; bordering it was a weed-choked background beneath which a bearded creature crouched and gazed apprehensively up towards the framed dwelling.

Waverly flipped the volume open to a coated page bearing a photostatic reproduction of a letter sheet covered with handwritten notations.

"Look at this," he said. "A ground floor plan of Lovecraft's study, dated May 2nd, 1924, in his own hand." Waverly turned the pages to other photostats—a pen-and-ink sketch of a house, with writing beneath—a postcard—a hand-drawn map—a specimen page of a story revision.

Keith glanced skeptically at his companion. "I admit the writing seems similar, but you can't rule out the possibility of forgery."

"Look at this paper." Waverly held the torn sheet to the light.

"Yellow and crumbling. See how the ink has faded? This letter was written more than fifty years ago, when Lovecraft was unimportant and unknown. Why should anyone want to forge his handwriting then?"

"Perhaps it was done recently," Keith said. "Somebody got hold of a blank sheet of old stationery—some practical joker—"

"We're not dealing with a joke here. There's nothing funny about a savage and perverted murder." Waverly's sensitive eyes blinked behind the dark glasses as he stepped back from the harsh glare of the light overhead. "The killer—or killers—had a deadly serious purpose."

"To rob the store?"

Waverly shook his head. "They weren't interested in antiques —they wanted those boxes Santiago bought from that old warehouse in Boston. And they wanted to get rid of him before he could reveal what he had, or where it came from. Remember how his file and desk were ransacked? I think they were after sales-slips, check-stubs, bills of lading—anything which indicated where the purchase had come from. And those empty cartons that we saw must have contained the material they were looking for."

"What kind of material?"

"I think it was the stored and unclaimed personal effects of R. Upton—his books and a collection of letters he'd received. Letters like this one, from H. P. Lovecraft." Again Waverly held up the fragment of stationery. "They must have torn and dropped part of a page which wasn't noticed, because the spindle fell and covered it."

Keith's forehead furrowed. "I can't buy that. Why steal some old books and correspondence owned by an artist nobody ever heard of?"

"Maybe to keep him from being heard of," Waverly said. "We'll find the answer—"

Keith rose abruptly, running a hand across his haggard face. "I've got to get some rest."

"Want to stay here? I can put you up in the spare bedroom if you like."

"No, I'll get on home."

"Sure you're up to driving?"

Keith glanced over at the window. "Still too early for morning traffic. I'll be all right."

Waverly led him along the hall to the front door. "Call me tonight. Then we can decide on our next step."

Keith shook his head. "I don't want to take any more steps," he said.

"We can't stop now!"

"Oh yes we can." Keith's voice was firm. "This is where I quit. I don't want to hear any more, I don't want to know any more." He opened the door and started across the threshold into the early morning light. "All I want is to forget the whole crazy business. And that's just what I'm going to do."

As Waverly stared after him, Keith strode down the driveway to his car.

There was resolution in his movements as he drove off; a fixed determination that overcame his weariness as he sped along the empty cross-town streets and threaded his way up the winding roads leading to the hilltop home above the canyon. Only after the Volvo was parked in the garage and the front door opened did he permit himself the luxury of relaxation.

It was good to be home once more in the hushed house. As Keith moved down the hall towards the bedroom, the events of the past twelve hours seemed like a bad dream, a nightmare from which he had at last awakened, safe and sound.

Then, passing the open doorway, Keith glanced into the den, and safety and soundness were shattered.

The den was dim. Nothing had been disturbed, and the room was still, but the table-top on which the ghoulish canvas had rested was utterly bare.

The painting was gone.

Twilight cloaked the looming hills beyond as Keith indicated the window of the den.

"They got in through here," he said. "See these marks on the lock where they forced the window?"

Waverly nodded, his eyes grave behind the tinted glasses. "You're sure nothing else was taken?"

"Positive." Keith gestured towards the jade and ivory figurines in the cabinet. "This stuff is worth a small fortune, but not a piece is missing. They came for the picture." He shook his head. "But who are they, and how did they know the painting was here?"

Waverly stepped back from the window. "The answer's obvious. They're the same people who went to Santiago's and got hold of his accounts records. He must have listed his sales for the day, including the painting. Then they found your personal check with your address on it."

Keith grimaced. "Didn't waste any time, did they?"

"It's a good thing you were still at my place when they came here," Waverly told him. "After seeing what happened to Santiago—" He broke off. "Have you seen the papers?"

"You've never been involved with the FBI, have you?" Waverly said.

"Of course not."

"Neither have I. So our prints aren't on record. We're home free."

"Free?" Keith stared at the table where the canvas had lain. "I don't think I'll ever feel free again."

"You will, when we find out what's behind all this."

Keith shook his head. "I told you I was calling a halt. Let the police handle it. And I still think we should tell them what we know."

"Tell them what? That you discovered a murder last night and failed to report it—but now someone has stolen a portrait of a ghoul and you want it back?"

"Then let's drop the matter, just as I suggested."

"It's too late for that now. Whoever did this knows who you are." Waverly took a deep breath. "I don't mean to sound like an alarmist, but if I were you I'd clear out of here for a few days. Take a room at a motel and keep a low profile. I don't think they'll come back now that they have the painting, but you never know."

"That's just it. We know nothing about these people—or this person, if there's only one involved. And we don't even have a clue."

"I think we can find one." Waverly moved to a chair and picked up a small parcel resting on the seat-cushion. Carrying it to the

table, he removed the wrapping to reveal a half-dozen books. "I
brought these along," he said. "You can read them at the motel.
But please be careful—no coffee-stains. Some of this stuff is
extremely valuable."

Keith moved to the table and sorted through the volumes,
reading off the titles to himself. *"The Outsider and Others—Beyond
the Wall of Sleep—"*

"Lovecraft's collected stories," Waverly told him. *"Marginalia,*
that one in the yellow dust-wrapper, you saw last night. The rest
are biographies and memoirs—de Camp's *Lovecraft: A Biography,*
Long's *Dreamer on the Night-Side,* and Conover's *Lovecraft at Last.* I
suggest you read the fiction first, then the factual material."

"But how will that help?"

" 'Seekers after horror haunt strange far places,' " Waverly said.
"That's what Lovecraft wrote in one of his stories, and I think
you'll find he was right. Somewhere in his work or in his personal
background we may come across the answer we're looking for."

"I'm not sure I want to find that answer."

"It's no longer a matter of choice." Waverly's face was grim.
"Our very survival may depend upon being able to discover
what's behind all this. Read these books, my friend. Read as if
your life depended upon them. Because it does."

The motel was everything Keith despised; a sterile functional
simulacrum of plastic comfort and impersonal modernity. But
during the next three days he scarcely noticed his surroundings,
for with the aid of the books Waverly had given him he was
exploring another world.

It was the New England world of the 1890s, into which
Howard Phillips Lovecraft had been born, the only child of gen-
teel parents whose fortunes declined. His father died when Lovecraft was eight, and he spent his formative years with a mother
whose eccentricities gradually lapsed into severe mental illness.
Poor health drove him to refuge in reading, so that he became
largely self-educated. As a young man he felt alienated from con-
temporary society and, identifying with the past, he affected the
outlook and mannerisms of the eighteenth century. An outsider
in his own time, he was still keenly interested in modern science;

he produced a journal of astronomy and involved himself with amateur press associations. Soon he began to correspond with other writers.

And when Lovecraft himself started a writing career, he chose the field of fantasy. His early poetry was modelled on classical lines, his early prose contained elements comparable to the work of Dunsany.

But in the 1920s, following the death of his mother, Lovecraft took up residence with two elderly aunts and the diminishing trickle of inherited income forced him to enter another world. He became a ghost-writer, revising the work of others, then began professional publication of his own stories.

Gradually he ventured forth into society. The solitary night-prowler of the streets of Providence now travelled along the Atlantic Coast to seek out ancient landmarks and took residence in New York. But after a few years, during which he married and separated from a successful businesswoman, he retreated again to Providence where he continued revision-work, correspond-ence and his own writings until death from cancer cut short his career in 1937.

In his lifetime Lovecraft's tales were little-known, for they appeared only in the pages of pulp magazines. No major publisher ventured to issue a novel or collection then or post-humously. Two younger writers, August Derleth and Donald Wandrei, finally formed a publishing house of their own to issue *The Outsider and Others* and *Beyond the Wall of Sleep* in small editions sold by mail-order. Still even in death fame eluded Love-craft; sales moved slowly and reviews were scarce.

But gradually stories were reprinted in anthologies. Derleth took over the publishing venture and put out volumes by other writers who had been members of the so-called "Lovecraft Circle" of correspondents, and belated recognition came. The work of the man whom his friends called "HPL" grew to become a sort of underground classic. The old magazines and early books containing his stories commanded fabulous prices as collectors' items. Finally, in the 1960s, Lovecraft moved into prominence, and the 1970s produced widespread critical attention here and abroad.

All this Keith learned from the biographies—which, in spite

of Waverly's suggestion, he read before turning to Lovecraft's fiction. And as he entered Lovecraft's private personal world, there were many elements with which he himself could identify.

Keith too had been an only child who scarcely knew his father—though divorce, not death, brought about that circumstance. He too had chosen the life of an introvert and had experienced a short-lived marriage and an amicable divorce. Fortunately his own health was good and his comfortable inherited income allowed him to live as he wished; to travel widely and indulge in collecting the curious and grotesque items which intrigued his fancy. Under similar conditions perhaps Lovecraft's life might have paralleled his own. Reading, Keith began to experience a strong sense of empathy with HPL.

But there were other aspects he couldn't understand. The three biographies were widely dissimilar. Willis Conover wrote a memoir of a man he'd corresponded with as a teen-age fan; a kindly, erudite grandfather figure. *Lovecraft at Last* was the Lovecraft of the 1930s.

Long's *Dreamer on the Night-Side* concentrated on the 1920s and the New York years when the two men spent time together. His tall, lean, lantern-jawed HPL was a father-figure, painted in the warm colors of affectionate reminiscence.

De Camp's lengthy book dealt with yet another HPL. The two men never met, but *Lovecraft: A Biography* was an intensive study of an entire life-span and life-style. His portrait of Lovecraft included warts and all; an examination of eccentricities and affectations which probed the psychological background responsible for the fantasies.

Taken together, the three books posed paradox and contradiction. And all three paled before the black brilliance of Lovecraft's fiction.

Keith read the early poetic efforts, but soon he found himself enmeshed in darker themes—the terrors of decadence in old New England towns, and the still more frightening decadence of their inhabitants.

Lovecraft had invented imaginary locales for his stories. Most disturbing was the witch-haunted city of Arkham, home of Miskatonic University. In its library reposed a rare copy of the

Necronomicon, a blasphemous book of black magic containing revelations about the evil powers that spawned and still secretly controlled our universe.

In the deep woods beyond the city, a strange recluse born during the eighteenth century prolonged his unnatural life through cannibalism; in the lonely hills near the village of Dunwich, an eccentric farmer practised wizardry, offering a feeble-minded girl to an alien entity and producing hideous off-spring, half-human and half-monster.

Other hybrids lurked in the abandoned port of Innsmouth, whose seafaring inhabitants had met and mated with creatures dwelling in the ocean depths of Polynesia where they were worshipped by the natives. Gradually the inbred offspring of these unnatural unions lost their human characteristics and became icthyoid or batrachian; in the end they developed gills and took to the sea. But meanwhile they hid in the crumbling houses of the forgotten town, serving the strange gods they'd found in the South Seas and disposing of intruders who stumbled across their existence.

In Lovecraft's domain, winged visitors from other planets haunted the deserted Vermont hills and mountain peaks. Aided by human allies, they plotted against mankind. Other humans formed a worldwide cult to serve Cthulhu—one of the Great Old Ones who ruled earth in ancient times and now slept beneath the sea in the sunken city of R'lyeh. When volcanic activity raised Cthulhu from the deep he slithered forth from his stone tomb, ready to reign and raven. Almost by chance he was seemingly destroyed and sank again into the stone city beneath the sea, but still he lives and waits the day when his followers will find the spell to call him up from the depths.

All of Lovecraft's later work fell into this pattern of legend; of a race of monsters who once ruled the earth and were expelled, yet live on outside or beneath it and shall return with the aid of human allies worshipping them with rites of secret magic. The Cthulhu Mythos reveals a world in which civilization and its technology is meaningless and ephemeral. Modern man, engrossed in pointless progress, cannot escape the power of the Great Old Ones who once ruled and will soon return to rule again.

For three days Keith lived in this world—the shadowy dream-world of Lovecraft's life and the nightmare-world of his stories.

Then Waverly's call brought him back to his own home, and to reality.

"Well, what do you think of Lovecraft now?"

Waverly settled back in his chair, brandy-snifter in hand, as the two men stared out at the sunset through the window of Keith's den.

Keith shrugged. "He had a terrific imagination, no doubt about that."

"None?"

"What's that supposed to mean?"

"Suppose he wasn't just writing fiction." Waverly leaned forward. "Suppose he was trying to warn us."

"About what? Don't tell me you believe in ghouls."

"Someone does." Waverly's eyes narrowed behind the dark glasses as he gestured towards the empty table-top. "Someone stole your painting. Someone killed the dealer who sold it to you."

"Is that what the police say?"

"The police say nothing." Waverly tugged at his beard. "There hasn't been a follow-up story on the murder—not a line in three days—and I don't think there will be. The killer left no clues. If we hadn't found that scrap of paper—"

"It proves nothing. Neither does the painting." Keith took a sip of brandy. "Many artists paint monsters, but this doesn't mean such things actually exist. Many people indulge in weird forms of worship; there might even be some sort of mysterious underground cult like the one in Lovecraft's stories. But what they worship is a superstition, pure and simple."

"I don't think it's pure, and I don't think it's simple." Waverly reached for the brandy decanter and refilled his glass. "Neither did Lovecraft—and all his biographers agree he was a strict materialist. I'm convinced he wrote fantasy to cloak fact."

"What sort of fact?"

"The fact of miscegenation." Waverly nodded. "Lovecraft had a puritan attitude towards sex, and yet this theme threads through his stories. Even in the early tales, his morbid dislike of 'foreigners' hints at something evil in the mingling of blood-lines, something that would debase civilized attitudes and drag mankind down to a pre-human level.

"Remember the degenerate underground race he describes in 'The Lurking Fear' and 'The Rats in the Walls'? In 'Arthur Jermyn' he told of the offspring of ape and human, but I think he was really getting at something far worse. Then, in 'Pickman's Model,' he openly spoke of ghouls—creatures who feast on the dead and presumably are born from a necrophilic union.

"But all this was only a prelude to the real horror—not the mating of superior with inferior, of man with animal, of the living with the dead, but something even more disturbing—the mating of man and monster.

"Consider Wilbur Whateley and his twin brother in 'The Dunwich Horror'—children of Yog-Sothoth and a human mother. Think about the villagers in *The Shadow over Innsmouth,* worshipping the Kanaka gods of Polynesia with sexual rites which spawned a race of beings that lived on land until they developed the 'Innsmouth look'—fishy-eyed, frog-faced mutations who finally wriggled back into the sea to join Great Cthulhu in the deep." Waverly gulped his brandy. "That's what Lovecraft was trying to tell us in his stories—there are monsters in our midst."

Keith set his glass down upon the table. "If Lovecraft really believed in such superstitious nonsense, then why did he write fiction?"

Waverly pursed his lips beneath the beard. "Your choice of wording supplies its own answer. From the beginning of time there have been accounts of such beings. Greek and Babylonian mythology gave us the Hydra, the Medusa, the Minotaur, dragon-men with wings. In the lore of Africa we find leopard-men and lion-men; the Eskimos speak of bear-creatures, the Japanese have their fox-woman, the Tibetans tell of the Yeti, the so-called Abominable Snow-Man. Europe knew the werewolf, the *lycanthrope*; our own Indians feared Big-Foot and the snake-people who whispered in the woods. Always a few have warned and some have worshipped as well—but the majority continued to speak in your voice. The voice of reason, which damns all this as superstition, and damns those who believe it as ignorant or insane. Lovecraft knew their fate and had no wish to share it. But he couldn't keep utterly silent; consequently he chose to hide behind the mask of fantasy."

Keith's hands formed the steeple to a temple of disbelief. "You keep saying Lovecraft *knew*," he murmured. "The implication is that he had access to some sort of forbidden lore, and spent years investigating the subject."

"Right," said Waverly.

"But that's absurd! The facts of Lovecraft's life are fully documented."

"Not all of them."

"What about the biographies I read, and the memoirs of Derleth and others?"

"De Camp didn't know Lovecraft personally. Long met him in New York and on other occasions—but he only saw what Lovecraft chose to reveal of himself. Conover saw him just twice, and Derleth never set eyes on him at all. Neither did most of HPL's correspondents or today's scholars. They rely on hearsay and the letters he wrote. Well, hearsay is inaccurate. As for the letters, what better way for a man to hide his real *persona* than behind a wall of words?" Waverly spoke softly. "I tell you the man was up to something—and into something."

Keith frowned. "But how did it all start?"

"We know HPL was fascinated by old New England and its historical landmarks. He spent time with antiquarians and local historians in the cities. Maybe they put him onto something. He began visiting the backwoods, the almost-forgotten little hamlets with their deserted, boarded-up houses he wrote about so frequently in his stories. But suppose he wasn't just sightseeing. Perhaps he was looking for something. Something he found in an ancient attic or crumbling basement—an old diary, a manuscript, or even a book."

"You think the *Necronomicon* really existed?"

"I wouldn't go that far." Waverly shook his head. "But there were actual witch-cults in New England, and they did use volumes of so-called black magic. If Lovecraft discovered one of these it may have started him thinking seriously about the old legends and tracking down the truth behind them."

Keith poured himself another brandy. "When do you think all this happened?"

"It must have started about 1926, after his marriage broke up and he left New York to live in Providence again with his two old aunts. There was a lot they didn't know and were in no position to guess." Waverly cleared his throat, his voice hoarsening. "All this stuff about HPL being a noctambulist, prowling the streets at night. Do you really believe he just wandered around aimlessly, or did he have a destination? I think he must have. And it was then, of course, that he met Upton—the Richard Upton Pickman of his story."

Keith gestured in interruption. "We still don't know there even was such a person. Just because you picked up a scrap of paper—"

Waverly chuckled, but his features remained immobile. "On the basis of that scrap of paper I've had a very busy three days, calling people back East. Let me tell you what I found out. First of all, there *was* an artist named Richard Upton. Born in Boston, in 1884. Died there in 1926."

"I suppose you're going to tell me he disappeared from the basement of a weird old mansion in the dead of night?"

"Nothing of the sort. According to newspaper accounts, on December tenth he returned from a trip—to Providence, mind you—to discover his studio had been broken into and his entire collection of paintings stolen. That evening, after reporting the theft to the police, he shot himself."

"Motive?"

"He left no note. The paintings were never recovered, and if the police ever learned anything it wasn't made public." Waverly leaned forward. "But I found out something they didn't know. A week earlier, before Upton made the Providence trip, he crated up one painting, boxed his books and correspondence, and sent them off to the North End Warehouse and Storage Company. The stuff laid there unclaimed—probably forgotten—all these years. Until Santiago bought the lot."

"How'd you trace this down?"

"I told you I have contacts. Beckman suggested getting hold of a Boston phone-directory and calling storage firms to inquire

about any recent sale to Santiago; that's how I got the information."

"Beckman?"

"A book-dealer I know here in town. Specializes in first editions and rare items. Naturally he was interested in anything to
do with HPL. He thinks it's quite possible that Santiago might
not have gotten all of Upton's material—there could be more
still in the warehouse, including correspondence from Lovecraft.
Such letters fetch high prices nowadays. Anyway, he was willing
to make a deal with me."

"What sort of deal?"

Waverly rose. "I'm going to Boston at Beckman's expense.
Whatever I find to buy, Beckman sells—and we split fifty-fifty."

"When do you leave?"

"There's a flight in the morning." Waverly moved to the door
of the den. "If you plan on being home, I'll give you a call tomorrow night around eight and tell you what I've learned."

"I'll be waiting," Keith said.

They came out of the darkness and the depths, capering,
crawling, creeping in response to the faint, eerie piping of an
unseen flute.

Those that capered were human, or humanoid; they danced
in the flickering flare of fires set about the ancient stones high
on the lonely hilltop, and Keith heard their shrill and cadenced
chanting. *Iaa! Shub-Niggurath! The Black Goat of the Woods with a
Thousand Young!*

And then came the response—the buzzing drone that was
not a human voice or a human sound or even an imitation of
human speech. But there were words he recognized—*Yog-
Sothoth, Cthulhu, Azazoth*—and their utterance rose from the
shadow-shapes that crept and crawled in the lonely night beyond
the circle of firelight.

None could be seen clearly, and for this Keith was grateful,
but the flames glinted to give glimpses of massive, monstrous
mountains. Heaving, quivering mountains alive with the movement of myriad ropy tentacles; mountains covered with bulging
eyes opening and closing spasmodically and hundreds of gaping

mouths from which issued the hissing and croaking horror of words not shaped by mortal tongue.

It seemed to Keith as though the very hills shuddered to the fearsome echo of that guttural response, and then the scene faded and he was back in his own room once more. He realized he had dreamed and was still dreaming as his bed shook as though an earthquake assailed it.

Now, as his dream continued, the shaking ceased, but the memory of the creatures persisted, and with them the memory of all that Waverly had hinted at.

Fear came, and then resolution.

In his dream, Keith fancied he reached for the phone-book on the nightstand and fumbled through its pages until he found the listing for *Beckman, Frederick T., rare books*. He imagined that he dialled the number, listening to the faroff sound of the ringing phone—the lifting of the receiver on the other end of the line—and his own voice whispering, "Mr. Beckman?"

Then came the reply: deep, hollow, unearthly, but distinct. The voice that said, *"You fool—Beckman is dead!"*

It was then that Keith opened his eyes to find himself sitting on the side of the bed, phone in hand, listening to the click that cut off the connection—the click that told him he had not dreamed.

At 7:30 that morning Keith picked up his newspaper from the front driveway. A boxed-insert story above the fold on the front page caught his eye:

3.5 QUAKE JOLTS L. A.
Little Damage Reported

That much, at least, had been real. Keith scanned the story—a story familiar to every Los Angeles resident—noting the usual references to the San Andreas fault and the establishment of the quake's epicenter in the Lancaster area. Seismologists were repeating their warning that the temblor might signal a major upheaval to come, but that too was a standard ingredient of any such account.

Keith read the story almost with relief, and it wasn't until he turned the page that he found the item which really jolted him. Again it was boxed and brief, as befitted a last-minute insertion of late news:

GLENDALE BOOK-DEALER SLAIN

Police are investigating the murder of Frederick T. Beckman, 59, who was stabbed to death last night in his home at 1482 Whitsun Drive, Glendale. The body was discovered by sheriff's deputy Charles McLoy following a neighbor's call reporting sounds of a disturbance next-door. Presumably Beckman's assailant entered through an open bedroom window and attacked him while he slept. Beckman, a dealer in rare books and manuscripts, kept his large stock on the premises in a wall-safe which was apparently undisturbed.

Keith's hands shook as he put down the paper; they were still shaking as he dialled Waverly's number and listened to the echo of repeated rings.

Obviously Waverly had already left home for his early flight to Boston, but there might still be time to catch him at the airport. Keith called L. A. International to have Waverly paged, but the courteous voice on the other end of the line informed him that the Boston flight had departed on schedule half an hour ago.

So now there was nothing to do but wait.

First, however, Keith checked the windows and locked the doors. He felt self-conscious as he did so, here in the dazzling morning sunlight of a bright autumn day, yet the solid click of bolts and latches sliding into place was reassuring.

Reassuring—and disturbing. For the sound brought back memories of another click; the click of the receiver in a dream that was not a dream.

Or was it?

Several hours passed before Keith nerved himself to pick up one of the books Waverly had loaned him—the thick, well-thumbed copy of *The Outsider and Others.*

He turned the pages until he found the story he remembered only too well; "The Statement of Randolph Carter." It was a brief account of a midnight trip to an ancient graveyard by the narrator and his friend, Harley Warren. Warren's purpose was to open an old tomb which, he hinted, contained strange secrets—something to do with corpses which never decayed. It was a typical early tale, written in the florid style which Lovecraft then employed and which certain critics condemned as overblown. And yet the very excesses of its imagery evoked an aura of nightmare; the sense of being in the presence of things larger than life—or larger than death. It was a feeling Keith had experienced last night, and now, recapturing it in broad daylight, he was again apprehensive.

He forced himself to read on, to the point where the huge slab above the sepulcher was removed, disclosing a stone staircase leading down into the black opening beneath. It was then that the narrator's companion, Warren, descended alone—after first setting up a portable telephone as an instrument of communication. Warren disappeared into the darkness, trailing a reel of wire from his own receiver, while the narrator waited on the surface of the graveyard until a clicking signal summoned him to pick up his two-way phone and listen.

Keith found himself almost unable to read the rest—Warren's shocked whispers of dreadful discoveries in the pit below—his mounting alarm as he went on—and then, his frantic warning that commanded the narrator to replace the slab and flee for his life.

Suddenly Warren's babble was cut off. And as the narrator called out to him there came a clicking on the wire and the sound of another voice—the deep, hollow, unearthly voice which said, *"You fool, Warren is dead."*

Beckman is dead.

That's what the voice had told Keith, and it hadn't been a nightmare. The nightmare was here and now, in the realization that he hadn't dreamed.

The book slid to the tabletop and Keith shuddered. *You fool—*

Maybe he *was* a fool after all. There had been such a voice, and presumably it belonged to Beckman's murderer. But Beckman had died of stab-wounds in his own bed, not in an imaginary pit beneath an imaginary tomb, the victim of an imaginary monster.

His killer was human, and his choice of words had not been

accidental. Obviously the murderer was someone familiar with Lovecraft's writing.

But what sort of human could kill a harmless elderly book-dealer in cold blood, then calmly answer his telephone and utter a mocking paraphrase from a story? What insane impulse prompted such ghoulish humor?

Ghoulish. Pickman's Model. A world-wide cult, preserving the secrets of ancient monster-gods and dedicated to their return.

Waverly seemed to believe it, and he was nobody's fool. Did he know more than he'd already told? And did Beckman have such knowledge too, knowledge which could only be erased by his death?

If so, if someone suspected Beckman's awareness and destroyed him, then perhaps Waverly was in danger. What would he find in Boston—or what in Boston would find him?

There were no answers to these questions; only silence. Silence in an empty house, silence which Keith eventually drowned out with the mindless chatter of television soap-operas and the artificial frenzy of afternoon game shows. The early evening news offered no further enlightenment on the earthquake and no mention at all of Beckman's death.

For this Keith was oddly grateful, just as he was grateful for the mere sound of the newscasters' voices portentously proclaiming the posturings of politicians and sports-figures. The very banality of their statements was somehow reassuring; a reminder that in the real world life was proceeding in its usual pattern—three minutes of actual events followed by three minutes of commercials.

Time ticked by and darkness deepened. Keith switched off the TV set and switched on the lights. Suddenly he realized that he'd eaten nothing all day; he went into the kitchen and prepared a breakfast in place of his dinner meal.

He was just finishing up when the phone rang.

"Keith, are you all right?"

Something lifted from Keith's shoulders as Simon Waverly spoke. "Of course. What about you?"

"A bit tired—been running all day, but I'm back at the hotel now. Good thing I got here when I did, because Oliphant tells me they're starting actual demolition tomorrow."

"Oliphant?"

"Fellow who owns the warehouse. Inherited it from his uncle and he doesn't seem to know too much about the business. Acted pretty cagey until I identified myself, but then he cooperated. Took me all through the place this afternoon."

"Did you find anything?"

"According to the inventory listings, Santiago bought up the entire consignment of Upton material. But just on a hunch I asked to see the area where the stuff had been stored. You wouldn't believe how filthy it was—the old man, the uncle, let everything run down over the years. And of course the rats had gotten in. Apparently they'd been carrying off papers and using them to make nests. That's where I found it—in a corner—and if it hadn't been wrapped in oilskin, they'd probably have destroyed it."

"What are you talking about?"

"You'll see. I just sent it off to you, special delivery, registered. You should have it in the morning."

"Aren't you going to tell me what it is? Why all the mystery?"

Waverly's soft voice slurred into a whisper. "I have my reasons. Oliphant said he had several phone-calls from unidentified parties inquiring about Upton's material, wanting to know who'd purchased it. Naturally he didn't give them any information, but in view of what we know, someone must have found out."

"You told him what you suspect?"

"Not all of it—just enough so that he'd realize my motives were legitimate. He says he thinks whoever called tried to break into the warehouse afterwards, but the security patrol came by and scared them off. And he's noticed strangers hanging around the parking lot on several occasions, as though they were keeping an eye on the place. Of course he may just be imagining things, but you never know. So just in case someone may have spotted me, I thought it best to mail the item off to you immediately rather than risk carrying it myself."

Keith hesitated a moment, then took a deep breath. "Maybe it's a good idea, after what happened to your friend Beckman."

"Beckman?"

"He was killed last night." Keith told him about the murder, and his own experience.

When he finished there was a long silence at the other end of the line until at last Waverly found his voice. "We must talk about this further, just as soon as I get in. I booked a return flight for noon tomorrow, so I'll be home by evening. I'll call you then."

"Good enough."

"Meanwhile, I want you to promise me two things. First of all, stay put until you hear from me."

"Okay, will do. What else?"

"That item I'm sending you. Sign for it when it arrives, but don't open the envelope until we're together."

"Any particular reason?"

"I'll explain when I see you; then you'll understand. And Keith—"

"Yes?"

"Be careful."

Keith was very careful; careful about double-checking the doors and windows, careful to listen for any unusual sound in the night. But all seemed safe and silent, and when finally fatigue forced him to retire he slept surprisingly well, without disturbing dreams.

In the morning he maintained his vigilance, opening the front door only once, at noon, in response to the postman's ring.

He was relieved to sign for and receive the number-ten manila envelope Waverly had sent him from Boston, and immediately placed it in his jacket-pocket for safe-keeping, despite the temptation to break the seal and examine its contents. Waverly must have had good reasons for wanting him to wait, and in just a few hours they'd be together.

There were many questions he wanted to ask, and the thoughts which prompted them were unsettling. It seemed to Keith as though he himself had been living in some sort of envelope all these years, moving through life with the special handling accorded the fortunate few whose means insulate them from unpleasant contacts and conditions. Then, a week ago, the seal had somehow been broken and he'd suddenly been exposed to—what?

Certainly not reality. For recent events coincided with no concept of reality as he understood it. But perhaps most people, rich and poor alike, lived in sealed envelopes; narrow, almost two-dimensional confines which constricted their vision and afforded no glimpse of the world outside or what was actually happening to them. Sped through life by mechanical means they couldn't imagine or comprehend, sorted and handled by entities whose very existence was undreamt of, they travelled through space and time to unguessed destinations.

But now, outside the protection of the envelope, the narrow view widened, revealing limitless vistas, and the paper-thin sheet on which sanity is lettered was exposed to great winds blowing from gulfs beyond the stars.

Keith shook his head. This kind of thinking would get him nowhere; it was time to rely on common sense. There had to be a logical explanation for what happened and he hoped Waverly could provide it; if not, he'd go to the police.

Once he made the decision he felt relieved. He spent the afternoon picking up the threads of everyday existence, calling his broker, checking his bank-statements, making an appointment to bring the Volvo in for a tune-up, phoning an agency for domestic help to come in and clean the house on Friday. Then he inventoried his refrigerator and freezer and made out a shopping list.

The prosaic nature of such activities was in itself a calming influence, and by evening Keith was his own man again. He prepared and ate dinner, cleared the table, put plates and utensils in the dishwasher. Then he rewarded himself with a drink and settled down in the den to await Waverly's call.

Here in the dim lamplight the ivory and jade figurines leered silently, the tribal masks grimaced, and the shrunken head dangled; its lips seemed sewn into a grin that mocked his pretensions of ordinary tastes and interests.

But not necessarily. After all, didn't everyone respond to the weird and fanciful aspects of existence? The sophisticated artists who fashioned these grotesque figures, the primitive craftsmen who carved the masks, even the debased savages responsible for shrinking a human head—all were motivated by imaginative impulses which sought an outlet for expression. Just as he, in collecting such bizarre artifacts, fulfilled his own urge towards the fantastic.

And such urges weren't confined to artists, craftsmen or collectors. All humanity shared a need to indulge in flights of imagination—though their vehicles of escape were merely motion pictures, television, or comic-books. Even the illiterate knew the lure of the unknown; no one who shares the human condition, however humbly, is insensitive to the eternal enigma of life and death. There is something in all of us which seeks the strange, the abnormal, the inexplicable. And in so doing, propitiates its power over our minds. It's the hardheaded realist, the self-professed skeptic and scoffer at all mystery, who is most vulnerable to madness.

Keith stared at his collection with new awareness. These objects he'd accumulated were not just an expression of an eccentric taste; they represented a need to surround himself with fearsome symbols until the frightening became familiar. Once accepted as commonplace, they no longer disturbed him. It was, in a way, magic; a means of overcoming inner dreads. Just as Waverly exorcised his personal demons by reading fantasy, and Lovecraft—the realization came clearly—had done so by writing.

Keith was just freshening his drink when the phone jangled. He picked up the extension and smiled, reassured by the sound of Waverly's voice.

"Good evening. Did the package arrive?"

"The envelope? Yes, it's here."

"Fine. You haven't opened it?"

"No."

"Good man. Sorry I'm late in calling—I ran into problems."

"You sound like you had a cold."

"It was raining in Boston, and like a fool I didn't bring a coat. But that's not important. It's my damned foot—"

"What happened?"

"I tripped coming down the ramp after we landed here. Broke my bloody ankle."

"Good God!"

"Serves me right for being in such a hurry. Flight attendants got me into an ambulance and over to Dr. Holton's office. He took X-rays and put on a cast. Drove me home himself. I can't get around without crutches but Holton is sending a practical nurse to look after me for a few days."

"Then we won't be seeing each other tonight."

"Don't worry, I'm all right. Come on over and bring the envelope."

"Can't we get together tomorrow instead? You need some
rest."

"Look, I think I've found the answer to all this, and I want you
to hear it before I lose my voice entirely. How soon can I expect
you?"

"Give me an hour."

"I'll be waiting."

The night air was oppressively warm and still. Keith loosened
his jacket as he drove along Melrose, then turned south into a side
street where old frame bungalows rose box-like from the shadows of weedy and untended lawns.

Waverly's house was larger and better-preserved than its
neighbors, set well back from the sidewalk in a fenced yard, but in
the moonless dark it looked no more inviting than the surrounding structures. Keith parked behind a white van, puzzling at its
presence until he remembered Waverly's mention of a practical
nurse.

Thus he was prepared when, in response to his ring, the front
door opened and a stranger's voice asked him to enter.

Moving into the hall he confronted a smiling young black man
in a leisure suit. "Mr. Keith?" said the nurse. "I'm Frank Peters."

"Pleased to meet you." Keith lowered his voice. "How's the
patient?"

"A little under the weather. He's been taking some of those
pain-pills the doctor left, but his throat's giving him a hard time.
I phoned in a prescription for cough medicine—now that you're
here I'll run down to the pharmacy and pick it up."

"Good idea."

"He's waiting for you in the study. Try not to let him talk too
much."

Keith nodded and started down the hall as the young man left,
closing the front door behind him. "See you later," he said.

The study was dim and it took Keith a moment for his eyes
to adjust to the semi-darkness; the lamp on the desk had been

turned down to low. Waverly sat in a big chair at the far corner, his left foot resting on a hassock and encased in a plaster cast. Despite the stifling warmth he wore a long-sleeved woolen bathrobe and a neck-scarf, but that portion of his pale features not covered by the beard bore no trace of perspiration.

He nodded as Keith entered. "Thanks for coming—it's good to see you."

"Sorry I can't return the compliment." Keith surveyed his host. "You look like you've had a rough time of it. And you sound awful."

"Never mind, I'll be all right now that you're here. Help yourself to a drink if you like."

"No thanks." Keith seated himself in a chair beside the desk. "I'm not staying long—you're supposed to take it easy."

"Then I'll be brief." Waverly blinked at his visitor from behind the dark glasses. "Did you bring the package?"

Keith extracted the brown envelope from his jacket.

"Good." Waverly nodded his approval. "You can open it now. We're safe here."

Taking a letter-opener from the desk-top, Keith slit the flap and extracted a yellowed oilskin, sealed at one end. Waverly watched, expressionless, as the opener slashed and the oilskin fell away, exposing a single creased sheet of folded notepaper.

Placing the sheet on the desk, Keith unfolded it and stared down.

"Well?" said Waverly, softly.

"It's some sort of map." Keith frowned. "I can't make out the details—the ink is faded. Mind if I turn up the lamp?"

"The details aren't important." Waverly shook his head. "What I want to know is—do you recognize the handwriting?"

Keith squinted, then looked up in surprise.

"Lovecraft's!"

"You're sure?"

"Of course. Nobody could duplicate his penmanship. I saw specimens in that book you showed me—*Marginalia*. Didn't that include a map too?"

"Yes. A street-plan of Arkham." Waverly cleared his throat, then chuckled hoarsely. "Can you imagine drawing up such a thing, inventing all those street-names and then lettering them in just as though they actually existed? The man had a strange sense of humor."

"You think he did this as a put-on?"

"Of course." Waverly peered at Keith through the dark lenses. "Remember the letter he wrote giving another author permission to use him as a character in a story? He even included signatures of imaginary witnesses, written in German, Arabic and Chinese. Then HPL compounded the fake by writing a sequel to the other author's story—killing *him* off. He even used his own home in Providence as the setting, just to make it seem more authentic. Lovecraft was an inveterate and elaborate practical joker. Once you realize this, it explains everything."

"I don't follow you," Keith said. He picked up the creased sheet of notepaper for a closer inspection, but Waverly's words distracted him.

"That picture you bought—Upton painted it, but that didn't inspire Lovecraft's story. I think it was the other way around. The story was done first, and then HPL had Upton illustrate what he'd written. How he would have laughed if he knew the way we were taken in! For a while he almost had us believing in ghouls and all that morbid nonsense in the Cthulhu Mythology he invented." Waverly chuckled again. "Don't you see? It's all a hoax."

The air beneath the beamed ceiling was close. From somewhere down the hall came the faint sound of footsteps—probably Peters had returned from the pharmacy with the prescription.

Keith ignored the sound, staring at the figure seated in the shadows. "You're forgetting one thing," he said. "Santiago and Beckman were murdered. It can't be a hoax."

"Yes it can." Waverly's voice rose suddenly, sharp and shrill. "Peters—get the map!"

Keith turned.

The black man advanced upon him from the doorway. He wasn't smiling now, and he held a revolver in his hand.

"Give it to me," he said.

Keith took a step backwards, but Peters bore down upon him, his weapon aimed and ready to fire. "Give it to me," the black man muttered.

Then the hand holding the revolver began to shake.

There was a rumbling, and the whole room shook; the walls, the ceiling, the floor. Keith felt the house shudder and sway with a sudden cracking sound that merged with the black man's scream as the overhead beams started to fall.

Keith turned, clutching the map in his hand, and ran for the doorway.

Then the rumbling rose to a roar, the ceiling came crashing down, and he knew no more.

When he opened his eyes again, all was silent. Silent and dark and very still.

Earthquake. They'd predicted another one, and it had come.

Keith stirred cautiously, relief flooding through him as he discovered his limbs moving without pain. There was a numb sensation behind his left ear—he must have been struck by a piece of rubble from the ceiling. Large chunks of plaster weighed heavily against his chest; he pushed them aside and sat up. The crumpled map was still clutched in his right hand.

But the black man no longer held the revolver. He was lying behind Keith, pinned under a huge beam, his skull crushed to a pulpy mass.

Keith rose, turning away from the sickening sight. He groped his way through the debris littering the floor, searching for a glimpse of Simon Waverly in the shadows at the far corner of the room.

Miraculously, the chair had not been damaged. But it was empty now—or almost empty.

Through the darkness Keith stared down at the things which rested on the seat. They were three in number; three objects furnished with metal clamp attachments.

Three unmistakable objects—the face and hands of Simon Waverly.

The nightmare didn't end.

It continued in the street, where dazed figures stumbled from partially-demolished bungalows or frantically fought to re-enter them in search of the missing.

Numbed by shock, Keith noted that the white van no longer stood at the curb before Waverly's house. But the Volvo was there and apparently undamaged; he turned the key in the ignition and it started up immediately.

Keith drove into a night that was now neither dark nor still. Shattered dwellings turned to torches, lighting his way through a city that screamed in pain.

He was not alone; traffic constantly increased as others commandeered cars to escape from conflagration or explosions generated by leaking gas-mains. Water-pipes had burst and flooded Melrose, and Keith skirted the arterial until he found a safe crossing-point. He turned west at Fountain Avenue, swerving frequently to avoid hitting those who ran or plodded or merely stood stunned and irresolute in the street.

Highland Avenue was clogged with northbound vehicles headed for the freeway; on La Brea the sirens wailed as police cars, ambulances and fire-trucks raced on emergency errands.

But as he drove further west there was less evidence of violent destruction. Apparently the quake had hit hardest at the central city, and Keith offered a silent prayer that his own area might have escaped the worst tremors.

How long it took for him to move through canyon traffic he did not know; by the time the Volvo started to climb up into the hills he was soaked with perspiration. But there was little sign of the quake's effect visible here—the houses stood firm on their hillside slopes and only a few trees had fallen to partially block the roadway. Keith drove around them, noting gratefully that there was no sign of brush-fires, and the shriek of sirens had here subsided to a distant echo.

When at last he reached home he breathed a sigh of relief; the house seemed untouched. Keith parked the Volvo and went inside, sniffing for possible gas-leaks. Detecting none, he switched on the hall-light and found it worked. The curious numb feeling persisted, but he forced himself on a tour of inspection, checking for possible damage.

A few glasses had broken in the kitchen cupboards but the refrigerator's contents were intact. The electric stove worked, and the faucet in the sink operated normally. Only the jagged crack in the wall above it gave evidence of the quake's impact here.

In the den, figurines had toppled inside their cabinet; Keith didn't bother to inspect them. Several of the tribal carvings hung askew on the wall, and the shrunken head no longer dangled.

As it grinned up at him from the floor with sightless, slitted eyes and mocking mouth, another image suddenly superimposed itself upon his vision—the flabby, hideous mask of human flesh that was the face of Simon Waverly.

Then numbness gave way to panic. Turning, Keith opened the liquor-cabinet and groped amongst the unbroken contents until he found a brandy-bottle.

He carried it into the bedroom, switching on the light to assure himself no harm had been done here. Kicking off his shoes, Keith sank down upon the bed, twisted the seal from the bottle and, for the first time in his life, drank himself into merciful oblivion.

It must have been close to noon when he awoke with a pounding head and a consuming thirst. Aspirin and water helped ease physical distress, but the feeling of panic remained.

Emerging from the bathroom, he went to the night-stand and picked up the phone. He'd already started dialing the police number before he realized the line was dead. Apparently the quake had knocked out service in the area.

Keith moved into the living room and turned on the television set. It functioned, and after a moment of warm-up the welcome image of a commentator filled the screen. He congratulated himself on finding a news broadcast so quickly, then decided that every local channel must be carrying continuous reports of last night's disaster.

During the next hour he learned enough to piece together a coherent account of the tragedy which struck the city with 7.1 force on the Richter Scale.

The major effects were felt in the downtown area, where great shards of window-glass had razored down from tall buildings and shattered store-fronts. Luckily the inner city was practically deserted at the time, and few were killed or injured in the streets. But panic prevailed in theatres as fixtures and chandeliers fell;

scores had been trampled in the rush to escape. Several hospitals were scenes of calamity, and the destruction in private homes was severe. Fire-damage was considerable, although no widespread conflagration was reported. Los Angeles County had been officially declared a disaster area and the National Guard was assisting in the search for victims amidst the hazards of escaping gas and fallen electrical-power lines.

Keith turned the volume down and went into the kitchen to make coffee. His head was hurting again, but this was probably due to last night's blow from falling rubble.

The realization brought with it what he had thus far succeeded in forestalling—a full recollection of the happenings at Waverly's house.

And with recollection came recognition.

Those final moments in Waverly's study paralleled Lovecraft's story, "The Whisperer in Darkness."

Even the situation had its similarities. Lovecraft's narrator became involved with Henry Akeley, a scholar who believed that winged creatures from another planet were hiding in the lonely Vermont hills near his home. Confiding his fears in correspondence, he invited the narrator to visit him and bring along the photographic and recorded evidence he'd sent as proof. When the narrator arrived he was met by a stranger claiming to be Akeley's friend, and taken to the house where the presumably-ill scholar awaited him to whisper reassurances in darkness. Realizing at last that Akeley's supposed friend was a human ally of the winged creatures who lured him here to get hold of the evidence, the narrator managed to escape. But before leaving, he too made the shocking discovery of a human face and hands resting on the chair his friend had supposedly occupied.

There were differences, of course. In the story it was implied that the dead scholar had been impersonated by one of the winged creatures wearing human hands and face in a dreadful disguise.

Keith shook his head. He felt certain he had not been deceived by some monstrosity from outer space, whispering to him in imitation of human speech. But using Lovecraft's story as a guide, it seemed alarmingly simple to surmise what really happened.

Whoever was watching the warehouse in Boston had learned of Waverly's presence and the discovery he made there. His phone at the hotel had been tapped, so that they knew about the mailing of his find to Keith.

Perhaps Waverly had been followed on the plane to Los Angeles; more likely word was passed along and someone awaited his arrival here. Keith remembered the black man and the van. How simple it would be to draw up alongside Waverly unnoticed in the darkness of the huge, sprawling parking-lot and strike him down, then thrust his body into the back of the waiting van.

Then the phone-call to Keith—the hoarse voice impersonating Waverly, fabricating the story of an accident and asking him to come to the house with the envelope.

The rest fell into place; the black man posing as a male nurse, and his confederate masquerading as Waverly in order to obtain the envelope.

But why hadn't they killed him immediately? Why the elaborate impersonation, and the false explanation given by the whisperer?

A possible reason came to mind. Keith remembered the voice on the phone had spoken of a "package" rather than an envelope. So they weren't sure of just what Waverly had found in the warehouse; more importantly, they weren't aware of precisely how much Keith might know of the discovery. That's why the black man left, or pretended to leave—giving Keith a chance to open the envelope and reveal his reaction. Before killing him they had to make certain that he hadn't passed along news of the finding to anyone else.

Once assured of this, the black man was ready to act. But the quake which struck him down to death and stunned Keith had offered Waverly's impersonator his chance to escape. Probably he thought Keith was dead too; in any event he'd taken off in the van. Understandably, the sudden panic which prompted his flight had caused him to forget about securing the envelope's contents.

But what sort of people could conceive and carry out the multiple murders of Santiago, Beckman and Waverly? Was there really some sort of cult like the one in Lovecraft's stories, worshipping evil presences still secretly surviving here on earth?

Keith carried his coffee-cup into the living room as he sought a more rational answer.

Suppose there was a hoax—not perpetrated by Lovecraft, as the whisperer had clumsily suggested, but by fanatical and unbalanced followers of his writings?

Keith recalled news stories of ritual slayings carried out by Satanists who attempted to make their atrocities appear to be the Devil's handiwork. It would be characteristic of similar deranged devotees to emulate elements found in HPL's fiction, plotting deaths to duplicate those in his tales. Hadn't Waverly once mentioned some sort of society called The Esoteric Order of Dagon—the name used by the horrible piscine-faced cultists in *The Shadow over Innsmouth;* the humans who mated with undersea monstrosities, and whose offspring developed the "Innsmouth look"? Lovecraft's Cthulhu Mythos seemed to attract a certain segment of disturbed youth; there had even been a rock group named *H. P. Lovecraft* some years back. Hallucinogenic drugs might heighten the intensity of HPL's weird imaginings and inspire unbalanced addicts to translate them into hideous realities.

Neither solution, however, would explain the painting from "Pickman's Model" or the existence of the artist Upton, the actual prototype of the character in the story. That picture had been painted in 1926—before Lovecraft had written openly of the Cthulhu Cult, and before any member of today's counter-culture had been born.

Another possibility occurred. In letters and conversations, Lovecraft had often spoken of finding the plots for his stories in dreams. All his life he was subject to vivid nightmares, beyond the wall of sleep.

What really lay behind that wall? Did HPL wander there in other dimensions, a parallel universe? Could he have travelled through time and space in his dreams, travelled to witness visions of the past few days? Had he seen what happened and merely translated it into his fiction, changing the characters and settings?

It was a fantastic hypothesis, and yet if Keith rejected it he faced a final and still more frightening alternative.

Once he'd compared himself to Lovecraft. But suppose there

was another comparison? Suppose Keith was like one of the typical characters in Lovecraft's stories?

He recalled the narrators of such tales; introverted, imaginative, highly neurotic. Often they doubted the validity of their own experiences—admitted that they might be hallucinating, or actually insane.

Was that the real answer? Was all this a product of his own paranoid misinterpretation of normal happenings? How much of what Keith remembered had actually occurred?

There'd been an earthquake, no doubt about that, and he'd sustained a blow on the head while visiting Waverly's home. But maybe he was suffering from a concussion—in which case he might still be disoriented and imagining past events.

It wasn't a pleasant theory, but at least it was medically possible—and, if true, there'd be medical help for his condition. Far better that than facing a world of monster-gods and a black brotherhood dedicated to bringing them back to life. In a curious way the conclusion offered comfort, a sense of potential security.

Then Keith's hand found its way into his jacket-pocket, and when he withdrew it all comfort and security vanished.

For here was proof that last night had not been fantasy: he was holding Lovecraft's crumpled map of the—

"*South Pacific*—"

The phrase was barely audible as it issued from the mouth of the newscaster on the television screen. Quickly Keith turned up the volume and listened.

"—where latest bulletins indicate earthquake activity equal to or greater than our own disaster last night. Although the shock was felt in Australia and New Zealand, little or no damage has been reported. Seismographs indicate that undersea volcanic eruptions centered in an ocean area south of Pitcairn Island and southeast of Tahiti, approximately near the junction of south latitude 45 and west longitude 125—"

Keith glanced down again, scanning the margins of the map where numerals indicated latitudinal and longitudinal degrees. Then his eyes sought the point where the marked lines intersected.

Even before he found it he knew what he would see. Beneath

the crude cross marking the spot, Lovecraft had scrawled a single word—*R'lyeh.*

Wealth offers certain advantages, particularly in times of stress. Despite the disruption of normal business routine in the quake's aftermath, it took Keith less than thirty-six hours to set his affairs in order and board the Air France jet for Tahiti.

He'd left the house immediately, packing what he thought he might require and taking refuge in the Bel-Air Hotel. Here he felt safe against intrusion while he made the necessary arrangements with a travel agency and the passport people. His bank sent over the drafts he requested, and through its recommendations he engaged a property-management firm to close the house and maintain its upkeep during his absence. By the time he left, Keith was reasonably certain of security.

Apparently the recent disaster had caused cancellations of many vacation-plans, and once airborne, Keith found himself occupying the first-class section of the flight with only a single companion.

His fellow-traveller was a middle-aged Englishman whose stiff reserve seemed as much a part of him as the ruddy complexion, the striped old-school tie and the copy of Sotheby's auction-catalog on which his eyes were resolutely fixed.

But the persistent hospitality of the stewardess brought inevitable results, and by the time both men sampled their third drink they had moved into the comfort of the forward lounge and exchanged introductions.

The Briton's name was Abbott—Major Ronald Abbott, late of the Fifth Royal Northumberland Fusiliers, now retired and a resident of Tahiti.

"But only for six months out of the year," he said. "Can't stay longer without taking out citizenship papers—the French aren't about to let anyone poach on their private preserves."

"You heard about the earthquake?" Keith asked. "Do you think there's been damage done?"

Abbott shook his head. "Not to worry. It hit open water hundreds of miles south and east. Always the chance of a tidal wave, but there's not been a bloody word about that. I'm certain you'll find Papeete quite safe for tourists. You are on holiday, I take it?"

"Not exactly." Keith glanced up at the stewardess, grateful for the interruption and for the fresh drink she proffered. But that, plus the effects of altitude and fatigue, served to loosen his tongue. Almost before he knew it he was discussing his self-appointed mission, and while he took care not to spell out either its nature or his motives, he spoke freely of his hasty preparations for departure.

"Sounds as though you had quite a lot on your plate," Abbott commented. "All that rushing about." He gave Keith a shrewd glance. "Not in some sort of legal jam, are you?"

Keith smiled. "I'm not an embezzler, if that's what you're thinking. But I had to get away immediately, once I realized—"

He broke off, studying Abbott's stolid features, weighing caution against the urge to confide. One thing was certain; he'd need help if he intended to fulfil his purpose, and a man like Abbott was in a position to know his way around local rules and regulations.

But what else might he know?

Taking a deep breath, Keith made the plunge.

"Are you by any chance familiar with the work of a writer named H. P. Lovecraft?"

Abbott stirred his drink. "Don't know the name. Friend of yours?"

"No—but there's something he wrote, a story that explains what I'm hoping to do. If I could impose on you—"

"Let's have a look at it," Abbott said.

"I forgot." Keith frowned. "I'm afraid it's in with the luggage."

"No problem. Give it to me after we land and I'll have a fast read."

At the airport, following customs-inspection, Keith located *The Outsider and Others* in one of his bags and indicated the story in question.

" 'The Call of—what?' " Abbott broke off, puzzled.

"I think it's pronounced 'Cuth-uul-hoo,'" Keith told him. "Anyway, that's not important. Just read it and let me know your reaction."

Abbott nodded. "Where are you putting up?"

"The Royal Tahitian."

"Good. I'll ring you tonight at the hotel."

The Royal Tahitian was a relic of an earlier era, before the jet-borne tourist invasion. Old, rambling, and utterly charming, the main structure was surrounded by spacious grounds dotted with individual cottages. Here the traditional *tamaré* was danced, and as Keith explored the garden area he discovered a giant stone phallus which might well have served as an object of worship in ancient times. He smiled at the sight, then sobered as he pondered what else the Polynesians worshipped in those days—or what some of them might worship still. Not here, of course, in a Papeete hotel, or anywhere near roadways strident with motorbike traffic and the sound of transistor-radios.

If olden customs and beliefs persisted, they'd be found in the interior where wild pigs rooted on the hillsides and huge land-crabs still scuttled over rocky peaks. More likely some remnants of the primitive past might remain on the outer islands, Moorea or Bora-Bora, or in the lonely Marquesas to the north. It was hard to believe these smiling, friendly people had once formed part of a warlike society which practised infanticide, ritual cannibalism and ceremonies of sex-magic. But that was a matter of public history—and there might be a private history as well. Keith remembered the Kanakas who mated with the fish-creatures in *The Shadow over Innsmouth*. Perhaps he should have also indicated that story to Abbott, but there was a limit to his trust. As it was, he had taken a calculated risk in showing him the other tale, and after dinner in the open-walled dining room he found himself waiting impatiently for a phone-call.

Instead, Abbott made a personal appearance. He arrived around nine, and Keith found himself confronting a changed man. Gone were the tweeds, the shirt, the old-school tie: Abbott was wearing colorful shorts and a tank-top. His bare limbs were bronzed and muscular, and the ruddy complexion now seemed indicative of outdoor exposure rather than alcoholic indulgence.

But the greatest change was in his manner. Clutching the book firmly in his right hand, he led Keith out of the lobby and into the grounds beyond.

"Where's your bungalow?" he murmured. "We've got to talk."

Keith escorted him there and, once inside, offered him a drink.

"No time for that." Abbott set the book down on the coffee-table then tapped the cover. "Good Lord, man—you're really onto something here."

"You mean you understand?"

"Perfectly. It's not fiction, right?"

"I didn't say that."

"You don't have to. The thing speaks for itself." Abbott flipped the book open, turning pages until he found the line he sought. "He even gives the exact location—Latitude S. 47° 9', Longitude W. 126° 43'. And the date, way back in March of '25. It all fits."

"Fits with what?"

"I've done my share of nosing around these parts over the years. Picked up a bit of the lingo and made it a point to be friendly. Takita was a great help."

"Takita?"

"My wife. No Church of England ceremony, but you might call her that. Poor old girl—she died last year." For a moment Abbott fell silent, then continued. "Anyway, I got to know her people. Family still lives out in the Rapa Islands. Her grand-father—God knows how old he was, but he looked to be pushing ninety at the very least—had some very curious yarns to tell. Not just the usual native superstitions, but things he swore were true. That earthquake Lovecraft mentions; it really happened, you know. And there was a lot of talk about some sort of creature or creatures living at the bottom of the sea."

"Could we visit him?"

"Hardly. He's been dead for donkey's years." Abbott set the book down. "No matter—after reading this I've a pretty good notion of what you're after. You'd like to go out there and have a look around, right?"

Keith nodded. "That's more or less what I had in mind. Do you think I could get cooperation from the local authorities?"

"Hardly. The territory's outside French jurisdiction. And you know the bureaucratic breed. I take it that's why you haven't talked to your own chaps."

"Exactly." Keith frowned. "But something has to be done, and quickly, and I'll need help."

"Say the word."

"I was thinking, if I could fly over the area—"

Abbott shook his head. "There isn't a charter plane on the island that could make the distance."

"What about hiring a boat?"

"It would cost you a packet, what with crew and all."

"That part's no problem."

"Getting clearance might be a bit sticky." Abbott pursed his lips. "Best way to swing it would be to set Pitcairn as your port-of-call—tell the Frenchies you're working up a book about the descendants of Fletcher-bloody-Christian and the *Bounty* mutineers. Then, if you're blown off-course, it's not your fault."

Keith leaned forward. "Is there anyone you might recommend for such a trip?"

"I'd have to ask around, see what's in port and available. You'll need a skipper who knows how to keep his mouth shut, and that sort isn't likely to be running a floating palace." Abbott gave Keith a level look. "But before we go any further, you'd better tell me the rest. You didn't come all this way just to make a tour of inspection. Suppose you find what you're looking for—then what?"

Keith hesitated. "I'm not sure. But if it were possible to get hold of some kind of explosive, depth-charges perhaps—"

"Full marks." Abbott smiled. "Of course you can't expect to pick up that sort of thing on the open market. There's all sorts of ammo and weaponry in the local ordnance, but getting one's hands on government property takes a bit of doing. I'd have to grease a few palms."

Keith shook his head. "I wouldn't expect you to take such a risk."

"The whole business is risky. Forged ship's papers, bribing military personnel, handling live depth-charges." Abbott grinned. "Just the ticket for toning up a sluggish liver. With your permission, I'd like to sign on for the duration."

"You'd come with me?"

"I'm tired of batching it alone, and you're going to need someone who knows how to set off those charges," Abbott said. "I had a crack at it a few years back, in 'Nam. Harbor duty with a demo outfit." He sobered. "Besides, if there's any chance that what we both suspect is true, the job has to be done."

"It could be dangerous."

Abbott shrugged. "Frankly, I think you're a bloody idiot. But that makes two of us. With your leave, I'll get cracking on it first thing tomorrow morning."

It took three days to complete the preparations. Because of their nature, Abbott avoided using the phone to detail his progress. Several times he invited Keith to come out to his home in the black-sand beach area on the far side of the island, but Keith thought it best to avoid comings and goings which might attract attention. Accordingly, Abbott reported to him in person at the hotel, and made the necessary arrangements with the cash Keith provided from his bank-drafts and stock of traveller's checks.

On the fourth day they were under way at last. The sea was calm and this proved to be a blessing, for the *Okishuri Maru* was an old tub, and Captain Sato—as Abbott had predicted—did not extend himself in keeping a tight ship. But no one could fault his seamanship, and Abbott seemed satisfied to leave matters in his hands once the course was set.

Keith saw little of the eight-man crew and made no attempt to communicate with them when their duties brought them above-deck. "They don't speak English," Abbott said. "Pretty scruffy lot, but the best we could scrape together on short notice. I didn't want local people, for obvious reasons—these boys are out-islanders, from Tuamota. Sato picked up the steward and the cook; he swears they're reliable and we'll just have to take them on trust. At least the grub's not too bad."

"How much does Captain Sato know?" Keith asked, as they sat over coffee and cognac the first night out.

"A bit more than I'd prefer." Abbott lowered his voice. "He's nobody's fool—at first he must have reckoned we had some sort of smuggling operation in mind, and didn't turn a hair. Then, when we took the depth-charges aboard, he got the wind up. I had to tell him a cock-and-bull yarn about you being an oceanographer, and exploding the charges to bring up rare deep-sea specimens."

"Did he buy that?"

"Hard to tell. But he knows we're up to something illegal, and set the price accordingly. When he sees what we're really after, you may have to part with a bit more of the ready."

"If we do find something." Keith glanced out of the cabin porthole, watching the sunset rays striating the smooth surface of the water with multicolored flames. "You know, I never dreamed it would be so peaceful. Hard to believe there's anything out there that could possibly harm us, let alone what Lovecraft warned about."

It was not until the morning of the fifth day out that Keith's calm was shattered.

When Abbott pounded on the stateroom door and roused him to come out on deck, the sight which greeted his eyes rendered him speechless.

Shuddering, he stared at what lay off the starboard bow. It was horrifyingly familiar, and for a moment he thought he was experiencing *déjà vu*. Then he realized that he was gazing at what Lovecraft had so vividly and accurately described in his story— the tip of a single muddy peak upthrust from the ocean depths, atop of which towered a mountainous mass of masonry rising to a monolith formed by gigantic blocks of slime-green stone.

It was R'lyeh, and it was real.

The swarthy crew-members jabbered and pointed beside him on the deck. Captain Sato appeared from the bridge, scowling and squinting against the sun at the incredible immensity of the structure rearing above the oozing surface on which it rested and reared in dizzying, distorted angles that defied gravity and sanity alike.

Now at last Keith could believe it all, for here before him was the ultimate proof—proof in a form more frightening than anything hinted at in words or the imagery of nightmare.

Staring at this horror from the depths he knew its power—the power to make its presence known in the dreams of men halfway around the world. It was in dreams that Lovecraft had seen it long ago, and wakened to set down his warning.

And the cult was real, too; the cult whose prayers and invocations had willed the coming of the quake—the long-awaited eruption which had once again raised dark R'lyeh from the vasty deep where Great Cthulhu slept deathless and eternal, sending forth his commands.

Commands. Keith was vaguely aware of Abbott beside him, snapping orders at Captain Sato. The launch was to be lowered at once.

"Make sure to take along a couple of charges," Keith said. "If we can get that door open to drop them in—"

Abbott nodded quickly, then relayed instructions to Sato.

During the ensuing activity Keith continued to stare at the cyclopean citadel which gradually took comprehensible shape; at the huge, crazily-angled stone staircase that was not meant or fashioned for mortal tread, and the great acre-wide door to which it led. Even at this distance he could see the carvings of strange shapes crawling across its surface—tentacled, twisted, and utterly terrifying. And behind that door—beyond and below—was the reality they represented.

"Are you all right?" Abbott was shaking him by the shoulder.

Keith nodded; glancing down he saw that the launch was now bobbing beside the ship, manned and ready.

"Come on, then." Abbott clambered down the rope-ladder and Keith followed clumsily until he reached the safety of the boat below. Then they cast off, with Sato at the tiller.

Once again Keith's eyes returned to the mud-caked, weed-festooned mountain looming ahead, and the massive stone monstrosity which crowned its crest. "Look," he said. "He wasn't lying—the way those stones are set all askew, like something from another dimension, and yet they fit."

Abbott nodded impatiently. "No time for geometry lessons. Let's get astern."

The launch was already slowing before the sloping base of the emergent peak. Captain Sato shouted orders and anchor-lines went out. Keith noted that the chattering crewmen showed no fear—but then they did not know what lay ahead, hidden and waiting in the darkness behind the great door above the oddly-slanted stairs. And that was just as well.

Keith slipped and stumbled up the slope behind Abbott. The crew, he knew, would be lugging up the depth-charges behind him, but he did not glance back. His heart was pounding, not merely with exertion but with anticipation and expectation.

At last he and Abbott reached the great door above, set in ornate stone molding which did not yield to pressure at any point.

Then recollection came. "Remember the story?" Keith murmured. "It's like a panel, balanced on top."

Abbott crawled up along the carven side, then pressed the slimy surface of the stone lintel at a point high above. The door tilted inward, and as he slid down the stile, the gaping aperture widened to reveal the ebon depths beyond.

From the opening issued an odor of corruption which stunned the senses, a stench so overpowering in its intensity that Keith almost fainted.

Gasping for breath, he regained control and saw that Captain Sato and the members of his crew had now reached the top of the stairs and stood empty-handed beside him.

He frowned at Abbott. "The depth-charges—where are they?"

"In the bloody ordnance depot at Papeete," Abbott said. "You didn't think I'd actually pinch them, did you? There's been enough trouble as it is—if you'd only gone round to my place as I wanted, we'd not have needed to go through with all this." He shrugged. "Then again, I'd have had to come out here anyway to open the door."

Keith gasped, then turned to Sato. As he did so, he heard a sound of squishing movement from deep within the darkness beyond the gigantic doorway.

Sato heard it too, but his expression did not alter. Instead he inclined his head. The crew's mate, a burly dark-skinned native, moved up to peer intently at Keith from unblinking eyes set in a widemouthed face.

Captain Sato nodded at the man. "Him b'long Cthulhu," he said.

Then the crew was swarming around Keith, clutching at him with clammy hands to lift him up and over the yawning opening of that demon-fashioned doorway from which something was rising, reaching.

Keith could not bear to behold what lurked below; his eyes closed as he fell forward into the blackness.

His final glimpse was of the crew-men's fish-eyed faces. Too late he recognized the Innsmouth look.

II

LATER

"I'm afraid there's no doubt about it," said Danton Heisinger. "He's dead."

Kay Keith didn't answer. She sat there in the bank manager's office, inventorying her reactions. Kay was acutely aware of the chill from the air-conditioner, the reek of Heisinger's cigar, the squint of his astigmatic eyes imprisoned behind the thick barrier of bifocal lenses, the rustling of the papers he shuffled as he peered down upon them on his desk-top.

Her responses seemed to be in order—auditory, tactile, olfactory, visual.

But the actual news of Albert Keith's death produced no conscious reaction at all.

"Here are the reports from the Consulate," Heisinger was saying. "Eye-witness statements by the Captain and several members of the crew. They were questioned separately by the police and French governmental authorities, and their stories check in every detail." Heisinger pushed the onion-skin carbon copies forward. "If you'd like to examine them—"

Kay shook her head. "I'll take your word for it. But getting drunk and falling overboard on a boat in the middle of the South Pacific—that doesn't sound like Albert. Are they sure the identification is correct?"

"Positive." Heisinger stubbed the cigar-butt in his ashtray, much to Kay's relief. "They've traced his movements all the way back to the time he bought the airline ticket here."

Kay shook her head, then brushed back the blond curls with a self-conscious sweep of splayed fingers. "It's just that it doesn't seem like something he'd do. Running off to the middle of nowhere. I can't imagine Albert acting on impulse."

Heisinger shrugged. "Frankly, neither can I. Your ex-husband struck me as a very methodical man."

"So there must be a reason—"

"I'm sure of it." Heisinger nodded. "The point is, we'll never know just what that reason was. He didn't consult me before his departure. All I can tell you is that he announced it when he came in, immediately following the earthquake. He arranged to withdraw twenty thousand dollars in traveller's checks, and asked the bank to help cut through the usual delays and red-tape involving his passport renewal. We also helped him find a property-management firm to look after the house while he was away. He paid them for the first month in advance and said nothing about being gone any longer, so we can assume he intended to return within that time. And that's all I've been able to learn."

Kay frowned. "But why Tahiti, of all places? And what was he doing on this Japanese boat, hundreds of miles from land? He wasn't a fisherman. He wasn't a lush, either. The last time I saw him, when we had lunch together and discussed the divorce terms, he didn't even take a drink."

"That was almost three years ago, as I recall," Heisinger said. "People change." The little bank official smiled hesitantly. "Not entirely, of course. You can take comfort in the fact that your ex-husband never drew up a new will. You're still inheriting the estate. As his executor, I'm arranging for an immediate inventory. Which reminds me—"

Heisinger opened his upper right-hand desk drawer and produced a key-ring from a manila envelope. "Here you are. Duplicate keys to the house, front door and back, plus another for the garage. I thought you might like to take a look."

"Thanks." Kay put the keys in her purse.

"I must instruct you not to remove anything without consulting me."

"Of course." Kay pushed back her chair and rose. "Is there anything else I should know?"

"Not at the moment. I've kept the key to his safety-deposit box, of course. Apparently he didn't carry insurance."

"He must have let the policies lapse after the divorce went through." Kay sighed. "There wasn't much point in keeping them up any more, was there?"

For the first time, as she spoke, Kay felt a surge of sentiment, although she couldn't identify its precise nature. Sorrow because Albert was dead? No, in utter honesty, she was unable to summon anything as strong as grief. Perhaps pity was a shade closer to the truth—pity for a man who died so far away and so utterly alone. But then Albert Keith had always been far away and alone, even when they were married. If she'd pitied him then, if she'd been able to understand, perhaps he might still be alive. Damn it, she did recognize her emotional reaction now—it was *guilt!* If guilt is an emotion. No matter, she had no reason to feel guilty; ex-husband or not, she'd never really known Albert; she couldn't mourn him either for what he was or for what he might have been.

With a start, Kay realized Heisinger was speaking to her, had been for some time.

"—once the inventory is completed I'll have the attorney draw up the necessary papers for probate. We'll be in touch."

"Thank you again for all you've done."

"No trouble." Heisinger rose and escorted Kay to the office door. "We're here to serve you."

His thin lips relaxed in a fraction of a smile; Kay found herself translating it into decimal terms as she nodded and stepped out into the corridor.

Five per cent of a smile for five per cent of the estate. Fair enough, she supposed. She still retained ninety-five per cent of everything—including the responsibility of finding out just what might have happened.

But she *wasn't* responsible, Kay reminded herself. The divorce put an end to that, and she had the papers, the legal documents which proved it. If legal documents can really prove anything. Damn it, why was she feeling so guilty?

The smart thing to do would be to walk away from the whole affair. Let the executor and the attorney and the tax people make an inventory and a settlement, then pick up her ninety-five per cent and enjoy. She didn't love Albert, he didn't love her. And even if they'd had the greatest relationship since Romeo and Juliet, Antony and Cleopatra or Sonny and Cher, it didn't matter now. Albert was dead, she couldn't bring him back again, and if there was something fishy about the way he died—

Something fishy.

Oh Jesus, *that* was it!

Hurrying out of the building, emerging into the warm sunlight, the cold chill struck.

Kay trembled, and remembered.

Remembered the little girl, five years old, standing on the bank of the Colorado River before the picnic grounds and watching the state troopers dragging the *thing* up from the shallows and across the sand. The grappling-hooks had left their marks, but that wasn't what left the mark on her memory, scored it and scarred it over all these years. It was the *absence* of marks which had haunted her nightmares; the swollen smoothness of the *thing* that flopped wet and dripping upon the bank. Long immersion in the water had eroded all resemblance to humanity; the bloated flesh was muddy-gray, arms and legs were flopping flippers ended in fingerless, toeless blobs, and fish had feasted on the face.

That was the horror; the thought of the feasting fishes. The five-year-old girl had stared and screamed, and now that scream still echoed through the long corridors of memory.

Yes, the smart thing to do was to walk away.

But Kay's legs trembled until she was safely seated in her car, pulling out of the parking-lot. And she couldn't walk away— couldn't run away, because she wasn't five years old anymore— couldn't get away from the thought of Albert. Albert's death and how he died; drowning there in the deep where the fish swarmed and the serrated teeth tore into the foundered flesh—

She couldn't walk away. Nor drive away, either.

Turning west at the corner, the car headed toward the haze-shrouded hills.

Entering the canyon, Kay found herself gradually relaxing, as though the decision itself had put an end to both guilt and memory. In their place, however, came something very much akin to *déjà vu*.

She had taken this route many times before, but not during the past few years, and true memory was dimmed. Twice she lost her way in the winding confusion of dead-ends and roadways which circled back upon themselves; the late afternoon shadows were lengthening and blending into dusk when finally she drew up before the place she had once called home.

Or had she? Again the *déjà vu* feeling. She recognized this house and yet she didn't truly associate it with past reality. Perhaps she'd dreamed of living here; perhaps she shared someone else's memories and mistook them for her own.

Heisinger was right. People change.

Albert had changed, no doubt about it. She remembered best his brief bravado before their marriage, a sort of dominating demanding which hinted at the strength of his desire. It was, of course, nothing of the sort; merely an indication of a perennially-spoiled child's need to possess whatever he found attractive at the moment. But she'd *wanted* him to be possessive, she'd needed the feeling of belonging to someone. Unfortunately, his urge, or instinct—or collector's mania, perhaps that's what it really was—proved to be a temporary phenomenon. Children tire of toys, however attractive, particularly when owning them involves responsibilities. Albert soon lapsed into his habitual pattern of introversion, and this was the chief factor leading to their separation and divorce.

But she had changed too. As Albert's alienation increased, her own gregarious inclinations expanded. At the time of their marriage she'd been a timid, inhibited loner, unsure of her ability to cope with day-to-day contact with the business world and even less sure of her sexuality. From her early teens onward men had found Kay attractive, but her self-image was always that of an ugly duckling. More to the point, she'd never consciously yearned to become a swan.

And Albert Keith, ironically enough, had awakened her. The physical relationship of which he so quickly seemed to tire had brought her to self-awareness and the need for fulfilment.

But Albert didn't respond. His demands on her lessened; she might just as well have remained an ugly duckling because his lifestyle didn't even impose the necessity of pretending swandom. No need to act the well-groomed, stylishly-accoutred and totally artificial product of Women's Lib.

Perversely, however, this was exactly the image Kay set out to establish. The extension-courses she took out of boredom led to the modelling classes and the classes led to the professional assignments.

The rest was inevitable. From model to muddle in one easy step. Or one uneasy year. The divorce, when it came, was amicable—that was the word Albert used; he was always so good about finding the right word for the wrong action—they had gone their separate ways.

Her way had not been easy, but during the past few years it had led her, step by step, towards emotional maturity. Kay knew that now, and was content.

And yet she found herself wondering. Which way had Albert gone?

Opening the front door, stepping into the living room, Kay confronted the answer.

More exactly—more exotically, there in the gathering darkness—the answer confronted her. From the window beyond, the last red rays of the setting sun dappled the bulging eyes and snarling mouths of the masks mounted on the walls.

For a moment she stood startled, but she was not afraid of what she saw; the shrunken head dangling in the dusk and the figures crouching in the Chinese cabinet held no horror.

These were toys, not terrors. The kind of thing little boys order by mail from the ads in the back-pages of the comics magazines. Although the masks were authentic rather than plastic replicas, their menace was synthetic; the shrunken head, whatever its origin, could not harm her.

But could it have harmed Albert? Harmed him because his interest in such things became obsessive, because it led him to retreat into a world of childish make-believe?

I grew up, Kay told herself. *Albert grew down.*

Why? What had happened to cause his withdrawal from reality?

I happened to him. Our marriage happened. He couldn't cope, so he got out. He couldn't face me, so he surrounded himself with what he could face. Masks that do not see, do not speak; eyes and mouths that hold no criticism or contempt. A shrunken head with a shrivelled brain that thinks no secret thought to threaten one's self-image.

Kay shook her head. *Since when did you become a parlor psychoanalyst? But maybe it's true. The world seems to be full of people nowadays who can't cope with their problems. Drugs and alcohol help blur the distinction between reality and fantasy, but it's not enough. Not enough to forget the fears, remove the rage, exorcise the daily demons. So they hit balls instead of faces, smash bowling-pins instead of heads, and wallow in vicarious violence while staring at a screen.*

Albert hadn't gone that route, but then he didn't have to. He had enough money to purchase perpetual privacy; here in his hideaway he could surround himself with the symbols of security. If you're afraid to live with people, then live with things instead. Dead things, things that remind you of death but do not threaten your existence because they can be controlled. You *own* them, and they can't harm you.

You're making him sound like a candidate for the rubber room, Kay told herself. *He wasn't crazy.*

It was what happened to him that was crazy. The way he dropped out, disappeared, died.

And yet there might be a rational explanation for this too; an explanation which tied in directly with his desire to escape. Suppose he'd gone to Tahiti seeking some spot physically remote from the everyday world, searching for the simplistic solution which lured Gauguin to the islands? Perhaps the earthquake triggered his sudden decision to take off.

If so, even the mystery surrounding his death could be easily evaporated. Albert might have found the Tahiti of today a tourist-trap; chartering a boat, he decided to look for a more isolated island setting. As for the drinking, it might merely have been an antidote to the heat. He wasn't used to liquor, she remembered, and the combination of sun and alcohol could have been enough to make him careless.

Careless.

She was the careless one, standing here in this empty house and daydreaming.

Nightdreaming, rather, because the sun was gone now, and the shadows were everywhere. Creeping out of the corners, slithering from the walls, crawling across the floor, looming all around her. In the shadows the masks could move their mouths, the figures in the cabinet stared through the glass, the face of the shrunken head contorted in a ghastly grin. Logic blossoms in the light of day, but when the night comes it withers quickly at a shadow's touch. Then the darker flowers bloom and writhe, pouring forth the perfume of fear. They sway in the shadows, and the shadows sway with them.

Jesus, where did that come from? Kay smiled self-consciously, then moved toward the wall-switch. All that stuff about maturity sounded good, but here she was, little scaredy-cat, afraid of her own shadow.

Only it wasn't her own shadow.

This shadow moved.

It emerged from the hall doorway, coming towards her.

"Good evening, Mrs. Keith," said the shadow. "Turn on the light."

Kay pressed the switch and the shadow disappeared. In its place she saw a stockily-built man of perhaps thirty-five. Short hair, high cheekbones cushioning slitted gray eyes, barrel-chested body almost bursting the conservative confines of a brown business suit. That much she noted at first glance, but it wasn't enough to offset the prickle of apprehension caused by his presence. She tried to keep her voice calm.

"Who are you—what are you doing here?"

"Ben Powers." The man nodded casually. "Didn't Heisinger tell you?"

"Tell me what?"

"I'm with the bank. Estate and trustees department." He reached into his jacket, producing a wallet, then flipped it open to display a card behind a glassine holder. Kay waved it aside impatiently.

"How did you get in here?"

"The same way you did, I imagine." Powers's hand dipped into another jacket-pocket and emerged holding a key. "We all have duplicates."

"We?"

"It's a team operation, Mrs. Keith. We're taking inventory

here—got to make up a list to submit when we file for probate."

"At this hour?"

"I've been here most of the afternoon. Back in the bedrooms. Guess I didn't hear you come in." Powers grinned. "When I did, I got a little spooked—thought maybe it was some prowler. That's why I sneaked up on you."

"How did you know who I am?"

"From your pictures. Found an old photo-album in one of the drawers."

"What else did you find?"

"Not much. Your ex-husband apparently wasn't the type who keeps careful records."

Kay frowned. "I don't understand. What would that have to do with an inventory?"

Ben Powers gestured at the artifacts in the cabinet. "Might give us some idea of what he paid for all this stuff. And where it came from. Would you happen to know—"

"Sorry." Kay shook her head. "Most of these things were purchased after I left." She glanced at her watch. "Which reminds me—I'm leaving now."

"So am I. Didn't realize how late it is." The appraiser moved to the front door. "Let me see you to your car." He flicked off the light.

They stepped out into the darkness and Ben Powers locked the door behind them. Kay moved to the side of her little red Honda, then glanced at her companion. "Where are you parked?" she said.

"Down the street." He smiled at her. "In this business it pays to keep a low profile. Neighbors might get uptight seeing a strange car pulling in here day after day."

"How much longer before you're finished?"

Powers shrugged. "Another session should do it. With your help."

"Mine?" Kay fished the car-key out of her purse. "I have no intention of coming back here again."

"I wasn't thinking of that. Just a few questions and answers—"

"But I've already told you. I don't know anything about what Albert bought during the last three years."

"There are other things you could tell me. The price of the

house is recorded, but not the cost of the furnishings or what improvements you may have put in." Ben Powers smiled again. "Look, I've got an idea. Why not have dinner with me tonight and get it all settled?"

"Really, Mr. Powers—"

"It's to your advantage. The sooner I can submit a report the sooner the estate can go up for probate. I assume you'd like to have this over with as quickly as possible."

Kay hesitated. Powers nodded at her. "It won't take long, I promise. Besides, you have to eat anyway. Why don't you just follow me on down?"

"Where to?"

"There's a place on Burton Way—Maxwell's—"

"I know it."

"Good. See you there."

Ben Powers turned and disappeared into the shadows.

Maxwell's parking lot was brightly-lit, but the shadows were waiting in the restaurant. Powers peered through them as they were seated and noted Kay's frown.

"What's the matter?"

"Nothing." She glanced down at her menu. "I'd forgotten this place specializes in seafood."

"You don't like fish?"

"Not particularly."

"They have good steaks here. And good drinks. I recommend one of each."

The drinks came first. And over them Ben Powers smiled amidst the shadows.

"Your late husband," he said. "Did he hate fish too?"

"Why do you ask?"

"Just curious. From the reports I gather he might have been on a fishing-trip when the accident occurred." Powers's smile faded into the shadows. "*Did* he hate fish, Mrs. Keith?"

"I don't know. I never served seafood during our marriage, but that's because of my own feelings about it."

"Allergy?"

"No. It's something which goes back to my childhood—" Kay

broke off, frowning. "What has all this got to do with inventory-ing the estate?"

"Sorry. But I guess I'm interested in what the report had to say. Or what it didn't have to say, rather. Didn't it strike you as funny that there was so little actual information? In my business you tend to be a stickler for details."

"I can give you details about the price we paid for furnishings, carpet and appliances," Kay said stiffly. "Suppose we stick to that and just leave my husband's likes and dislikes out of it."

"My apologies." Powers produced a notebook and pen. "Let's get started, then, before our dinner arrives."

His questions were routine, her answers mechanical. Gradu-ally her initial irritation faded; now that she'd had the sense to put him in his place there were no further problems.

Powers pocketed his notebook as salad and steaks arrived. The food was good and somewhat to her surprise Kay realized she was actually enjoying herself. Ben Powers proved to be a very pleasant dinner companion now that he'd stopped playing inquis-itor. By the time their meal was finished, sitting over coffee and an after-dinner liqueur, Kay felt totally relaxed. She caught herself wondering if Ben Powers was married.

"Feeling better?" He smiled at her through the shadows.

"Much, thank you."

"Thank you for coming! You probably saved me from a fate worse than death."

"Such as—?"

Powers shrugged. "Ever notice how our society penalizes single customers?"

He's not married, Kay told herself—then quickly refocused her attention on the sound of Powers's voice as he continued.

"Take those come-on ads for the Vegas hotels. Bargain rates spelled out big on top—but when you get down to the bottom line, they always specify double occupancy. And when you go to a restaurant alone, no matter how good it is, they seat you at a little deuce-table right next to the kitchen."

"That's why I avoid seafood places," Kay said. "Every time the waiters come through those swinging doors I get a whiff of frying fish."

"Lovecraft hated it too," Powers said.

"Who?"

"H. P. Lovecraft. The writer."

"Never heard of him."

"Are you sure?" Ben Powers leaned forward.

"Of course. Why should I?"

"I thought perhaps your late husband may have told you. It seems as if he and his friend Waverly were really into the whole Mythos."

"Mythos?"

"Forget it." Powers sat back and lifted his liqueur glass.

"Not until you tell me what this is all about." Kay put her own glass down and stared at his shadowed face. "How did you know Albert and Waverly were friends? And what's that got to do with my husband's estate?"

"Nothing. Guess I made a mistake."

"I'm the one who made the mistake." Kay rose, gripping her purse.

"Now wait a minute—"

Ben Powers started to rise, but Kay gestured quickly. "Don't bother to see me out," she said. "And in the future, don't bother to see me, period."

"Mrs. Keith—please—"

But Kay was already moving through the shadows, and she didn't look back.

Shadows stalked the streets through which she drove, shadows crouched in the gloom of the garage beneath her apartment-complex and hovered in the halls.

Still more shadows awaited her when she entered the living room, and these she dispelled with light. But light did not disperse the others she carried within—the shadows of suspicion and uncertainty.

Kay entered the bedroom and dumped the contents of her purse on the bed, searching for the slip of paper on which she'd scribbled Danton Heisinger's address and phone numbers. As she recalled, there were two of the latter, and the second would be for his home.

When she found what she was looking for Kay made the call.

"Mr. Heisinger?"

"Yes."

"Kay Keith. I'm sorry to bother you at this hour—"

"Quite all right. What can I do for you?"

"I'd like some information about the gentleman who's handling the inventory of Albert's estate."

"Who?"

"Ben Powers. He was at the house when I went up there this afternoon, and—"

"At the house?" There was a momentary pause, and somehow Kay sensed that Heisinger must be shaking his head. Then he spoke again. "But that's impossible."

"What do you mean?"

"I'm positive he wasn't at the house because I went to see him right after you left my office this afternoon."

"Where was he?"

"Pierce Brothers Mortuary. He died of a heart attack two days ago."

The lights stayed on in Kay's apartment all through the night but the shadows remained. Shadows of doubt, deepening when she closed her eyes and tried to sleep.

The shadows were still there, in her eyes—and, what was worse for a professional model, under her eyes—as she kept her appointment next morning in Danton Heisinger's office.

"Please don't look at me," Kay said, shifting self-consciously in her chair. "I know I'm a mess, but I didn't get much rest."

"Neither did I." Heisinger tapped the note-pad resting before him. "Just got back from Pierce Brothers. Everything seems to be in order. Aside from myself and a few people here at the bank, no one else signed the visitors' book. Ben had no relatives as far as they know, and his effects are still in the safe there. That includes his wallet and identification. It's virtually impossible for anyone to have had access to them. Are you sure that's what you were shown?"

Kay shook her head. "The truth is, I only glanced at his wallet for a moment. How was I to know he was an impostor?"

"He counted on your not knowing, of course. Or else he

wouldn't have risked such a deception in the first place. From the description you gave me, there's no physical resemblance between this man and the real Ben Powers. He must have felt very sure of himself to take that chance with you."

"But why?" Kay frowned. "I didn't know he was there. If he intended to burglarize the house, all he had to do was stay hidden until I left."

Heisinger nodded. "Exactly. I think we've both ruled out burglary as a motive for his being there. And that leaves us with some interesting questions. How did he know your name? What prompted him to invite you to dinner? And just who is this H. P. Lovecraft he kept asking about?"

"I don't have any answers," Kay said.

"Well I have one." Heisinger glanced down at his notes. "According to the reference clerk at the Main Library, Lovecraft was a writer of fantasy and horror stories. Born in Providence, Rhode Island, in 1890; died there in 1937. His short stories were first collected posthumously in—"

Kay gestured quickly. "But I've never heard of him! That's what I told the man who claimed to be Ben Powers."

Heisinger looked up, nodding. "Maybe that's what he wanted to find out?"

"I'm not following you."

"Suppose he arranged the whole thing—getting into the house, introducing himself as an appraiser, inviting you to dinner—just to discover how much you might know about Lovecraft."

"Why should he think I knew anything? There's no connection."

"Perhaps Albert Keith is the connection." Heisinger sat back. "Was he interested in reading or collecting fantasy?"

"I never saw any books of that sort around the house, and he never discussed such things."

"But he did collect those masks and figurines."

"Not while we were together."

"I see." Heisinger glanced down at the note-pad again. "Well, let's try another approach. Had he ever lived in Providence?"

"No."

"Visited there?"

"If so, I'm sure he would have mentioned it to me."

"Did he have friends in Rhode Island, anyone who might have written to him?"

Kay frowned. "I realize what you're trying to do. But there's just no link between Albert and a man who lived and died three thousand miles away and more than fifty years ago."

Heisinger sighed. "I'm afraid you're right. It looks like Lovecraft isn't the key to the problem. And speaking of keys—"

Kay watched as the little man lifted a phone-book from his desk-drawer. "What are you going to do?" she said.

"Locate a locksmith. Whoever this intruder may be and whatever he's after, a change of locks will keep him from getting into the house again. And while I'm at it, I suggest you put a new lock on your own door."

"Don't you think you're over-reacting? After all, I'm not in any danger."

"We can't be sure of that."

"Then why not go to the police?"

Heisinger smiled bleakly. "I've already over-reacted to that extent. Earlier this morning I talked to a Sergeant Schneider. He's with the Burglary Section downtown." The eyes behind the thick bifocal lenses consulted the note-pad. "Here we are—Ralph Schneider—the number there is 485-2524, if you want to copy it down. He suggested you might like to stop by and go through what he called their rap-sheets, to see if you could identify the suspect."

"Is that all?"

"Frankly he didn't seem too excited about what I told him. Since nothing appears to be stolen, it's not really burglary. There isn't even any proof of breaking-and-entering, so that leaves only trespass and false identification."

"Then they aren't going to do anything."

"He's forwarding the information to the Hollywood Division. Patrol cars will keep an eye on the house. And he made the suggestion about changing locks. Once they're installed I'll see that you get a new key."

"Thanks." Kay rose.

"Are you going downtown?"

"I'll think about it." She gestured to the little bank official.

"Don't bother to see me out. But if you hear something—"

"Don't worry, Mrs. Keith. I'll be in touch."

Heisinger's smile of farewell faded as the door closed behind Kay. For a long moment he sat there listening to the receding clatter of her footsteps in the hall beyond.

Then he reached for the phone.

Kay picked up the phone in her apartment and dialed her answering service. There was a message waiting—call the Colbin Agency.

She did, and Max Colbin was his usual charming self.

"Where the hell you been?" he greeted her. "Never mind with the explanations, it's noon already and you're due at two."

"Due where?"

"1726 South Normandie. The Starry Wisdom Temple."

"The what—"

"Starry Wisdom Temple. One of those freak outfits, advertises in the shopping throwaways. They want somebody for straight head-and-shoulders stuff—no high fashion, no jewelry, just street clothes. Bedard's already talked to them and if you get it he'll handle the shooting. But they'd like to see you first."

Kay sighed. "Couldn't you just show them the album? You know how I hate these auditions."

"Look, baby, your end is three bills for an hour session, plus the usual step-up if it goes into overtime. For that you can suffer a little, so just get on down there. Ask for Reverend Nye."

It was exactly two o'clock when Kay's car pulled up and slid into the vacant parking-slot in front of 1726 South Normandie. But for a moment she hesitated before dropping her dime into the meter.

The large wooden sign above the wide doorway of the two-storey building plainly read Starry Wisdom Temple but it was obviously a recent addition, as were the heavy red drapes covering the big windows on either side of the entrance. Kay guessed that the stone structure had formerly been a temple of Mammon—most likely a local savings and loan establishment which had vacated a neighborhood no longer considered worth saving or loaning to.

But someone inside had three hundred dollars to spend for a one-hour stint. Duty called, and Kay dropped her dime.

Duty calls. Is that the way a call-girl feels about her assignments? Driving up to a strange address to keep an appointment with a strange man who will rent her body for three bills an hour?

Moving up to the doorway, Kay reminded herself that there's a difference between photography and pornography, at least in degree. Of course she'd had her share of passes and propositions; it was, after all, an occupational hazard in the profession. But she didn't do lingerie-shots or nudes, and so far there'd never been any real problem. Voyeurs, weirdos who were into S-M and bondage no longer hired models; they did their shopping in local massage-parlors or even the corner tavern.

Kay smiled self-consciously. How quickly she'd become inured to her present life-style! *If Albert knew what I was thinking he'd turn over in his grave.*

Her smile faded as swiftly as it had come. Albert would never know anything again, and he wasn't even in a grave. He was thousands of miles away, thousands of feet below the sea, and the fish—

Quickly Kay tugged at the doorknob. It held firm; the door was locked. Perhaps this was an omen and she could leave now with a clear conscience. Then, ready to turn away, she saw the buzzer set beside the door frame. *Duty calls.*

She pressed the buzzer and waited.

A chime sounded faintly from somewhere within the building. A sharp click of the lock echoed in response.

Kay grasped the knob; it turned now and the door opened. She stepped into a dark entryway extending to a curtained inner chamber. Beside it, to her left, a stairwell slanted upward. From above a male voice sounded.

"Mrs. Keith?"

"Yes."

"Please come up."

A light flooded the stairway.

Kay climbed the flight, peering ahead for a glimpse of the man who had called her. But the hall at the head of the landing above was empty. To the right of the stairs additional light fanned forth from an open doorway.

"I'm in here," said the man.

And he was.

Kay entered the small office, marvelling at its musty clutter. All four walls were flanked with bookshelves and their contents had overflowed onto the uncarpeted floor. Cartons of hardbound volumes and paperbacks, magazines and newspapers, stood in the corners and ranged in random rows on either side of the desk at the center of the room.

The bookworm seated behind the desk nodded a greeting.

"Peace and wisdom to you," he said softly. His voice had a lilting accent she couldn't quite place.

"Reverend Nye?"

He rose, holding out a white-gloved hand.

Kay shook it, wondering if her surprise was noticeable; apparently so, because he smiled.

"The gentleman at the agency should have told you," he said. "You didn't expect me to be black."

That, Kay decided, was the understatement of the year. And even if Max Colbin had told her, she wouldn't have been prepared—not for this.

Because the Reverend Nye was *cliché*-black, as in coal, or the ace of spades. The accent could be West Indian, probably Jamaican. But with his jet coloring, dark suit and the incongruous white gloves he looked like the end-man in an oldtime minstrel show.

Kay managed to return his smile. "The gentleman at the agency should have told *you* something," she said. "He happens to be black too."

"*Touché.*" Reverend Nye chuckled. "Well, one lives and learns." He stepped around the desk and pushed a large cardboard carton of books to one side, revealing a small cushioned stool which had been hidden behind it. He gestured to Kay and she seated herself.

"Sorry about the accommodations," he said. "I keep promising myself to get this place straightened up but there never seems to be enough time. Too busy living and learning." Reverend Nye moved back and eased himself into his seat again. "A pity we must make the distinction. Living and learning should be one and the same thing, don't you agree?"

"I've never thought about it."

"Few ever do." He nodded soberly. "They must be enlightened, and that is the purpose of my ministry. Are you familiar with the teachings of the Starry Wisdom?"

The question caught Kay offguard. "Not really. I mean there are so many new movements these days—Hare Krishna, Scientology—"

The soft chuckle sounded again. "I assure you there is no resemblance. And the Starry Wisdom is not new. Its ancient teachings antedate all other living faiths. But that's the point, of course—other faiths aren't actually living, because they aren't learning. They're dead and done for, victims of today's technology. What did the Buddha know about electricity? Did Mohammed prepare us for the Space Age? Could Christ cope with the computer?

"The Bible, the Koran, the Talmud are all out-moded. Their lore and laws were suited to the life-style of desert nomads leading an earthbound existence with no thought of cosmic realities beyond. Today we scan their pages and find nothing pertinent to present problems.

"That's why these new movements, as you call them, are arising. But most of them offer the same old answers in different terms. Meaningless answers. The complexities of today's existence require mediation, but they teach meditation. And all their metaphysical trappings and psychological frills add up to the weary platitude—*Know Thyself.* But even if that were possible—and it isn't, not in any meaningful sense—what's the point of self-awareness? Our sole hope of salvation lies in knowing the world outside ourselves, the world of space and the stars. Don't you agree?"

Kay nodded, wondering what he was driving at. Reverend Nye was a preacher, no doubt about it, but why preach to her?

"Once, long ago, mankind knew the truth about itself, about our place in the universe. Are you familiar with Wegener's hypothesis that at one time all of earth's land-masses formed a single continent which fragmented and drifted apart over the ages? It's considered a relatively new concept, but the Starry Wisdom knew the truth long ago. Just as they knew the reality behind so-called UFO phenomena, and what we term radio-signals from outer space—"

A flying-saucer nut, Kay told herself. *This man's not a preacher, he's a fanatic.*

Once more the soft chuckle sounded. "Sorry, Mrs. Keith. I tend to get carried away."

By the men in the white jackets. Kay's thought echoed a completion of the sentence, but that was not what Reverend Nye had in mind.

"It's merely that familiarizing yourself with our postulates will be of help to you in your assignment," he was saying.

"I was told you just need some straight portrait shots," Kay said. "Newspaper ads, I assume."

"Correct." The man behind the desk gestured with a white-gloved hand. "But needs are one thing; wants are another. And I want something more than mere photographs of an attractive, smiling face. I want that face to mirror sincerity, enlightenment, real understanding."

Kay nodded, painfully aware that her face mirrored none of these things at the moment. The musty smell of old books rose around her, and this kinky character in the white gloves was really turning her off. But—*duty calls.*

"Al Bedard's a good man with a camera," she said. "I'm sure he can deliver."

"Only if your own eyes are open and aware," said Reverend Nye. He leaned forward, studying her. "For that reason, I've a request to make. There will be a Starry Wisdom lecture in the Temple this evening at eight. You'll have an opportunity to listen and learn, an opportunity to understand. Will you come here again, tonight?"

No way, Kay told herself, rising quickly.

But when she spoke aloud, the words were different. "Of course I will," she said.

Somehow she got out of the office, down the stairs, through the doorway, into her car. Even as she drove off into the slanting sunlight, everything still seemed blurred.

Everything, that is, except the vision of what had caused her to abruptly change her mind about returning—what she glimpsed when she stood up and glanced down at the carton of books beside the desk.

The title of the topmost volume meant nothing to her—*The Outsider and Others.* But the author's name was H. P. Lovecraft.

"You gotta be kidding." Al Bedard squinted sourly through the grimy windshield as he steered his VW on a clattering course down South Normandie with Kay beside him on the sagging seat. "Dragging me down into a place like this after dark. It's not safe—"

As if to confirm his words, a pile of rubble loomed ahead, barricaded by yellow sawhorses to indicate ongoing street repairs in the aftermath of last month's earthquake.

Bedard swung out to pass the obstruction on the left, shaking his head disgustedly.

Kay smiled at him. "You wouldn't want me to come alone, would you?"

"I don't see you coming at all," Bedard told her. "What's your cut on this job—two-three hundred, maybe? It's not worth the aggravation."

"Trust me," Kay said. She nodded toward the curbing at her right. "You can pull in here."

"I don't trust anybody in this neighborhood," Bedard muttered. "They'll have the car stripped five minutes after we park."

But he angled into a space alongside the curb and rolled up the windows as Kay stepped out onto the sidewalk. Locking the doors, he joined her as she stood staring at the building across the street.

The drapes were still drawn tightly to mask the windows, but the front door was open. Light from within illuminated the wooden sign above the entrance.

Bedard peered up at it as they crossed the street. "Starry Wisdom Temple," he said. "What is this, some kind of revival-meeting?"

"We'll see." Kay glanced at her watch. "Come on, it's past eight. They've already started."

Approaching the doorway she was aware that sound as well as light poured forth from within—a shrill piping which seemed vaguely familiar. Then, as deeper bass notes mingled with the melody, Kay recognized the theme. It was something from Holst—*The Planet's Suite*—the movement called "Uranus, the Magician." Hardly the musical setting for a revival-meeting.

But then, as they passed through the entryway and the opening between the curtains beyond, it became instantly obvious that this was no ordinary gathering of Born-Again Christians.

Kay had formed no preconceptions; even if she had, there was no way for her to have anticipated what waited within.

The meeting-hall was larger than one would have guessed; an inner chamber extending the full length of the building, with walls completely covered by black, velvet-textured drapery from ceiling to floor. Perhaps it had come originally from a church, along with the heavy old pews of dark oak which served to seat the audience. Certainly a church-supply house was the source of the incense that burned in tall wrought-iron braziers set along the side-walls, suffusing the air with a cloying, sickly scent which evoked a disturbing association.

Al Bedard noticed it too, and his nose wrinkled. "Smells like a funeral parlor," he murmured.

Kay nodded, eyeing the occupants of the pews. The presence of blacks came as no surprise, but she was puzzled by the large number of Latin-Americans and orientals; the ethnic groups seldom mingled for any reason, let alone religious observance.

In the back of her mind she sensed some common denominator here and tried to identify it. Not economic status, surely— some of these attendees were conservatively well-dressed and others were tank-topped street-people. Then she realized the single attribute all shared in common; it was youth. A high proportion of the group seemed to be teen-agers, and no one looked older than thirty.

Oddly enough, the crowd was decorous, with no evidence of the noisy restlessness generally associated with a gathering of young militants. One and all sat listening intently to the music pouring from overhead speakers, staring through the faint radiance which emanated from a row of dimmed spotlights set on both sides of the elevated stage at the far end of the hall.

The stage itself was curtained on either side of a central

narrow opening which revealed the presence of a large lectern. The area behind the lectern was steeped in shadow.

Bedard gestured to Kay. "Let's sit over here," he murmured, indicating the vacant rear row of pews. Kay nodded and they took their places near the central aisle.

As they did so the music changed. Once more she was surprised to recognize the source, as Holst gave way to Vaughn Williams—the final movement of his Sixth Symphony.

Perhaps Reverend Nye was right about her coming here to listen and learn. In so doing, she'd already discovered that he knew something about music—and its effects. The eery quality of muted strings evoked images of other worlds, lifeless planets, dead and distant suns, moving like motes of dust in the empty infinity of outer space which in itself was dying. This is the way the world ends—not with a bang, not even with a whimper, but with a whisper. A whisper lost in darkness.

Then, in the silence, the lights went out.

There was a rustling, a murmuring from the crowd. They too had felt the touch of eternal emptiness and now, for an instant, they were a part of it.

But only for an instant.

The clang of a gong shattered eternity, and the livid light blazed forth above the platform as the red-robed figure stepped forth from the shadows.

"Peace and wisdom to you!"

Reverend Nye's voice boomed. He raised his arms from beneath the scarlet cloak and evoked the echo from the audience.

"Peace and wisdom!"

"Starry Wisdom!"

"Starry Wisdom," came the echo.

Invocation and response. *Why, it's just show-biz,* Kay told herself.

But it worked.

Worked like magic, because it *was* magic. Music and incense, darkness and light, robes and ritual—it worked now and it had always worked. Wizards and warlocks chanted their spells at the Sabbat, druids recited their runes before the dolmens, witchdoctors gibbered in the jungles, and magic *happened.*

Reverend Nye, in his red robe, was no witch-doctor. But when he raised his white-gloved hands in an ancient gesture before a modern microphone, there was a happening. Individuals became merged into the greater whole of an audience; audience became followers; followers became believers.

He spoke, and Kay saw it happen, heard it happen. Again, as in the aftermath of her interview of the afternoon, sight and sound seemed oddly blurred.

But though the precise substance of his words often eluded her, the sense was crystal-clear, evoked in images which flared fitfully through the blur and summoned by the deep drone of his voice.

Azathoth. Yog-Sothoth. Shub-Niggurath. The words were nonsense-syllables but the nonsense-syllables were names; names formed by human lips in feeble effort to identify the realities they represented.

The realities of the Great Old Ones spawned in outer space who came to reign over earth before mankind rose from primal slime—rose at their bidding, to serve and succor their desires. Man was created to worship and obey the Great Old Ones who gave the gift of life, and there is proof of that relationship. Proof in the legends of all lands, recently resurrected by Velikowsky's theories of "astronauts" from other planets and Van Daniken's "chariots of the gods"—symbols of the journeyings of the Great Old Ones through space and time.

Even bits of physical proof remain and may still be found, for it was with the wisdom and direction of their immortal masters that men reared the towering temples on Atlantis, Lemuria, Mu and the lost lands of prehistory and the biblical Babel which was destroyed by flood.

It was the flood—product of upheavals which shattered and submerged continents in convulsions caused by the passing of huge comets—that tumbled the temples of the Great Old Ones, trapping them beneath the crushing weight of roiling oceans or mountainous masses of polar ice.

Somehow a minute portion of humanity survived; survived in brutish squalor over interminable epochs of glacial drift and only gradually evolving into a semblance of civilization once again.

But amongst the new cultures some of the past was preserved in myth, distorted to form the basis of emerging religions. Some of the knowledge was preserved also; enough to account for the fashioning of Stonehenge, Zimbabwe, the Mayan temples, Angkor Wat, the Great Pyramid.

New priesthoods ruled here, perverting the ancient wisdom to their own ends. They denied the very existence of the Great Old Ones, masking their memory in the guise of demons—Ahriman, Set, Baal, Satan.

But they could not mask the racial memory which still rises in men's dreams and is mirrored in their art-forms today. Always the collective unconscious has retained a hint of the truth and it exists in altered fashion even now. What is astrology but a symbolic account of the influence of the stars—the stars from which the Great Old Ones issued forth to rule our destinies?

Always the priestcraft has sought to discredit truth, to dismiss awareness as evil. Man fell, they say, because he tasted that which is forbidden—the fruit of the Tree of Knowledge. And it was the priests' gods, singular or plural, who sent floods and cataclysms as punishment. Always the self-appointed spokesmen of the new gods maintain that theirs is the only wisdom, their rituals of worship the only way.

Hence sects and schisms, wars and conquests, division into nations, rivalry of doctrines born in fire and blood—the destruction of the many so that the few may rule. Hence, too, the persecution of the faithful.

Yet the faithful remain. Always there have been a chosen few, the initiate, who were not deceived by the distortions and deceptions practised by their mortal masters. They remember the Great Old Ones.

And the Great Old Ones remember them.

For they have not died. Entities capable of crossing the vastness of outer space are immortal. Buried they may be under titanic immensities of ice or immured in great stone citadels beneath the surging sea—buried, but still sentient. Sleeping throughout eons that are to them only an instant; stirring in their slumber to send forth dreams. Dreams which invade the minds of unbelievers in the guise of nightmares—but to believers they bring fresh faith, fresh hope of a day when the Great Old Ones shall arise and reign again.

In sunken R'lyeh, Great Cthulhu lies waiting; waiting for the time when the stars are right and the power of release returns. That time is close at hand and the power is potently preserved, set down in secret writings which the faithful have guarded through the ages. It is this power, this knowledge, which is embodied in the Starry Wisdom.

"I bring you tidings," Reverend Nye intoned. "The weary waiting is at an end. The constellations cluster in their cosmic courses. Last month's earthquake was a token of that which is ordained. Forces form to fashion the future. Soon mountains will be as motes of dust, the icy barriers dissolve, the sea surrenders its secrets.

"Many will perish—the priests of false faiths and their false prophets whom men call scientists, together with all those who follow them. There will be times of terror for them, my friends— and times of triumph for us. Those who believe shall survive."

The gloved hands rose, weaving before the dark face in slow patterns contrapuntal to the woven words. "To some, I know, this seems the sheerest nonsense. To others it is blasphemy, or at best the stuff of superstition. And you say to yourselves, who is this charlatan?"

The cadence of his voice changed abruptly. "Or do you say, rather, who is this turkey and what's with all this far-out jive he's laying on us? Man, we don't dig what's coming down, we got too many smarts?" Reverend Nye smiled and shrugged. "Well, however you phrase it, a doubt is a doubt. It stands in the path of truth and must be removed.

"So now is the time of truth."

As he spoke, the gloved hands dipped beneath the rear of the lectern and rose again, holding a box or chest.

Kay stared at the rectangular container; it was perhaps a foot wide and eighteen inches in length and depth, formed of a yellowish metal tarnished with age. Its outer surface was etched with designs of writhing figures only half-visible in the shadows and the lid was ornately carved.

Reverend Nye set the box atop the lectern; the crowd murmured

and then fell still. Kay sensed an urgency, and expectancy, and from
the warmth of their huddled mass rose a hint of chill which carried
the scent of fear. Once again everything seemed to blur.

Then the Reverend Nye pressed against the box on its far side.
The lid sprang open and out of the blur came a lance of light—
dancing, dazzling light from within the metal container.

Nye's face was suffused in its glow as he stared over the opened
box. His arms extended and his voice rose with the gesture.

"Behold the gift of the Great Old Ones, risen from the sea as
they themselves shall surely rise! Behold the gift of truth, sent
down from the stars to set you free!"

He tilted the box forward to show the source of the light
within—a huge crystal, set and suspended by horizontal metal
bands extending from the sides and base of the box's interior, its
surface carven into fiery facets which poured a luminous radiance into the eyes of the audience.

Kay tried to turn away from the blinding brilliance but there
was no escape; the glare magnetized vision. The light was everywhere and the voice was everywhere.

The voice was part of the light and the light was part of the
voice and the whole was part of a dream. And in the dream Kay
herself felt fragmented, fragmented like the facets of the crystal.
A part of her watched and a part of her listened and yet another
part participated in what she saw and heard.

For the voice was chanting now, chanting in a strange tongue
which evoked a strange response from the crowd below the platform. Deep guttural growls blended into a buzzing noise, then
gave way to shrill sibilant sounds which bore no resemblance to
human voice or human speech, and yet somehow she seemed
to sense the meaning of the words, if words they were. It was
indeed like a voice heard in dreams, a voice resonating in the
echo-chamber of a sleeper's skull. And despite its strangeness it
was familiar; despite its dread it compelled complete attention
and the power that it proclaimed held the promise of reassurance. *Listen not to the words but to meaning; open your eyes to truth.
Abandon fear for faith, out of the unknown comes understanding.*

And in the nightmare, in the dream, in the reality, Kay heard
the voice exhorting believers to come forth. Come forth and

be cleansed in the crystal's eternal light, come and be healed of sorrow and of suffering by the shining power of truth.

There was a murmur and a movement; shadowy shapes rose and converged towards the base of the platform beneath the crystal on the lectern. The lame, the halt and the blind were summoned by the voice and drawn by the radiance. Slowly they limped and groped their way forward to stand, each in turn, before the outpouring rays, there to be bathed in sound and shimmer, then departing with straightened limbs and opened eyes while the crowd exulted and exalted in the—

"Come on, let's get out of here!"

Someone was shaking Kay by the shoulders and she opened her eyes. Funny, she thought her eyes had been open all along—but now she blinked and saw Al Bedard standing over her, peering down anxiously.

He muttered something else but she couldn't make out the words; they were lost in the shrieks and moans of those about her. And over all rose the chanting and the greenish glow pouring from the crystal in the box.

Bedard gripped her arm and helped her rise. As she turned away from the clamoring crowd Kay caught a last glimpse of the faces bathed in the crystal's light—the pale and swarthy and saffron faces, the bearded faces, the faces with pinpoint-pupilled eyes and opened mouths which wailed and panted and pursued her with echoes of ecstasy as Bedard guided her out of the chamber and into the quiet darkness of the deserted street beyond.

She was still not entirely aware; there were moments when the blurred feeling returned. The sound of the motor starting dispelled it and she found herself seated beside Al Bedard as the car pulled out into the street in a U-turn and headed back north on Normandie.

All the while he was talking to Kay, telling her to snap out of it, get herself together. She tried to concentrate on what he was saying.

"Hypnotist, that's what he is, a goddam hypnotist! I remember when I was a kid, my folks dragged me down to see Sister Aimee at her Temple. She used an organ and light-cues, but it worked for her too—"

Mass-hypnosis, that was the answer, Kay told herself. Bedard kept on talking.

"—phoney hype with that crystal—he must have rigged up a battery-powered light behind it in the box—"

Very possible. Kay nodded, welcoming the common-sense explanation.

"—all those faith-healers depend on the same thing—pitching a line to a bunch of hysterical freaks so that they come to Jesus and throw away their crutches. Of course he could have used stooges too, planted them in the audience. Whatever his gimmick is, I'll bet he sure as hell winds up with a big collection tonight after the way he turned them on. Did you get a good look at those kids? Half of them stoned out of their skulls on smack. And that damned incense smelled like hash to me. He set them up for a real trip."

Kay nodded again. It made sense, the kind of sense she desperately desired. Hard drugs could help explain the audience response, and it explained the makeup of the audience too. She strained to remember what she had seen and heard, as though groping amidst the fading memories of a dream. And the bits and pieces came in flashes, in facets like the facets of the crystal. *Staring eyes. Shrieking mouths. The white, black, brown, yellow, youthful faces.*

But something still eluded her, something important, something she knew she must recall. It was back there in the dream, back there in the blur, back in the chanting and the chamber. A glimpse of what didn't belong with the others—the youthful ones.

Then it came.

When she stood up and walked out; that's when she'd seen the face. The face off in the shadows on the far side of the hall—the face that wasn't young.

The face of the man who called himself Ben Powers.

After Bedard dropped her off at the apartment, Kay took one of the little red pills.

Ordinarily she avoided them; as a matter of fact she'd made a point of hiding the plastic container at the back of the top shelf in her medicine-cabinet, so as to minimize temptation. *Red devils, get thee behind me.* But there were times when sleep refused its summons, and then it became necessary to seek slumber in capsule form. Every model Kay knew did the same; they were all Sleeping Beauties whose very existence depended upon awakening refreshed after a long rest. Without sleep the beauty faded and the telltale evidence of fatigue would be detected by the camera. The camera was today's Prince Charming, awakening the modern Sleeping Beauty with a click instead of a kiss.

Last night she'd faced her insomniac problem without a chemical solution and without success. A repetition of that was out of the question. Out of all the questions—*who was this man who shadowed her and why, who was Reverend Nye and what did he want?*

Kay took the pill and the questions vanished. Vanished in the darkness of her bedroom, in the deeper darkness of her descent into oblivion, nepenthe, the little death.

But in her sleep she was shadowed still—not by the man who called himself Powers but by a crazy Irishman named O'Blivion. He stood watching as the Reverend Nepenthe gave her the potion to drink, the potion that brought peace and forgetfulness. Only she did not forget—she remembered. Remembered the haunting chant that echoed through the deeper darkness. *"That is not dead which can eternal lie. And with strange eons, even death may die."*

She knew what it meant now. It meant that Albert wasn't dead. He was merely asleep, as she was asleep, resting beneath the roiling waters until death died and he could rise again, a red devil rising from the deep blue sea when the Great Old Ones came forth from stony sepulchres and icy tombs to claim their own. Their eyes were watching her, millions of eyes opening to hurl their hunger in a stare; millions of mouths opening to appease that hunger; millions of tentacles groping to grasp her, draw her closer to the hungry eyes and gaping maws, and as the chanting rose she drowned it out with a scream.

And sat up, blinking in the morning sunlight.

Kay needed no mirror to tell her that she hadn't rested. A glance at her alarm-clock, which she'd forgotten to set, was sufficient to provide the other information she required.

Ten o'clock. She'd overslept, but that was good. It meant the agency was open and she could call Max, tell him to cancel the model session with Reverend Nye.

Kay thought about it as she bathed, dressed, fixed breakfast. Max was going to need a good excuse before he dumped the deal, but what could she tell him? Certainly the truth wouldn't do—the truth was only a dream.

Or was it?

One thing was very real—her glimpse, last night, of the man who pretended to be Ben Powers. But that wasn't Max's concern. This particular bit of information must be passed along to Danton Heisinger.

Perhaps she'd better talk to him first. And meanwhile she could be thinking about what to say to Max. Maybe Heisinger could come up with a suggestion, something she could use to get off the hook.

But right now the first thing to get off the hook was the telephone itself.

Kay picked up the receiver and dialed the bank number, but with no result. The line was silent. She tried again, then realized the phone was dead. But it couldn't be! *That is not dead which can eternal lie—*

She cradled the phone, frowning at the thought which came unbidden. Here in the sunlight the dream dissolved; panic was not a practical response to reality. The thing to do was go down the hall, see if a neighbor was home and would let her use the phone to call the telephone company for repair service.

It wasn't the end of the world; lines get out of order every day. The time had come to stop the paranoid *shtik* and get her act together.

Kay rose and crossed to the living room door, just as the knock sounded.

"Yes?" she called. "Who is it?"

"Pacific Telephone. Your line's not working."

"How'd you know?"

"Landlady phoned in a complaint. Mind if I check it out?"

"Right."

Kay opened the door for the repairman.

And the stranger who called himself Ben Powers moved into the room.

*

There was no way of getting past him; Kay could only retreat as he closed and locked the door.

"Don't panic," he said.

"I just might." Kay kept her voice steady with an effort, eyeing the canvas repair-kit which the intruder gripped in his left hand. Or was it a repair-kit?

Now he advanced to the coffee-table and placed the bulging bag on its surface. Kay took another step back, wondering if she could make a break for it, run into the bathroom and lock the door. The stranger glanced up and shook his head.

"Hold it," he said, unzipping the bag. "I've got something for you."

Now his hand dipped into the bag. Kay took a deep breath, ready to expel it in a scream when the knife came out.

But it wasn't a knife.

Instead the emergent hand clutched a book. Kay couldn't read the title; all she glimpsed was the spine lettering of the book which revealed the name of its author.

"H. P. Lovecraft?" Kay murmured.

"Here." The stranger held the volume out to her. "Read this."

"Why should I?"

"Because it's important for you to understand what's happening." He thrust the book into her hand. "Read it now."

Kay shook her head. "The answers I need aren't in a book. Who are you? What do you want? Did you kill Ben Powers?"

The intruder grinned. "You've got the right questions, but in the wrong order. First of all, I had nothing to do with Powers's death—he had a heart attack and you can check on it if you don't believe me. I think you've already figured the rest out for yourself. I used Powers's name to get to you, see what you knew about your late husband and his possible involvement in this affair."

"How'd you know something was wrong with my phone this morning?"

"Because I cut the line." The stranger raised his hand to silence Kay's response. "I figured you might do something hasty—like canceling your modeling appointment or talking to that bank manager."

"Why shouldn't I?"

"We'll get to that later—after you've read the book."

Kay hesitated. "You still haven't told me who you are."

"My name is Mike Miller. That's not important."

"You could have told me that to begin with. Why all the secrecy?"

"Security measure."

"You're some kind of government agent?"

"Not officially."

Kay met his gaze. "Look, Miller—if that's really your name. You admit you've been lying to me all along. And there's no proof you're telling the truth now. Why should I believe you?"

"I don't give a damn if you believe me or not. Just read the book."

He picked up the canvas bag, turned, moved to the door. He nodded at Kay as he unlocked it. "Don't waste time. I'll be back this afternoon. You'll get your phone connected again after we talk."

Then he was gone.

Kay stared at the closed door, forcing herself to wait until he'd had time enough to reach the street outside the building. Then she crossed to the window and glanced down. To her relief she recognized his car as it pulled away from the curb, and caught a glimpse of him behind the wheel. At least he'd told the truth about leaving. And now, if she acted quickly—

Kay turned, tossing the heavy book on the coffee-table as she passed it on her way to the front closet. She scooped up her purse from the shelf, then moved to the front door. Opening it, she started across the threshold.

A man blocked her exit.

She couldn't see his face in the shadowed hall, but it didn't matter. All her awareness was centered on the little snub-nosed automatic that seemed to suddenly materialize in his right hand.

"Sorry, lady," he said softly.

Kay stepped back, slamming the door in his face. She locked it, turned, set her purse on the table and picked up the heavy copy of *The Outsider and Others*. When reading is inevitable, lean back and enjoy it.

Settling down on the sofa, she glanced at her watch. Eleven o'clock.

Then she opened the book.

The next time she looked at her watch was at five P.M. and somebody was knocking on the door.

"You've read the book?" Mike Miller asked.

Kay nodded. "Most of it."

"And—?"

"He was quite a writer, if that's what you mean. Frankly, I've never been much interested in fantasy."

"Neither have I."

"Then what's the point?"

"Suppose Lovecraft wasn't writing fantasy?"

Kay frowned. "You don't expect me to believe those stories, do you? I can see now why you wanted me to read them; they're the source of Reverend Nye's whole crazy cult. He even took its name—the Starry Wisdom—from one of Lovecraft's yarns."

" 'The Haunter of the Dark.' "

"Yes. And that's where he got the idea for that crystal gimmick he rigged up. Lovecraft called it the Shining Trapezehedron, didn't he? Nye must have copied it from the description in the story."

"Pretty effective, wasn't it?" Mike Miller said.

"Very. He had that crowd sold, no doubt about that."

"What about your reaction?"

"Mine?" Kay hesitated.

"I watched you during the faith-healing session. You couldn't tear your eyes away from the crystal."

Kay shrugged. "Of course it was all mass hypnosis."

"And just what is mass hypnosis?"

"Why, you know—it's like the Indian Rope Trick. The magician fools the crowd into seeing something that isn't there."

"How?"

Kay gestured impatiently. "Don't ask me. I'm not a psychologist."

"Right." Mike Miller smiled. "Psychologists discarded that nonsense about mass hypnosis long ago. They know a magician can use misdirection and mechanical devices to create illusions. But they also know that no one person can hypnotize an entire group. It's always a one-to-one transaction. There are people

who, for various reasons, are exceptionally susceptible to suggestion. If they're in the audience when a subject is placed under
hypnosis on the stage, they might react themselves in the same
way. But such people are the exceptions, and they respond only as
individuals. There's no such thing as mass hypnosis."

"Then what did happen in the Starry Wisdom Temple the
other night?"

"Something the psychologists can't explain."

"Suppose Reverend Nye was using plants in the audience, fake
cripples who pretended to be healed?"

"It's possible. But what about the phenomenon—the blurring,
as though you were caught up in a dream? You felt it, didn't you?"

"Yes." Kay frowned. "But why weren't you affected too?"

"Because I came prepared for what I'd see. Because I'd read
Lovecraft and knew what to expect."

"You're telling me the Reverend Nye used the actual Shining
Trapezehedron—that what Lovecraft wrote about was true?"

"Not was. *Is.*"

"And all that wild stuff about the Great Old Ones—is that supposed to be for real too?" Kay frowned. "I don't believe it."

"Don't—or don't want to?"

"You're putting me on."

"You're putting yourself on." Mike Miller rose, pacing as he
spoke. "Not that I blame you. Most of us try to avoid any reality
that's unpleasant. We know it's there, but we don't want to face
it—out of sight, out of mind.

"We're willing to admit that we eat meat, but we'd rather not
carry the thought any further. We don't want to enter a slaughterhouse and see animals butchered to satisfy our appetite.

"We accept the presence of mental disturbance, terminal
illness and death, but we avoid talking or even thinking about
such things. We stay clear of asylums and hospitals, and there are
millions of people who won't attend a funeral.

"We're conditioned to turn off on anything that's even mildly
disturbing. We'd rather not listen to 'other people's troubles' or
'complaints'. There's a whole widely-accepted school of thought
that rejects so-called 'negative thinking', including criticism of
the *status quo*. Panglossian philosophy prevails."

"Whatever that is," Kay murmured.

"Sorry." Miller halted, smiling self-consciously. "I know I'm hung up on all this. But I get so damned tired of the way we turn our backs on anything that might upset us, drown out our inner voices with stereophonic sound, deaden them with drugs and—" He took a deep breath. "No point in making speeches. Maybe that's my way of avoiding reality."

"Seems to me that your idea of reality is pretty weird," Kay said. "You're saying that somebody who wrote for the pulp magazines fifty years ago was actually revealing the secrets of creation for a penny a word. That a phoney cult-leader is using those secrets to fill his collection-plate."

"You think that's all he's doing?"

"What else could it be?"

"That's what you've got to find out."

"Why me?"

"Because you're the only one who has a chance to take a look at what's going on behind the scenes."

Kay shook her head. "I thought you security people had agents for that sort of thing."

"We do. Twice within recent months we've managed to plant operatives with Nye's group—one black, one Chicano—as converts to his sect."

"What happened?"

"I wish we knew. They've disappeared."

Kay stared at Mike Miller. "And you expect me to take the same risk?"

"For you it wouldn't be the same. You've got a legitimate *entrée*. And you didn't approach Nye—he came to you."

"Just what makes you think I could come up with anything if I did go through with this?"

"I'm not saying you can. But at least there's a chance. For one thing, we want to find out where Nye bases his headquarters."

"Doesn't he live upstairs from the Temple?"

"That's only a front. Our people did manage to give us a few reports before they dropped out of sight. Nye was giving them indoctrination—said they'd be taken to a special place for initiation into the higher orders of the cult when they became worthy.

Since they vanished, we've kept a stake-out on the Temple, waiting for Nye to leave. He did go out once, last week, and he was followed."

"Where?"

"To an office-building downtown, with underground parking. Either he switched cars there or managed to sneak out through the building itself. Anyway, we lost him."

"You never thought of just going in and raiding the Temple?"

"Damned right we have." Miller's voice was harsh. "When our people disappeared I had a hell of a fight on my hands to keep the team from doing just that. But it's a last resort. Once we made the move, we'd be blowing our cover. And unless we managed to break Nye or some of his followers, we'd be right back where we started. It's my hunch that there's no way to make anyone talk."

"But I've read about these new brain-washing techniques. If you grabbed a couple of young people from his group and deprogrammed them—"

"Look, we're not dealing with some ordinary religious fanatic here. The man we're up against has his own ways and means of controlling converts. He has to, because he's playing for higher stakes."

Kay glanced up. "If you're so sure of that, then you must have some idea of what's really going on."

Mike Miller nodded. "That's why I wanted you to read those stories. Do you remember some of the things Lovecraft wrote about the messenger of the gods? How he'd appear amidst earthquakes and disasters to predict the end of the world? He would be a black man wearing a red robe, speaking of science, inventing strange instruments, giving demonstrations of power. Doesn't that remind you of someone?"

"Reverend Nye—"

"Nyarlathotep."

"Now wait a minute. I'm not going to buy that!"

Miller shook his head. "Of course not. But others do. Obviously this man took the name of Nye deliberately—and my guess is that he tells the inner circle, the most devoted of his followers, that he really is Nyarlathotep."

"All this nonsense, just to con a bunch of street freaks out of their money?"

"I wish it was that simple." Mike Miller resumed his pacing. "But as far as we know, the people in the inner circle have no money. They're mostly just youngsters from the *barrio* and the black ghetto, hooked on drugs."

"But if he's not after their money, what does he want?"

"Power." Miller's eyes narrowed. "You ever hear of the Sheikh al-Jebal?"

"Who?"

"The Old Man of the Mountains. He built a fortress called Alamut back in the days of the Crusades. Nobody dared touch him—not even the armies of the Crusaders or the Saracens. They paid him tribute and obeyed his commands because he had the power. The power of life and death. You may not have heard of him, but the name of his followers has come down through history. They were called Assassins.

"The word comes from the Arabic. *Hashshashin*—the same source as the word hashish, because that's what they were into. The Sheikh recruited young men, hooked them on hash, told them he could grant eternal life if they obeyed his commands. Then he gave them a taste of it.

"After a drug session, when they passed out, he'd take them into his secret garden on the mountain-top. When they woke up they thought they were in paradise—he psyched them out with music, lights, perfume, feasting, drinking, and a harem of beautiful girls and young boys. When they came back from their trip they got the word—this was only a sample, but if they followed orders it could be theirs forever, even after death.

"Those who believed became the *fedais*, the faithful ones, and were trained in all the ways of secret murder. Then he sent them out to kill, slipped them into courts or military camps to knife or strangle their chosen victims in the dead of night.

"Believe me, it worked. Worked so well that hundreds of leaders and officials died, and thousands of others paid tribute to save their own lives. It worked then and it still works today."

"What's all this got to do with Nye?" Kay said.

"We're not sure it's Nye. But somebody's using these tactics.

Terrorist activities—if you knew how many key people have been hit in the past few months—"

"How come I *don't* know? I read the papers."

"It isn't in the papers. If it was, we'd have panic in the streets." Mike Miller scowled. "We've got to back up our suspicions about Nye with solid evidence, and do it quickly. No point in just bringing him in on a phoney charge—we need to find out what's behind this, see if there's someone higher up calling the shots. That's the important thing."

"Maybe to you, but not to me." Kay shrugged. "Not important enough to put my life on the line."

"I think it is."

"Give me one good reason."

"All right." Miller stared at her. "I think one of this man's victims was your ex-husband, Albert Keith."

Kay's phone rang at precisely six o'clock.

It startled her and she looked up at Miller in confusion.

"I told you service would be resumed," he said. "Go ahead, take the call."

"If it's Nye—?"

"You know what to say."

Kay hesitated, wondering if Miller had told her the truth. Or all of the truth. Then, as the phone shrilled its imperative, she lifted the receiver.

"Miss Keith?"

"Yes."

"Good evening. This is Reverend Nye."

Kay nodded at Miller and silently mouthed the name of her caller. Then she listened.

Miller watched, unable to interpret her occasional monosyllabic responses to the caller. When at last she replaced the receiver he gestured impatiently.

"Well?"

"He wants to set up the photo session with Bedard for tonight. I agreed."

"What time?"

"Eight-thirty."

"Where?"

"I presume it's his home. The address is four hundred Lampton Drive."

"Never heard of it."

"He says it's off the Pacific Coast Highway, north of Malibu."

Mike Miller frowned. "For someone who's covered his tracks as well as Nye did, he's pretty careless about giving out his home address. Either that, or pretty sure of himself." Miller picked up the phone. "Let's see what we can find out."

He dialed a number, then waited.

"Eighteen," he said. "Unmonitored request for information— description of property occupying address. Four hundred Lampton Drive. Malibu area."

Now it was Kay's turn to watch as he waited, then listen to his terse affirmation of what he heard. When the receiver was back on its cradle he turned to her with a nod.

"Just as I figured. He doesn't live there."

"How do you know?"

"Because four hundred Lampton Drive isn't a home. It's a private museum."

"Museum?"

"Like Getty's place, a few miles south. But this one's brand new. Built by something called the Probilski Foundation, whatever that is—and not supposed to officially open until next month."

"I don't get it."

"Obviously Nye's meeting you at a switching point. You'll go there and he'll pick you up, then sneak you off to somewhere else." Miller anticipated Kay's reaction with a reassuring smile. "Now don't worry, we're not going to lose him this time. I'll set up tight security—stake out both ends of the street and any back exit will be covered too. If he takes you out, you'll be followed. And you won't be going in alone."

"Bedard?" Kay shook her head. "What makes you think he'd be any help in something like this?"

"Bedard won't be with you."

"But—"

"I've already talked to Max Colbin, told him just enough to make sure he'll keep his mouth shut and cooperate. He's will-

ing to let me replace Al Bedard with one of our people. Fred
Elstree—I think you've already met him."

"Where?"

"In your hall here, just after I left this morning." Mike Miller
gestured towards the front door. "Don't worry—he's not a professional photographer but he knows enough about cameras to
fake your session. If anything comes up, he can handle it, but I
don't anticipate problems. All you do is keep your eyes and ears
open, stay on the good side of Nye, see what you can learn about
his operation."

"That's all," Kay murmured. "Just be a good little fly, walk
right into the spider's parlor, and don't forget to smile pretty for
the camera." She faced him furiously. "Anything else you want
me to do?"

"Yes." Mike Miller nodded gravely. "I want you to remember
Albert Keith."

It was difficult for Kay to realize that only twenty-four hours
had passed since her trip to the Starry Wisdom Temple with Al
Bedard.

In a way this evening's journey was almost a repetition of last
night's experience; almost, but not quite. Now the car was head-
ing west to Santa Monica and the Coast Highway below, and Fred
Elstree did the driving.

Kay was grateful for his presence, grateful that he was aware,
alert and armed. Her gratitude emphasized the difference
between tonight's journey and that of the previous evening.
Then she'd merely been curious about their destination and what
they would find there. Tonight she was afraid.

Miller's advice about remembering Albert Keith was no help;
in a way it only made matters worse. If Reverend Nye was in
some way responsible for Keith's death, then what comfort could
she take in knowing she was en route to meet her ex-husband's
murderer?

She took what comfort she could from Fred Elstree's silence.
It suggested competence, the self-confidence of a man who had a
job to do and knew just how to go about doing it.

Elstree drove well. As the car turned sharply and descended

the ramp leading down onto the highway there was no awkward cornering to dislodge the bags of camera equipment resting on the back seat. Kay was suddenly certain that he'd be equally expert in the use of that equipment when the time came; he'd probably carry off his role as a photographer without any hitch. So what was there for her to fear?

"Fog," said Elstree, as they headed north. "Where'd it come from?"

It came from the sea, of course, and that's what Kay was afraid of—the sea, and what it spawned. Drowned things stirred beneath the waters, slithered to the surface, lurched onto the land. Drowned things lurked behind the fog that swirled across the highway ahead as it rose to form a billowing curtain of ghostly gray. Drowned things. Was Albert Keith one of them?

Kay blinked in unison with the car's headlights as Elstree dimmed them and slowed their progress to a cautious crawl. "Better take it easy," he said.

She nodded. *Yes, take it easy. Forget Albert Keith. He's dead and you're alive. That's the important thing.*

The car moved north as traffic thinned and fog thickened. To the right the high cliffs loomed, but no lights were visible from the windows of the houses perched atop them. Other dwellings lined the seaside at the left, but their lights too were hidden behind a gray shroud. The air was clammy and chill; Elstree rolled up the car window on the driver's side as he noted Kay's reaction. But it wasn't the dampness that made her shiver.

"Hang in there," he said. "Shouldn't be much further now."

She stared through the windshield as they looped past the rows of beach cottages and onto the stretch beyond where the land at the left dropped off steeply to the water, now far below the road. No homes down there, nothing but the fog, rising and rolling from the sullen, silent sea. And then, as they rounded a turn, a single structure loomed ahead, perched on the edge of the cliffside like—

"The Strange High House in the Mist," Kay murmured.

Elstree glanced at her quickly. "What?"

"Nothing." And it was nothing—only the title of one of the stories she'd read in the book. One of Lovecraft's stories about the old man in the old house who communed with the Old Ones from the sea.

Did Fred Elstree know those stories? She hoped not; better that he concern himself with carrying out a routine security assignment in a routine fashion. Showing her own unease might upset him and she didn't want that.

"You're all right?" he was saying.

"Of course. Once we get out of this fog."

"Here we are." Elstree spun the wheel and they turned left onto a narrow driveway. Parked beside it on the shoulder of the highway was a pickup truck. No one was visible in the cab, but as they passed it the truck's headlights flickered on and off quickly.

"Our people," Elstree said.

Kay frowned. "Just the one car?"

"One car means this is the only way in or out." Elstree smiled reassuringly. "Everything's been checked. If there's another exit we don't know about, Miller has it covered."

"Maybe further on," Kay said.

But they saw nothing else—nothing but the fog-swept vacancy of the bare parking area at the far end of the driveway. That and the strange high house on the rim of the cliff beyond.

Closer inspection revealed that it was not a house at all. The low windowless structure of white stone blended almost imperceptibly into the foggy background and it wasn't until they parked and climbed out of the car that Kay realized the roof was domed and the entrance raised above a row of steps. It did look like a museum now, and any further doubt was dispelled by the bronze plaque affixed to the dark oaken doorway.

Elstree lifted his two bags of photo equipment from the back seat, closed the car door, and came up beside Kay. He squinted at the plaque.

"Probilski Foundation," he muttered. "Hell of a name for a museum. Sounds like a Polish corset." His grin faded as he glanced at Kay. "Sorry. No time for ethnic humor, right?"

Kay nodded. "I don't like the looks of this place."

"Well, maybe this will help? We've already done some homework. The Foundation is legit—set up in 1974 by Donald Probilski, oil man from Shreveport, one of those tax-shelter deals. He died two years ago. His widow, Elsie, inherited, runs the Foundation as administrator. We've got the dates on when this land was purchased and who it was purchased from, plus the records of application and permits to build the museum. Outside of a few kickbacks, the usual setup, the deal looks kosher. J. C. Higgins handled the job—big construction firm working out of Long Beach. The place will be formally opened next month, with visiting hours four days a week. Curator's some guy they hired away from the library at the University of Wyoming. That make you feel any better?"

There was something very reassuring about Elstree's matter-of-fact tone and his matter-of-fact recital. Kay offered him a grateful smile.

"Yes, thank you. By the way, what kind of a museum is it?"

"We'll find that out in a minute."

Elstree pressed a buzzer beside the door. Chimes echoed from behind it, and his whisper sounded over them. "Stay cool now," he said. "Remember, there's nothing to worry about."

Except Albert Keith and what happened to him.

The young man who opened the door was a familiar figure. Over the years Kay had seen thousands just like him, on campus malls and city streets, dressed in jeans and jackets and sprouting hair from head, upper lip and chin. Not only did they look alike; they mouthed the same idiom, responded uniformly to the same stimuli, marched to the same drum—which, in their case, was an electronically-amplified guitar. And they shared another thing in common; each and every one prided himself on his unique individuality.

Thus it was that although Kay thought she could recognize this particular young man from the Temple audience last night, she could not be sure. Perhaps if she heard him speak—

But he didn't speak, merely nodded and gestured them forward through the lighted, unfurnished lobby to a wide double-doorway beyond.

There was little doubt about their being in a museum now; the lobby's atmosphere conveyed a characteristic coldness derived more from architecture than from temperature alone. Bare white marble walls and the stark formality of rising pillars created a visual vista of chill *déjà vu*. The final touch was the echo of their footsteps as they crossed the uncarpeted floor; Kay had heard that sound in every museum she'd ever visited.

But once inside the room beyond the double doorway, familiarity faded. The huge chamber was only faintly illumined by lamps recessed in panels bordering the high ceiling, and the ceiling itself bore no resemblance to the exterior outline of the building's circular dome. Instead it rose from the walls in four triangular stone panes which slanted sharply to meet at a common apex above.

They were standing in what seemed to be the interior of a hollowed-out miniature pyramid.

Kay glanced at Elstree, wondering if he had recognized the resemblance. Apparently so, for he grinned and whispered, "Wish I'd known. I could have brought some razor-blades to sharpen."

Her involuntary smile of response froze now as she glanced at the contents of the room itself. Any doubt about its architectural inspiration vanished in the shadows of the four walls and what waited there.

Glass display-cabinets mounted on marble slabs held objects which Kay had been only vaguely aware of through an elective college course in Egyptology, but now half-remembered words and pictures became recognizable realities.

In one cabinet rested a great stone stela bearing the sign of the asp; in another, wings outspread, stood Bennu, phoenix-symbol of resurrection; still others housed papyrus scrolls, bronze tablets, funeral urns. Here was a miniature model of the sacred barge which carries the spirits of the dead to the Underworld for final judgment, and here a full-size display of what the dead leave behind; four Canopic urns containing the liver, lungs, stomach and intestines of the deceased. The bodies from which such organs were drawn rested in mummy-cases, hearts still unremoved and intact through slumbering centuries, faces carefully preserved so that they could be recognized when confronting the forty-two Judges of the Dead.

And against the triangulated walls rose the great figures of brass and bronze and stone, the carven creatures with human forms and animal heads—the gods of Egypt.

Here stood bullheaded Apis, horned Hathor, saurian-snouted Sebek and Horus of the falcon-beak. Bast and Mother Sekhmet crouched, baring their feral fangs; the ibis profile of Thoth and the jackal muzzle of Anubis reared in the dim light. Beside them Nekhebet's vulture-visage gazed coldly down at the great ram-head of Amon, the scarab-skull of Khepri, the man-serpent Buto and the Typhonian animal countenance of Set, Lord of Evil. Rising above them all was the figure in the feathered robe, bearing the *uas* sceptre and wearing the *atef* crown—Osiris, King of the Dead.

He stared. And stirred.

Kay gasped as the figure advanced from the darkness, then realized it was not the statue which had moved, but the man who had waited unseen in the shadows before it.

"Peace and wisdom to you," said Reverend Nye. Nodding at Kay, he extended his white-gloved hand to Fred Elstree.

Kay made the introductions hastily, eliciting a polite smile from her companion and a fleeting, almost imperceptible frown from the black man. He glanced at Kay questioningly.

"This is not the gentleman who was with you at the Temple last night."

"No—he had to leave for San Diego on another account." Kay nodded at Elstree. "I think you'll be just as happy with Fred's work. When it comes to portraits he's really a better photographer."

"I'm glad to hear it. But is he familiar with the purpose of this assignment?"

"Yes. I've clued him in."

"Good." Nye gestured to the bearded young man. "You can go now, Jody." The young man stood motionless, his eyes fixed on the statuary against the wall.

Nye's voice firmed. "Jody—out!"

The glazed stare flickered and the young man's head bobbed quickly. He turned, moving to the door with a peculiar gliding gait which confirmed Kay's suspicions.

Freaked-out on something. Remember what Mike Miller said about the Assassins.

If Miller was right about that, then perhaps he was right about the rest. The museum here was just a switch-point; now Nye would try to sneak them away to someplace else.

"Well then, let's get started," Nye was saying. "If you'll set up your equipment—"

As he spoke, the Reverend crossed to the far wall and pressed a switch. Kay blinked at the sudden surge of light.

Miller was wrong about us being switched. And maybe he was wrong about the rest.

For a moment Kay surrendered to her confusion, but the light helped to dispel doubt as well as shadows. Its glow warmed the room, transforming sinister statue-shapes into harmless examples of the sculptors' art. While still grotesque, they no longer seemed menacing.

Perhaps that was the answer to the entire situation after all. *Grotesque but not menacing.* Everything was part of Nye's hype— window-dressing for his cult. Even the photos Kay was here to pose for were intended as advertising, mere make-believe to attract the gullible. Once again the thought crossed Kay's mind— this whole setup was just another form of show biz.

She glanced at Fred Elstree, wondering what he was thinking, but couldn't read his reaction. Already he was opening his two bags and lifting out portable lighting equipment. Extending the telescoped legs of the light-stands to support his spots, he unlooped the coiled wires attached to the units and strung them across the floor to plug into baseboard electrical outlets. He was doing the job like a real pro, and Kay's misgivings vanished; he made this seem like just another photo session.

To her further surprise, that was almost exactly what it proved to be.

Reverend Nye nodded approvingly. "All set? Fine. Now, before we begin, let me tell you why I picked this location. The lady in charge of the Foundation also happens to be a member of the Starry Wisdom and she was kind enough to give her permission. I think we can use these statues to good advantage, and if you don't mind I'd like to suggest a few poses."

"Go right ahead," said Elstree. "I'm just here to point the camera."

Nye took over, issuing instructions in a low voice. What he wanted, obviously, was a series of close-ups featuring Kay—head-and-shoulders shots. But each pose included a statue in the background; serpent-skulled Buto, vulturine Nekhebet, Osiris of the all-seeing eye. Again the emphasis on lighting and composition seemed routine; the difference lay in his instructions to the model.

"Remember last night," Nye murmured. "Remember how those poor suffering people looked when they approached the altar. That's what I want—the intensity, the complete concentration on the mysteries of Being and Becoming. I want you to see these statues for what they are, symbols of the gods who are in turn symbols of even greater powers. Look into the eye of Osiris and see what he sees—the secret of life which is the secret of death which is the secret of eternity. Renewal and recurrence, endlessly repeated. In the eye of Osiris you yourself are merely a reflection—and when the eye blinks, you vanish, only to reappear when he resumes his gaze."

Kay heard his voice droning from beyond the circle of light, drawing her into the darkness. Listening, she obeyed; obeying, she believed. As she stared she could almost sense that the eye of Osiris was returning her gaze with an awareness of its own. And if it blinked she would cease to exist.

Silently she gave thanks for the sound of the other voice; the voice which returned her to reality.

"Let's have a little more of the profile," Elstree was saying. "Raise your chin just half an inch now. There, got it—"

When at last they finished, Kay felt drained. She was oddly grateful to Elstree for turning off the blinding spots, and to Nye for dimming down the overhead lights so that the room was once again swathed in shadows. Now she didn't have to gaze at the grotesque gods, stare into the eye of Osiris and see it stare into her own.

Elstree was unplugging connections, coiling wires, dismantling and packing equipment. If they could get out of here—

He picked up his bags and nodded. "All set," he said.

"Thank you for coming." Reverend Nye walked with them to the door.

"I'll have prints ready day after tomorrow," Elstree told him.

"Excellent." Nye turned and rapped sharply on the door's upper panel. "Jody—open up!"

The door swung inward.

Standing on the threshold was the bearded young man. He was holding something in his hand, and at the sight of it Elstree reached quickly into his jacket pocket.

He yelled something—Kay thought it was, "Look out!" She couldn't be sure, because his voice echoed through the anteroom beyond.

But there was no echo at all as the bearded young man raised his revolver and blew off the top of Fred Elstree's head.

Kay felt the cool pressure of the stone floor against her cheek and her first reaction was surprise. *I'm not the fainting kind*, she told herself. Then she remembered what she had seen and the giddiness returned. *But it happened without a sound. He must have used a silencer.*

There was sound now; the low murmur of voices. Kay opened her eyes. From where she lay on the floor of the museum chamber she could see the bearded young man talking with Nye before the partially-open door. Kay couldn't make out what he was saying or what Nye replied, but she watched as he nodded and made his exit through the doorway, moving past Elstree's body on the tiles beyond.

Nye closed the door, then turned as Kay sat up. He came towards her, black face immobile, voice expressionless. "Are you armed?" he said.

Kay shook her head.

She flinched as he reached out, but he made no effort to touch her. Instead he picked up her purse from where it had fallen beside her. Opening it, he turned it upside down to empty its contents on the floor. Compact, keys, pen and pencil clattered in a clutter. Satisfied, he turned away.

As Kay raised herself on an elbow, Nye helped her to her feet. Before she could draw away, his gloved hands moved swiftly over her body with expert efficiency.

"I'm surprised they didn't plant a bug on you," he said. "Of course it wouldn't have made any difference."

"What are you talking about?"

Nye shook his head. "Don't waste your breath. Just be grateful you still have it. Jody wanted to snuff you too, like the others."

"Others—?"

"Those two in the pickup truck outside." He nodded. "I gather they were too busy listening to their intercom to notice his arrival. The silencer is a crude but useful invention."

"They're dead?"

"In the current idiom, blown away. Jody put the truck in gear and headed it over the cliff. I can't argue about the wisdom of disposing of any evidence, but I'd like to have examined the bodies and the intercom unit. Lacking that opportunity, I must depend on you. This was some sort of security operation, wasn't it?"

"I don't know."

"Then suppose you tell me what you do know."

Kay shook her head. "Nothing. All I did was come here on a job—"

"Elstree was on a job too." Nye's voice was level. "He doesn't work for Max Colbin—he was planted by someone to accompany you. Now who's responsible?"

"I tell you I—"

Even a gloved blow can sting. Pain coursed across Kay's cheek and temple.

"Sorry." Nye lowered his hand and his voice. "Under the circumstances, maybe it's asking too much for you to tell the truth. But I can guess. Some unidentified government agency has me under surveillance, on a trumped-up charge. Narcotics violations, smuggling, terrorist activities. They asked you to cooperate, find out what you could. Well, let me spare you any further doubts. All of the charges are true."

"You admit it?" Kay felt another surge of giddiness, fought it. "That means you're going to kill me—"

The ebon face was an enigmatic mask. "I admit it because it doesn't matter. Nothing could have saved those men. They would have died anyway, and so would all the others. Including Albert Keith."

"You know about him?"

"Of course. Do you think it was an accident that I tracked

you down, sought you out at the agency for a stupid modeling assignment? I don't need any pictures to advertise a phoney cult that has already served its purpose. This is all part of the pattern, the plan—"

"What plan?"

"To save your life."

"I don't believe you."

"Stop and think. Why all this? If it were merely to build the Starry Wisdom, there'd be no need of such drastic measures. But there's another purpose, a greater goal. I admit our methods are crude, our precautions flimsy and lacking in sophistication. But we must move quickly against the time when the stars are right, the time when the world ends."

Kay frowned. "You say the cult is phoney. But you're preaching to me just the way you preached to those people in the Temple."

"The cult is false, yes. But its teachings are based on truth. The world *is* ending—the world as you know it, the petty world of mind and morality and mankind. The Great Old Ones are already stirring, and the earth trembles in anticipation of their coming. Only the chosen will be spared—and you are one of them, destined to play a special role in what is to be. That is why I seek to save you."

Nye glanced up as the door opened. Jody entered, revolver in hand. The bearded man closed the door, then moved with Nye to the opposite end of the room where the statues brooded in shadow.

There was a whispered conversation; then Jody nodded and started towards Kay. He was still holding the weapon.

"Turn around," he said.

"What—?"

"Turn and face the door."

His voice remained level but the revolver was raised in command and Kay obeyed.

She stood there sensing Jody's presence directly behind her, then felt something cold and hard pressing between her shoulder-blades. *He's going to kill me,* she told herself.

Abruptly the pressure subsided. "No sweat, lady," said Jody. "Relax."

Kay turned as the bearded young man lowered his weapon. She glanced past him, seeking a glimpse of his companion, but all she could see was the semicircle of statues looming up from the darkness along the far wall.

"Reverend Nye—?"

"He cut out."

That was obvious. But how had he left? The door was locked and there was no other exit from the windowless room. Kay's glance met Jody's grin.

"Don't worry, he'll be back. Wouldn't split without you. No way."

No way. But there had to be a way. Kay forced her fear aside and concentrated on the reality. Nye was gone and Jody was here to guard her until he returned. And then—

"Where are we going?" she murmured.

"On a trip. You dig tripping, lady?"

He was stoned, no doubt about that. But she believed him. Nye would be back soon to take her away. He'd promised to save her—for what?

Kay didn't want an answer. But the only way to avoid it was to act now, before Nye returned. *There has to be a way—*

She peered down at the floor, then started forward.

"Hold it," said Jody. "Where you going?"

"My purse—here on the floor. I want to get my things." It was hard for Kay to keep her voice steady, hard to move. But she had to, and she did.

Stooping over the purse, she began to scoop up her belongings. Jody moved up beside her, watching as she gathered the scattered items which had spilled from it—handkerchief, compact, mirror, perfume, key-chain, pen, pencil, notepad—and dumped them back into the bag. As she did so she placed the heavier objects on top, unhooking the clasp of the compact with her fingernail. Obviously she had no weapon here and she could sense Jody relax as she lifted the bag and rose.

Then, turning, she swung the open bag forward, smashing it against Jody's face. A blinding spray of powder exploded from the open compact, and Jody's arm flew up to shield his eyes from the whirling keychain and the sharp points of the pen and pencil.

As he did so, Kay lunged against him to wrench the revolver from his grasp. Coughing, Jody clawed at her, his face contorted.

Kay wasn't conscious of pressing the trigger but she must have, because suddenly his face was gone; in its place, a gushing crimson mass receded as he toppled back to crash upon the floor.

Nothing had prepared Kay for the sight—nor for the smell—nor for her own reaction. She turned, stomach churning, the revolver slipping from her fingers as she gripped the side of a display-case for support.

For a moment she stood there until the retching subsided; then panic propelled her across the room to the door.

It was locked.

And the lock had no keyhole.

She stared down with numbing realization. Jody had closed the door when he came in; a deadbolt must be locking it from the other side.

There had to be a way. Carefully averting her gaze from the sprawling figure beyond, Kay turned to pick up the revolver from the floor, then moved to the door again. Standing at one side to shield herself, she took aim at the lock and squeezed the trigger.

Click.

Again she squeezed and again the clicking echoed. The revolver was empty.

No way.

She glanced across the room, staring into the darkness where the gods of Egypt crouched and stood, leered and mocked.

Slowly she crossed to them, peering at stone-snouted Sebek, bronze-beaked Horus, the metal maw of brazen Bast. And from above, on his high pedestal, Osiris fixed his eye upon her.

Nye had been standing here when last she saw him. Here, beside Osiris, Lord of the Dead.

The wall behind the statuary was solid and unbroken. Kay ran her fingers across the old stone surface and it did not yield. There was no secret exit here. *No way.*

She turned, gazing again into the eye of Osiris, Ruler of the Underworld.

Underworld.

Kay glanced down into the shadows behind the pedestal,

almost tripping over the projection before she saw it. The metal ring looped forth from the iron circle set flush with the floor.

Stooping, she grasped it; the heavy rounded lid was perfectly counterbalanced so that it rose swiftly, silently, effortlessly.

She dropped to her knees, staring into the dark opening below. This was the way Nye had left, through a trapdoor. No steps, just a series of rungs forming a ladder.

But where did it lead to?

Kay took a deep breath, then grasped the topmost rung. Slowly she began to lower herself into the Underworld.

Down. Down into darkness, down into dampness. Kay descended cautiously along the metal ladder, moving one hand at a time to establish a firm grip on either side, then lowering her feet to seek support on the next rung beneath. The rungs seemed to be spaced about two feet apart, their flat upper surface narrower than that of an ordinary ladder. *Thank God I'm not wearing high heels,* she told herself.

The light from the trapdoor opening above grew fainter as she continued her descent. She kept count of the rungs—*thirty-one, thirty-two, thirty-three*—wondering how much further there was to go. But knowing when they would end was of no consequence. It was *where* they would end that mattered.

For a moment she paused, clinging to the ladder in the sable silence. There was nothing to see, nothing to hear, and she felt lost; without sight or sound she could only rely on tactile sensation. The metal rungs were cold to the touch, and the air fanning her face and forehead was moist and chill.

The breeze billowing up from below had to come from somewhere outside the pit. If Nye had left by this route, it must lead to an exit.

Slowly, steadily, Kay resumed her efforts. The light from above contracted to a pinpoint, then winked out. She ignored its passing and concentrated on keeping count. And it was after reaching the sixty-sixth rung that her right foot moved down to rest upon a solid surface of stone.

This would be what—a hundred and thirty feet? But that's thirteen stories down! Kay tried to remember the height of the cliffside on which the museum rested. She must be at the base, close to actual sea-level here. And now, as she strained to listen, it seemed as though she could hear a far-off muffled booming, repeated at regular intervals; the sound of waves beating against rocky walls in the distance.

She had to be in a passageway of some sort, but there was no clue as to its dimensions or the direction in which it led. She could only follow the current of air moving directly across her face, follow it to its source. And if the booming sound grew louder it would mean she was coming closer to the exit.

Kay released her grip on the metal rungs and instantly regretted it. Now she stood alone in the darkness; once away from the ladder she'd never be able to find it again.

She turned and extended her arms, seeking to touch the sides of the opening in which she stood. Her left hand struck against something solid which projected outward at shoulder-level and Kay felt her fingers close around a knob or lever. It moved forward with a faint *ping,* and then she blinked as sudden light lanced her pupils.

A dim fluorescence flooded forth from overhead and she could see its source—the roof of the tunnel opening before her here at the base of the ladder.

The narrow aperture seemed to be cut from solid rock; it was perhaps four feet in width and six feet high. Tubular fixtures were set at regular intervals along a sheathed conduit extending along the ceiling of the passageway, revealing rough-hewn walls winding forward. Their rocky surface was moist and mottled by dank greenish patches of lichen growths.

It was a man-made cave, no doubt of that, and obviously an ancient one. But the lighting was just as obviously a recent addition, and the levered wall-switch she had brushed against was an incongruously modern fixture.

At that moment recollection flashed; the unbidden, unwelcome memory of the subterranean passageways in Lovecraft's story, *The Shunned House.*

Kay shook her head. It was time to focus on fact, not fancy, and right now only the air was important. The air flowing from the tunnel mouth and emanating from a source deep within. There had to be an exit beyond the passageway.

She moved forward without further hesitation. The corridor was clammy and the smell of the sea was everywhere. The echo of her footsteps blended with the cadenced booming of waves beating against the outer walls. As she had thought, the tunnel wound and twisted its way through rock; soon Kay lost all sight of the opening behind her. From time to time she encountered smaller openings on either side, as though the entire cliffside was honeycombed with caves and passages, but she ignored them and concentrated on following the central, lighted route. The constant draft of air from ahead held promise and she began to quicken her pace.

It was not until she was quite well upon her way that Kay sensed the gradual change in the *quality* of the sound. The echo of her footsteps remained constant, as did the muffled roar of the surf beyond, but now there was something else—something which filled the intervals between the pounding onslaught of the waves. It was a sound of movement; not from without but from *within*.

Kay paused, peering forward. The shadowed corridor stretched emptily ahead. She could see nothing moving there, but now as the rushing of unseen waves subsided, the ensuing silence was again broken by the other, fainter noise. What did that remind her of?

Rustling. Insidious scurrying. Racing rats—Lovecraft's words. And his story, "The Rats in the Walls."

Something cheeped and chittered in the distant shadows, but the noise came from behind her.

Kay turned, glancing back along the passage. The far-off floor was deep in shadow. But shadows do not slither and squirm. Shadows have no eyes.

She saw them now, darting in the distance; thousands of little red eyes glaring up from a moving mass covering the passageway behind, thousands of bloated black bodies scampering forward in a swarm pouring out of a side-opening to choke the central corridor. Now she could hear the sharp claws scraping against the stone, smell the stench of the wriggling horde padding down upon her.

Kay began to run, and the living shadow raced behind her,

tiny talons clicking. The creatures were gaining, coming closer; now they were only yards behind her, readying to pounce and leap. Fanged mouths opened, squealing in unison, shrilling their hunger. The hunger of the rats, the rats in the walls—

She saw the side-opening ahead just in time; the doorway set in a narrow niche to her left. As she raced towards it the frantic furry forms surged at her heels. Kay turned at the threshold, freezing in panic at the sight of slitted eyes, hairy muzzles, the pointed yellow fangs roped with strands of saliva. A great gray rat leaped forward, launching itself at her right leg. Kay kicked out, screaming, then ran through the aperture, wheeled and tugged at the heavy door which stood ajar against the inner wall.

For a moment it resisted and she fought to force it forward as the rat horde shrieked and scuttled across the threshold.

Then the door swung shut with a clang; behind it she heard the thumping of bodies, the mewings, the squeaking. But the door held firm. It was a very modern, man-made barrier of machined metal, expertly hung on shiny hinges. Kay stared at it for a moment, panting, fighting for breath and composure. Only then did she turn to gaze around the room.

And it was really a room she stood in now, not a natural cavern or hollowed-out cave. The squared-off walls of the huge chamber were obviously the work of skilled artisans, fluorescence poured from man-made ceiling slots set symmetrically overhead, and the humming which rose around her indicated the presence of machinery operating from some unseen source.

Air-conditioning? The notion seemed absurd, but that's what it sounded like—the steady, persistent drone of a giant air-conditioner at work. And it was cold in here, much colder than the damp corridor outside.

Pulse steadying, Kay found final confirmation of human artifice in the contents of the chamber spreading before her. The long open aisle leading to another door at the far end was lined on both sides with solid rows of metal boxes or compartments. Each was four feet high, two feet wide and perhaps seven feet long; their flat upper surfaces were covered by what seemed to be aluminum sheathing. At a quick guess there must be several hundred of the containers standing row on row.

As Kay started down the aisle between them she noted the snake-like coils of tubing winding through each box at its base, linking them together. The humming rose around her, drowning out the noise of the creatures in the outer corridor, but this new sound held a disquieting note of its own; a rhythmic pulsation like the deep throbbing of a gigantic heart.

Kay quickened her pace, doing her best to ignore the sound rising from either side. But she could not ignore the increasing chill and her sudden shiver of involuntary response.

The cold issued from the boxes—hundreds of refrigerated boxes like the storage units of some huge freezer-locker.

Impulse impelled her to glance at a unit to her right; curiosity brought her to a halt and caused her fingers to grip the icy metal handle extending from the thin aluminum sheath covering its contents. The sheath must have rested on runners at each side, for at her touch the covering rolled back to reveal what lay beneath.

It was only another protective layer, this time of thick, clear plastic, but it was quite transparent. And staring down she saw what was contained in the box beneath.

Winding wires, tangled tubes, spiralling through a cloudy liquid that bubbled and shimmered; the strands coiled and twisted to termination in clamps that clung to the form floating within—the smiling corpse.

It was the naked cadaver of an elderly man, gaunt and emaciated, lying face upwards in the milky solution that bubbled against the pipestem limbs, the bony rib-cage, the trailing fingers of fine white hair framing the sunken cheeks.

The box held death. Writhing amidst the wires like a monstrous marionette, the bobbing corpse grinned up through the seething swirl.

And its eyes were open.

Kay did not scream. She stood there, letting the cold flood through her, inhaling the ammoniac reek, as the senseless words burst upon her brain.

That is not dead which can eternal lie—

Lovecraft's phrase. And, again, his story. "Cool Air," that was the one, about the crude effort to prolong and preserve life by artificial refrigeration more than half a century ago.

Prolonging life—that was a theme he'd hinted at over and over again. That, and the theme of ancient survivors, resurrected or undying, in "He," "The Festival," "The Terrible Old Man." And that other old man, the cannibalistic creature of "The Picture in the House."

But this thing in the box was not nourished by blood, or by primitive methods of preservation. Here was the modern reality of cryogenics. Frozen flesh, thwarting decay in suspended animation, hibernating against the day of revival.

And in the other boxes—

Kay peeled away the sheaths of surrounding compartments at random, knowing what she must find; each box contained another corpse. Here was a middle-aged man, sleek and smiling, cheeks bulging with an obscene plumpness far more hideous than any emaciation. There, the tiny form of a child, twisting and turning amidst the tubes that fed its frozen veins against desiccation and decay. And a young girl, very much like herself; blue lips shaped in a secret smile, glassy eyes mirroring the dreams that come in death.

How many hundreds huddled here, cryonic captives awaiting the summons to rise?

Kay turned away, hastening to the door at the far end of the aisle, praying that it wasn't locked. Whatever lay beyond could be no worse than what lay here in this chamber.

To her relief the door responded easily to a tug at its handle, opening out to reveal another dimly-lighted corridor stretching ahead. She paused at the threshold for a moment, welcoming the flow of warmer air against her face.

And the air was indeed flowing. Which meant she was again headed in the right direction. Somewhere beyond the tunnel was the exit she sought.

Kay started along the passageway. Its dimensions were very much like those of the one she had traversed and the lighting was similar. As she hastened forward the humming sound subsided, and there was no repetition of the rustling. Again she found herself passing niches, other doors set in the sidewalls of the corridor. She tried to keep from thinking about what might lurk behind them and did not pause to investigate. Instead Kay centered her concentration on the moist breeze which filtered from somewhere ahead, moving towards it in eager expectation.

Now the corridor slanted off to the right and she followed it, noting that the pitch of the rocky floor was gradually slanting upwards. This had to be the way out, the path to final freedom. Kay hurried on, conscious of the sound of her own labored breathing. And then—

The *other* sound.

The muted, clanging echo in the distance. The clanging of doors opening on the sides of the corridor behind her.

Kay wheeled, staring back down the length of the corridor, towards the point where it twisted off. The expanse was empty, the distant darkness deserted.

But from somewhere beyond, somewhere past the turning point, the sound swept down upon her, changing even as it continued. The clanging had ceased, but in its place came an unmistakable thud and thump of movement. But, unlike footsteps or the padding of animal paws, the pattern of progression was irregular. The thuds and thumps suggested a sort of hopping, accompanied by other noises of dragging and scraping which held a hideous hint of things that crawled rather than walked.

And now, suddenly, Kay was aware of a rank, fishy odor—a reeking stench sweeping over her from the source of the sound as it grew louder. In a moment her pursuers would emerge into the straight length of the passageway behind, and Kay steeled herself for the sight of them.

Then the lights went out.

Darkness closed around her, and from it came the rising sound—the thumping, plopping, scraping sound of the unseen presences bearing down upon her. But that was not the worst.

The worst was the new element audible from the others, the unmistakable murmur of voices which bore no semblance of human origin; a bestial babel of baying, barking and deep, guttural croaking.

Kay turned and ran—ran blindly with arms outstretched to shield her from collision with the winding walls, feet pounding along the floor of the tunnel which rose at an ever-steeper slant.

The stone surface was wet and slippery now, treacherous with trickles of unseen moisture.

And from the darkness behind the sounds pursued; the flopping, the pattering, the thudding, interspersed with hoarse raspings and gaspings which told of increasing effort to overtake her. The din grew louder, the wave of detestable odor even stronger.

But there was light ahead. Dim light, from a circular opening above—the mouth of the tunnel.

Tensing with effort, Kay flung herself forward, racing to reach the exit's rim. Panting, she clambered up the final sloping stretch. And fell.

For a moment she blacked out at the shock of impact as her body slammed against the slimy stone.

Then consciousness returned as she felt the touch upon her shoulder.

She tried to squirm free, but the touch became a grasp, the grasp tightened to a relentless grip. And over the oncoming babble of wheezing croaks and savage snarls came the sound of the voice.

"Kay—don't fight me—for God's sake, hurry!"

She opened her eyes as Mike Miller pulled her upright and yanked her through the opening ahead.

The rest was a series of dazed, momentary impressions; lightning visions interspersed with darkness. A flash of the narrow rock-ledge from which the cave-mouth yawned down upon the sea below—a glimpse of the motor launch bobbing in the water—Mike's anxious face peering down at her as he led and lowered her into the boat—the feeling of vibration against her prone body as the engine revved and the launch began to move swiftly out into the sea beyond—a final glimpse of the cavern opening above as the shoreline receded.

Something filled that opening now, looming up from its shadows, flopping, hopping, croaking, bleating, and in a moment it would burst forth. But the moment never came.

Instead there was the roar of the explosion which rained rock and rubble down upon the cave entry from above as the entire cliffside seemed to shatter in a cosmic convulsion. Deafening sound, blinding light, and wrenching movement combined as Kay felt the boat spin violently in the trough of the swelling waves, felt Mike Miller's arms receive her as she fell back.

Then there was only darkness.

Twenty-four hours passed before Kay was fully conscious again, but there were fitful moments of awareness punctuating the period preceding. Memories of those moments consisted almost entirely of jolting movement and vaguely identifiable sounds.

The sound of the launch-engine wheezing its way to shore—the feeling of being led, half-stumbling and half-supported, to a waiting vehicle—the reassuring warmth of Mike's shoulder as she lurched against it in the seat of a speeding car—the sensation of being carried from that car into a place where other engines throbbed—pressure against her eardrums as the throbbing rose, and renewed pressure when it later descended to a drone—once more the feeling of being carried and of another ride in a vehicle with Mike beside her—finally, a reeling progress which ended as she sank onto the grateful softness of a bed. And now, inevitably—

"Where am I?"

Opening her eyes, Kay stared up at Mike as he stood beside the bed in a circle of lamplight.

"My place," he said. "You're in Washington."

"But how—?"

"We'll talk later. Right now Dr. Lowenquist wants you to rest." As he spoke, Mike took a bottle and glass from the end-table, pouring the contents of one into the other. "Here, drink this."

Kay drank and surrendered to slumber. This time there was no consciousness of sensation and, mercifully, no dreams.

When she awoke again Mike was there, and the end-table beside the bed held a tray of covered dishes. To her surprise she realized she was quite hungry, and perfectly capable of sitting up and feeding herself.

The meal further revived her strength and helped to clear her head for the conversation that followed. Together they fitted the events of the past two days into place.

Mike's surveillance team at the museum had indeed been

caught by surprise and disposed of, just as Nye had told her. But in spite of his precautions he'd not counted on anyone covering the site from the sea below, and thus Mike was able to locate the cave exit by launch and come to her rescue.

"And the explosion—?"

Mike shrugged. "Nye must have arranged to mine that passageway, planted some kind of triggering device to activate it under sufficient pressure. Lucky you avoided stepping on it yourself—when it blew, the whole cliff went up, taking the museum out too. I understand the force broke windows all the way from Santa Monica to Oxnard. There's a crew working at the site now, but they'll never dig down far enough under all those tons of rubble to find anything."

"What happened to Nye?"

"When he left you he must have gone straight to the Starry Wisdom Temple. A least that's what we figure, because just about the same time the cliff went up, all hell broke loose on South Normandie."

"Another explosion?"

Mike shook his head. "Fire. But so sudden, and so devastating that there's no doubt it was prearranged. The entire building was gutted in a matter of minutes. And this time there were casualties—at least a half-dozen bodies have been found, according to last reports."

"Including Nye's?"

"We don't know. The victims were incinerated, burned beyond recognition. Some of his people, no doubt about that, but I don't think Nye had any intention of suicide. He was just making sure that there'd be no evidence left behind."

Kay frowned. "Evidence of what?"

"We can use your help in answering that." Mike seated himself on the bed beside her. "Think you're up to telling me exactly what happened the other night?"

"I'll try."

"Good." Mike pressed against the surface of the drawer beneath the surface of the end-table. There was a faint clicking sound.

"What's that?"

"Built-in recorder. We've been monitoring you, just in case you happened to talk in your sleep." He grinned. "Sometimes this cloak-and-dagger stuff can come in handy. Mind if I start with a few questions?"

Kay nodded. "Go ahead. Maybe we can make some sense out of all this."

But what Mike asked and what she answered seemed to make no sense at all. Not until Kay herself took over the questioning— and then Mike's replies made the sort of sense she was not prepared to hear, let alone accept.

"You guessed right about 'Cool Air,' of course," he told her. "Whether or not he got the idea from Lovecraft, it looks like the cryonics installation was part of Nye's grand design. He must have promised some of his wealthier converts the gift of future resurrection and survival when the Great Day came. For example, we already know that Elsie Probilski disappeared shortly after donating the museum and cliff property to the sect. We've traced her as far as a private clinic outside Mexico City where she was undergoing some form of unorthodox treatment for terminal cancer. She left there suddenly several months ago and dropped out of sight completely. Chances are it was Nye's doing; I'd be willing to bet she was one of the cryogenics subjects in the installation you saw."

"And the rats—?"

"I'm willing to blame coincidence for that, rather than Lovecraft. Those tunnels were a natural sanctuary for them. From what you say, the entire cliffside must have been pitted with caves and passageways—Nye's people merely made use of a few and added the necessary improvements to serve his purposes. And again, according to your experience, it wasn't only rats that took refuge there. Those others who pursued you—"

"Please." Kay shook her head quickly. "I've been thinking about that. Maybe I was wrong."

"How so?"

"I told you how frightened I was. Perhaps it was my imagination, playing tricks. What I heard could have been some of Nye's people, assassins, as you call them, instead of—"

"Instead of what?"

"I don't want to talk about it."

"Then let me." Mike's face was grim. "You were thinking about Lovecraft again. About his story, *The Shadow over Innsmouth*. And the things rising from the bottom of the sea to mate with men and spawn half-human hybrids."

"But that's just a legend—like mermaids. No one has ever seen any creatures like the ones he described."

Mike shook his head. "Lovecraft said the offspring look human enough at first. It's only in maturity that the change begins and they're forced to go into hiding. Suppose that cave-riddled cliff beside the sea was such a hiding-place? A refuge for things that hop and creep and croak. You heard them—"

"I heard noises, yes. But I saw nothing."

"Be grateful for that."

Kay stared at him. "Meaning that you have?"

"Perhaps." Mike nodded slowly. "That explosion didn't go unnoticed. The whole cliff wall just sheared off and dropped into the sea. So there was nothing police or fire-fighting units could do when they arrived except to cordon off the area. Coast Guard cutters were alerted immediately for offshore patrol and they stood by ready to salvage whatever might float up to the surface. One of them got lucky—or unlucky—and found something.

"But before there was a chance for any flap to develop, our people took over. They confiscated the finding, packed it in dry ice, and flew it to our lab here for examination and testing. I had a look just a few hours ago."

Kay raised herself on one elbow. "What was it?"

Mike hesitated, then took a deep breath. "A body. Part of a body, to be exact. The head and torso were almost intact but arms and lower limbs were missing and the facial features had been blown away. What remained seems human, at first glance. It was one of the pathologists who pointed out the significance of the formations of either side of the neck. He identified them as rudimentary gills, then corrected himself."

"They weren't gills?"

"They weren't rudimentary." Mike nodded. "Tests indicate these organs were in a state of partial development, with evidence of continuing growth. Other tests showed blood characteristics which don't correspond to any known classification.

"The subject—that's the way they referred to it—didn't drown, but there was water in its lungs. And the lungs themselves don't conform to normal physiology; it's as though they were adapting to functional gills. There's a preliminary orthopedic report too, indicating other changes in bone structure. Anomalies, I think the technical term is, involving the spinal column. And something about atrophy of the rib-cage. Naturally there's hell to pay; right now everyone involved has his own theory. All I can say is thank God the face was destroyed.

"But they're ready to proceed with a full autopsy and dissection, and once they get a look at the heart and other organs I'm afraid there won't be any further doubt."

"What happens then?"

"Nothing, if we can help it. All the lab personnel will be detained under tight security. That may help us stall for time, but we can't keep the lid on forever.

"The news media caried the explosion story and it's taken a lot of doing to keep the area off-limits to television camera crews. The Coast Guard search is being conducted under wraps and they're still patrolling, though so far nothing else has surfaced. The next step will be to send down divers, though I've got a hunch they won't be able to get through the rock-slide. At least I hope so."

Kay nodded. "If you can keep the story from leaking there won't be any panic. And even if it does get out eventually, at least the danger will be over."

"I wish it was that easy," Mike said.

"What's that supposed to mean?"

Mike rose, moved to the end-table, extending his hand, and the recording device inside the drawer clicked off. "Dr. Lowenquist will be stopping by soon to check on how you're doing. See if you can sleep now until he gets here."

"Aren't you going to answer my question?"

"As soon as Lowenquist says you're ready to be up and around, we'll set up a meeting."

"Meeting?"

"With my people. That's why they wanted you here in Washington—they have questions too."

"But it's the answers I'm interested in."

"So are we." Mike nodded. "The problem is, there may not be any answers."

The next morning Dr. Lowenquist gave the word and Kay got out of bed, pleasantly surprised at how well she felt. She was even more surprised to discover that her clothing and personal effects had arrived, neatly packed, awaiting her needs.

Any irritation at the invasion of her privacy was soon offset by the pleasure of selecting a fresh outfit and making herself presentable for the coming meeting. Mike Miller had notified her to be ready by seven that evening; he arrived promptly after she finished the meal brought in by one of the security men an hour earlier.

Strange how quickly she'd become accustomed to their presence and to living under such measures. It was only thanks to such measures that she was living at all.

Kay was suddenly aware that she'd never fully expressed her gratitude to Mike; she wanted to do so now, but sensed he was in no mood to listen. After their initial exchange of greetings he led her downstairs to his car and immediately switched on the radio, as though deliberately creating a barrier of sound between them. Something was troubling him, no doubt about that, but whatever it might be he seemed determined to keep it to himself.

Rain pelted the windshield as they drove out of the city, and Mike devoted his full attention to the evening traffic inching along the slick-surfaced expressway. Settling back in her seat in seeming surrender to the soft sounds issuing from the speaker, Kay stole a sidelong glance at her companion.

Questions and answers. That had been the substance of their previous conversation together. But wasn't it the substance of all conversation—the substance, really, of all relationships? Life itself was merely a brief period of speculation between the two great unanswerable questions; the mysteries of birth and death.

Nor was conversation itself a satisfactory medium of communication. Take Mike, for example: like most people he had not one, but several, mutually distinct modes of speech. At times he used the vernacular, much as she did herself. But he was capable of employing a totally different vocabulary when discussing Lovecraft's work and Nye's involvement with it.

Nye had the same verbal versatility, ranging from street talk to evangelical oratory or the scholarly terminology of Lovecraft himself.

How differently people spoke in plays or films! There a character was identified by the uniform consistency of his conversational style. But in reality one's language, like one's thoughts—like one's actual personality-pattern—was infinitely more complex.

Words offered only a partial clue, and were equally useful as a cover-up. Reverend Nye was a perfect example, with his role-playing; she had no idea as to what motivated the man, how much of what he said was true, how much of it he really believed in himself. For that matter, the same applied to Mike. Hadn't he deceived her when they met? And later, pretending to be frank, he'd withheld most of what he knew about the danger.

But words aside, one thing seemed certain. The danger existed. And the question remained. Just what *was* that danger?

In Kay's preoccupation she'd neglected to notice where they were going. Glancing up, she was surprised to see that they'd left the expressway and moved presently along a rainswept country road. Looming in the headlights before them was a wire-fenced area behind which she caught a glimpse of a one-storey factory building. Now the car halted at a gate and Mike dimmed his lights in signal to the security guard who emerged from a cubicle to admit them. As the lights came up again they beamed across a wooden signboard lettered Pinckard Salon Furniture.

The car rolled up the driveway beyond to halt directly before the building entrance. Mike left the car and Kay joined him as he crossed to the door and pressed a night-buzzer. It swung open— activated, she realized, by electronic control—and he nodded at her to enter, taking her arm.

Again the thought of danger crossed her mind, but Mike's grip was firm. She stared ahead into bright light, steeling herself against anticipation of sudden shock.

To Kay's surprise she found herself in an actual furniture factory. There was no mistaking the nature of the lathes and machinery. Although the assembly-line was deserted, the smell of fresh sawdust attested to its recent operations, and behind a glass-walled section at her left she could see the cluttered confines of the upholstering department. Office cubicles lined the right wall, but Mike led her past them and down the aisle to a freight elevator housed in the rear wall.

"Aren't you going to tell me where we're going?" she murmured, as they stepped onto the platform.

"Down," he said.

The door clanged and they descended. Once more the question came—what was the danger?

Five levels below she found the answer.

The conference room was large, well-lit, and amply supplied with communications equipment. Kay noted the screen on the right wall for motion picture or slide projection, a screen on the left for closed-circuit television viewing. At the far end hung a huge map of the world; beneath it a recording console in which a tape-unit spooled silently.

The long plastic-topped conference table in the center of the open floor-space had individual microphones set before each of the twenty seats bordering its circumference. Eighteen of these seats were already occupied save for two near the head; when Kay and Mike took their places the last vacancies were filled.

The steady drone of conversation was not interrupted by their arrival, nor did they seem to be the object of any special scrutiny. No introductions were offered or exchanged, and Kay could only glance curiously at her companions.

The inspection added to her confusion. She found no consistency in the appearance of those present—they ranged from men of Mike's age to the very elderly, and there were two other women here, both gray-haired and rather dowdily-dressed. No one's garments offered any clues; if some of the men were scientists they weren't the pipe-smoking white-smocked types familiar to every viewer of monster-movies. Several of them had the rigid posture and stern expressions associated with high-ranking military personnel, but they wore no identifying uniforms. And at least three of the younger men were as hirsute as any of Reverend

Nye's followers; their jackets and jeans seemed as nondescript as the drab business suits of the others.

Now she turned to question Mike, preparing to raise her voice above the buzz of conversation around the table. But suddenly the sound subsided to an anticipatory hush, broken only by a few nervous coughs.

A tall, baldheaded man seated at the far end of the table beneath the wall-map now rose, rapping for attention. Any uncertainty as to his ranking position here was dispelled by the presence of an imposing array of file-folders and bound documents heaped on the tabletop before him, and his words affirmed his authority.

"Most of you don't know one another," he said. "And quite a few of you don't know me. But I'm not going to waste time on introductions."

"What's important is that I know you—from your reports, transcripts, taped conversations, depositions and dossiers." He gestured at the folders and documents stacked before him. "This is only a fraction, a small part of what we've processed over the past two years. The amount of material we discarded—the false leads, unsubstantiated testimony, hoaxes, crackpot ravings and outright nonsense—would probably fill this room, even on microfilm. But what remains has been studied, researched, computerized, subjected to every test of authenticity. And verified.

"That's why you're here. Because each and every one of you has contributed validated data to this investigation—an investigation many of you didn't even know existed."

The tall man's eyes moved from face to face around the table as he spoke. "Some of you have academic backgrounds in a wide variety of disciplines—literature, anthropology, archeology, astrophysics, geology, advanced parapsychology. Each of you has done individual research which has been brought to the attention of this agency. Because of the nature of that research, a number of you were called in, questioned, and asked to proceed with further study along the same lines. At the same time you agreed to refrain from airing or publishing your findings, to act in the utmost secrecy."

There were involuntary nods and murmurs from a number

of the listeners around the table as the tall man paused, then continued.

"Each of you who cooperated felt that your work was unorthodox, open to question by the so-called scientific establishment and, above all, unique in its field.

"And so it was. But what you didn't know is that your companions here this evening—other scholars and researchers, working in entirely different and seemingly unrelated areas—were engaged on similar undertakings. And that their theories, their experiments, their experiences, all had a bearing on the same subject."

More murmurs, this time indicating surprise, interrupted the speaker. He gestured for silence.

"One more thing your individual efforts had in common—the belief that you had, each in your own research, stumbled upon something not only new and unprecedented but also dangerous. In a word, a possible threat to national security.

"You were correct."

The murmur rose again and the tall man rapped for attention.

"This is not an opinionated value-judgment, a hastily determined conclusion. Your data, as it came to us and was fed through the computer, formed a growing pattern. But it was not a complete or even a recognizable picture. What we had, in effect, were a number of pieces of a jigsaw puzzle which seemed to fit together. Even so, there were gaps, blanks, missing portions.

"That's when the operation was upgraded, expanded to bring in military aid and the services of our own security personnel. What they found were the linkages—linkages in fields far beyond the scope of your own special attention. Linkages dealing with such seemingly disparate matters as international terrorist activities, political assassination, geophysical irregularity and upheavals, epidemics of psychosis, and the rise of religious cult-movements such as those described on the taped conversation between a young woman and one of our agents which was played for you here earlier this evening."

Kay felt herself reddening as she realized the reference, but Mike's hand on her arm offered reassurance.

"Two years of teamwork, two years of group effort, two years of fighting political and bureaucratic interference—but at last the pieces have come together and we've got a picture. A picture so disturbing, but so graphic and unmistakable, that there is no further doubt or dissent from official sources. They are fully convinced, as are we, that what has been shown them is the truth. A truth which must be faced without further delay.

"As a result you've been brought here as members of a special task-force, part of an all-out operation now officially designated as Project Arkham."

Arkham? Kay tensed at the sound of the word. Wasn't that—

"A stupid label." The tall man shrugged. "Then again, perhaps not. Because it symbolizes the work of Howard Phillips Lovecraft, whose name and writings are familiar to you all."

Again the speaker paused and again there was a reaction of surprise from his audience; a reaction shared by Kay. Was it true—did everyone here know about Lovecraft? And if so, how and why?

"From the very beginning some of you who were already familiar with his fiction noted certain parallels with the phenomena you brought to our attention. This was our first inkling that all of the data submitted seemed to be part of a larger pattern. As we proceeded, additional reports were offered by people who knew nothing of Lovecraft. It became our policy to see that his work was made known to them—because what they offered as fact corresponded to what he had written as fiction."

Kay glanced at Mike. He nodded, expressionless, as the speaker continued.

"Thus you're all aware that Arkham is the name of the New England town serving as the background for many of Lovecraft's stories. Like other place-names in his work—Dunwich, Kingsport, Innsmouth, Miskatonic University—it has no existence save in his imagination.

"The same holds true for the book of sorcery and black magic mentioned in his tales, the *Necronomicon*. Lovecraft himself denied its existence. But we cannot rule out the possibility that it did exist at one time—perhaps under another name, which Lovecraft concealed for obvious reasons. Of one thing we're quite certain; he wasn't writing fantasy, even though it appeared so at the time.

"Remarkable progress has been made in the physical sciences during the past half-century. Some of the people responsible for the most recent advances and discoveries are seated here at this table. Let me cite a few examples, without mentioning names.

"In his short novel, *At the Mountains of Madness*, Lovecraft describes an Antarctic expedition which stumbles on the ruins of an ancient city in an unexplored mountain area—a city once seemingly inhabited by alien creatures who came from the stars.

"When he wrote this tale, Antarctic exploration had scarcely begun, and there was no reason to believe any advanced life-form had ever flourished in this frozen wasteland. Since then we've learned a great deal more about continental drift—massive disturbances which in remote times caused actual polar shifts—glacial epochs involving tremendous changes in climate—periods lasting millions of years, during which Antarctica was a tropical region. It is now accepted that life may have indeed existed here in prehistoric times, and in forms completely alien to our own. More recent surveys reveal the possibility of warmer regions still to be found behind mountain barriers, perhaps even under the polar icecap itself.

"Lovecraft's city may be here, under the plateau he called Leng. The unexplored region of Australia he describes in 'The Shadow Out of Time' may offer up its secrets. As to the aliens he describes—in the light of unexplained but verified UFO sightings we've had access to, we can no longer dismiss the possibility of their presence, either in the remote past or today."

A pudgy little man whom Kay could only describe as thick—in form, features, and accent—shook his head impatiently from his seat across the table. "But Herr Lovecraft nowhere speaks of space-ships," he muttered.

"Not directly, perhaps," the tall man said. "Still, one must consider the implications." He turned to point at the map behind him. "The enormous so-called meteorite which theoretically exploded near the Stony Tunguska River on the Siberian plateau in 1908 left no crater at its impact-site and no traces of the fallen object itself were ever found. More recent investigation tends to confirm the theory that some sort of atomic-powered spacecraft may have exploded directly overhead when entering the friction of our atmosphere at high speed. Lovecraft himself used a meteorite as a possible vehicle for an alien life-form in 'The Colour Out of Space,' but perhaps he was purposely attempting to disguise what he knew. Other extra-terrestrial creatures are represented in his stories as flying to earth on membranous wings, their bodies impervious to the hazards of outer space, their minds sealed off for infinite light-years during the journey—surviving because of a different subjective time-sense, alien-structured physiological patterns, and a tremendously lengthy life-span.

"But there are other ways to account for interstellar or inter-galactic journeying, and Lovecraft didn't neglect them. He wrote about gateways between dimensions and of passages for return-ing to this dimension in other areas of space or time. The current constructs in astrophysics—black holes, white holes, anti-gravity and anti-matter—were apparently anticipated in his work.

"And maybe he wasn't anticipating. His story, 'The Dreams in the Witch-House,' links modern science to ancient witchcraft, suggesting that certain spells and incantations actually embody mathematical principles to bring about temporal and spatial interchanges. In other words, the alien life-forms once regarded as demons could be summoned, not from hell but from outer space, other dimensions, other points in time, by means of spoken rituals designed to alter the vibrational frequency and structure of matter and its interrelationships.

"Some of you here have done advanced work on field theory in this regard. Others have investigated parapsychological phe-nomena—even so-called black magic—which leads to the same conclusion.

"Through certain sources we were able to set up an exchange of information with the Soviet laboratories engaged in the same research, and their findings correspond to ours.

"So much for the scientific aspect of Project Arkham. If that was all we had to consider we might shrug it off as irrelevant. And, in passing, pay our respects to the intuitional brilliance of Lovecraft—that most aptly-named of all writers.

"Unfortunately, there's another angle we've pursued with our own people; one which involves the military, political and geo-physical disasters which threaten us in real life, today."

Ignoring the murmured response from his audience, the tall man picked up a sheaf of notes from the tabletop and turned to the map behind him.

"What I tell you now is classified information. Only a small portion of it has been reported in the news media during recent months, and in such instances the actual details were suppressed or glossed over. In many cases these details were not apparent until we investigated. Fortunately, no outside agency or observer has yet found the common connection between them all; it remained for us to establish the links."

His bony forefinger jabbed at various points on the map as he spoke.

"Item—terrorist activity." He read from his notes. "The assassination of Fuentes in Argentina on July 9th, of the Shah of Iran on the 23rd, the unsolved disappearance of the leaders of three African republics between July 15th and 27th. In August, the attempt on the life of the French Minister of Justice on the 1st, the apparent death by drowning of the putative heir to the Spanish throne on the 10th, the allegedly accidental death of two members of the Politburo on the 18th. The plane crash which wiped out the lives of five United Nations delegates from the so-called Arab oil countries on September 2nd, the September 11th report of the sudden death of China's Number Two man in the Peking government, the assassination of Hoffman in West Germany on the 25th and of Salvador's president on the 29th. The murder of India's conservative party-leader the week following, the supposed suicide of our own Senator Portright on October 8th—"

He paused as voices rose around him, then turned and rapped once more for order.

"I could go on, but I think these examples are sufficient. Apparent suicides, alleged accidents, unexplained disappearances, unsolved murders and outright assassination attempts. In only four of the latter instances were the perpetrators apprehended. Three were shot down on the spot and the fourth killed himself before he could be questioned. None were definitely identified, and no terrorist group has come forward to claim credit or responsibility for the crimes. The death of world leaders and persons in key governmental positions remains a mystery."

Kay glanced at Mike as the tall man moved to the map once again. Mike nodded, then directed his attention to the speaker.

"Item—the South Pacific. Volcanic activity reported or observed during the past several months in the area between the Equator and south latitude 46°, west longitude 131° to roughly 150°. I'll spare you the dates and cite only few major instances, for seismic disruptions occurred somewhere within these perimeters on an almost daily basis. A major quake, followed by unprecedented tsunamis, inundated the so-called Gilbert and Ellice Island group. Similar disturbance led to the Manihiki disaster and set off a chain of major destruction in the Celebes area, Ceram, Timor and Tuamoto. Renewed temblor and tsunami activity wiped out every man-made structure on Easter Island last week, tumbled every standing statue, and left no known survivors. This latter has not been publicly revealed—nor has the typhoon which hit Pitcairn two days ago. Early reports from rescue-mission flights have, and will be, suppressed. Over half of the population is dead, and the remainder either seriously injured or in a state of trauma which one medical officer equates with acute paranoid schizophrenia.

"Accompanying these phenomena during the same two-month period are other classified instances involving the disappearance of light planes, fishing boats, motor launches, and cargo vessels. Our present information is incomplete, but we have reports on no less than seventy-nine such occurrences."

One of the gray-haired women at the table looked up quickly. "The Bermuda Triangle!" she said.

The tall man shook his head. "I'm talking about the same Pacific area in which the quakes occurred. Of course the Caribbean could be one of their secret lairs too."

"Lairs?" A mustached elderly man frowned at the speaker, his eyes narrowing.

"I use the term advisedly. The Caribbean—Antarctica—the northern Siberian plateau—the Himalayas—underground caverns in our own state of Maine—Lovecraft hinted or specifically wrote about them all. But his main concern, and ours, is the South Pacific. The area he identified most precisely in 'The Call of Cthulhu.'"

"You're evading my question." The mustached man was on his

feet now, glaring. "These lairs you speak of—'advisedly', as you put it. What about them? Are we to presume you believe they are actually inhabited? And if so, by what? Aliens? Extra-terrestrials? The monstrosities that Lovecraft wrote about in his stories? You say his main concern, and yours, is the South Pacific. All right, let me put it to you straight and you can give me a straight answer. Are you saying that Cthulhu really exists?"

There was a moment of shocked silence; all eyes were on the speaker as he met the gaze of his challenger.

"We don't know," he said. "But that's why you're here, all of you. Because we've got to find out."

Suddenly the room seemed icy cold. Kay felt herself shivering; the shimmering effect began, and everything wavered as though seen underwater—far underwater, where the feasting fish fastened on the corrupt corpse-flesh, then fled before the coming of creatures neither fish nor men; they in turn circled and slithered off as the waters churned and the sea-floor shattered before the coming of Great Cthulhu—

She fought to focus her eyes and attention on the tall man as he continued.

"I brought you here because I need your reactions, your evaluations, additional data which you may have previously ignored but which may have a bearing on the problem, now that you understand its scope. I need your expertise, your cooperation, your help—and I need it now.

"Every one of you has been given a liaison officer and security protection. You have been individually assigned to custody situations throughout this area. For the time being I ask you to respect this arrangement. A few of you already know some of your companions because of previous professional contacts in the course of mutual research. But please do not identify yourselves to anyone else here at this briefing; do not fraternize or compare notes.

"I have scheduled separate interviews for all those present over the next forty-eight hours, and your liaison will be informed of the time assigned you. When we meet privately I trust you'll each be prepared to answer further questions in depth and offer any suggestions or additional data you believe will be of help. At such a time you may be asked to continue working alone, or in some cases, to join forces with others here. In the latter instance, the necessary introductions will be made then.

"This much I can tell you now. Whatever the nature of your particular professional function, its requirements have been anticipated. We have set aside the funds, the manpower and the physical equipment and will supply whatever is needed to carry on your efforts. The entire resources of this government are at your disposal.

"Now I'm going to ask you to return to your separate quarters and await further instructions. I think you've heard enough to understand the reasons for these precautions, the necessity for secrecy, and the urgency of our concern.

"Let me leave you with this final thought. What we know is called science. What we do not know is called magic. And what we must determine, in order to survive, is whether or not these two are actually one and the same."

Twenty-four hours later the tall man came to Mike's apartment for a private interview with Kay.

She still hadn't learned his name, and even now there were no introductions, though his manner was friendly and direct. Pulling a pipe from his pocket he settled in a wing chair, nodding at Kay and his host.

"Everything under control? Good enough. I know this arrangement's been awkward for you both, but it's important we keep a low profile." He smiled at Kay. "Putting you into a hotel would have raised a few problems—the minute anyone checks in with a security guard detail, the word is bound to leak out."

"I understand," Kay said.

"Then let's get down to business. You've been of great help to us, Mrs. Keith. From what we've been able to check out through your testimony, we're now satisfied that your ex-husband and his friend Waverly played the role of innocent bystanders in this affair. At least I can set your mind at rest on that point. What few indications we have seem to show that they got involved through accidental circumstances and were eliminated before they learned too much."

"Are you telling me that Nye killed them?"

The tall man lit his pipe. "We have reports on his whereabouts and activities during much of this period—enough to satisfy us that he was neither in Boston nor the South Pacific at the time they disappeared. But it's reasonable to assume he gave the orders to dispose of them."

"What could they possibly have known?"

"I have no firm answers. But we suspect Waverly went to Boston to investigate something concerning Lovecraft. And that made him a potential threat to Nye.

"As for your late husband, his trip to the South Pacific indicates that he knew or guessed a great deal more about the cult. We now think he may have actually been searching for R'lyeh itself. And that he was destroyed when he found it—just as Lovecraft's characters were destroyed when they found similar lairs in his stories. I refer you to 'Dagon,' and 'The Temple.'"

"I still can't accept it," Kay said. "Even knowing what happened to me."

"Then consider my position." The tall man puffed on his pipe. "How do you think I feel, standing up in front of hardheaded scientists and military personnel and admitting the realistic basis of black magic? Not just admitting, by God, but insisting that they believe?"

"And they do," Mike murmured. "Because of their own experiences."

"That's just it." The tall man nodded. "Everything ties together. And Nyarlathotep holds all the strings."

Kay remembered her earlier conversation with Mike. "Do you really think Nye is Nyarlathotep?"

"Consider the facts." The tall man tapped the residue from his pipe into an ashtray. "According to Lovecraft, Nyarlathotep is black, and the prophecy says he will come out of Egypt. We don't know Nye's origins, but we can't rule out that possibility. We do know he fits most of the description; red robes, strange devices and all, preaching the end of the world to people who come away not quite understanding what they've heard."

"So he created himself in the image of what he'd read."

"That's the obvious conclusion, and I wish I could go along

with it. But what about the rest of the circumstances—earth-quakes, tidal waves, all these sudden natural disasters combined with man-made disasters in the form of world-wide terrorist activity? It could be coincidence, of course, but it certainly sounds like Lovecraft's description of what will happen when the Mighty Messenger appears."

"Then you believe the rest will happen too—the end of the world—?"

"I didn't say that. What I do say is we must consider the possibility of what we're up against and prepare to deal with it, even if it means admitting that the legendary Old Ones may really exist."

"But I can't—"

"Why not? Think about it for a moment." The tall man pocketed his pipe. "Throughout recorded history mankind has had many cosmologies, many gods. I'm not talking of savages now but about our most advanced civilizations. The Greeks and Romans with their pantheons, the Egyptians bowing to their bestial-headed immortals, the devotees of a hundred Hindu deities—billions of true believers have worshipped outlandish entities. Let's get down to modern monotheism now. What do the Moslems actually base their beliefs on? Merely the word of a camel-driver who claimed Allah was the one true god and appointed him as the one true prophet. Much the same holds true for Gautama and Buddhism, Moses and Judaism, Jesus and Christianity. In most instances a nobody sets himself up as preacher, and either he or his followers incorporate the new religion in a book which they say is the product of divine dictation. And it works. Men do believe, millions upon millions of them.

"But where's the proof? These great religions were accepted almost entirely on faith. We have facts."

Mike faced the tall man. "Then what's the next move?"

"There are many moves. We're not neglecting any of them. One team has already been assigned to crack the linguistic problem—the words, phrases, place-names, proper names in all of Lovecraft's works. We've always assumed these were neologisms of invention—now we're not so sure. We're trying to relate them to possible parallel references in the standard grimoires and black magic rituals, spells and incantations in all known languages.

Maybe there's a common denominator and if so it would help if we could find it. The philologists on this project are using a computer backup because we need quick answers."

He nodded at Mike. "Your people, of course, are conducting the physical investigation, with full cooperation from CIA, FBI and public law enforcement agencies. Working under wraps we've pooled our data with Interpol to set up raids on known and suspected terrorist groups here and abroad. By tonight we'll have completed a full-scale sweep of Starry Wisdom members. I don't think we can net any of the principals but it's worth a try. What we're hoping for is that interrogation may give us a lead on Nye."

Mike shrugged. "You won't keep a lid on the situation if you go that route."

"We'll do what we can, but right now we're fighting the clock. Any public reaction to the raids is nothing, compared to the wholesale panic that could result if we don't take such steps to prevent what may happen next. If R'lyeh was thrust forth from the sea by these earthquakes and something slumbering there awakened, it must be stopped."

"How?"

"I've just cleared with Ermington at the Navy Department." The tall man glanced at his watch. "In exactly thirty-eight hours, our reckoning, a nuclear sub will be dispatched from a Pacific base. Objective, south latitude 47° 9', west longitude 126° 43'. Operational orders—seek and destroy."

Mike frowned. "Do they know what they're going up against?"

"The commanding officer will be briefed, of course, but we can't rely entirely on that. I've requested permission to assign an observer to the mission with special-consultant status."

"Someone you can trust?"

"I hope so." The tall man rose. "You'll leave for Guam in the morning."

The bedside alarm went off.

Kay stirred, then reached out and prodded Mike.

"Time to go, darling," she murmured.

Darling. A strange word, falling self-consciously from her lips. But as Mike turned and his arms tightened around her, the strangeness vanished.

What had happened last night now seemed both inevitable and very right. And what was happening presently seemed right too, except—

A sudden image rose unbidden; cattle moving up the ramp in a slaughterhouse, mounting one another blindly and compulsively even as they were driven to the death waiting within.

"No!" she whispered, pulling away.

"What's the matter?" Mike stared at her, puzzled. "Don't you love me?"

"You know I do." Kay freed herself and sat up quickly, hands cupped to push back her tumbling hair. "There isn't time."

Of course I love him, she told herself. Groping for a robe in the grayish light, rising, moving into the kitchen to put on coffee while he shaved and dressed, she repeated her affirmation. This was real, more than mere physical release, more than a one-night stand with some singles-bar stranger. But how did he feel about it; what did it mean to him?

She didn't have an answer, and she found none in his face as they sat at the breakfast table.

"Why so quiet?" he said. "Tell me what's bothering you."

"Nothing." She sighed. "Everything. I wish none of this had happened, that you weren't going—"

Mike's hand reached out to hers. "If it hadn't happened we'd never have met. And you know I have to go. But in a few days I'll be coming back."

"And then?"

He shrugged. "What do you want—a formal proposal?"

"Darling!"

This time the word came easily. And from then on, even at the last moment when she went with him to the door and he held her close, there was no longer any doubt.

But when he left the fear returned; returned and remained.

Not for herself—she was safe enough here and Mike's replacement lent a reassuring presence. He was a soft-spoken Southerner named Orin Sanderson, and Mike had greeted him warmly when he appeared to take up his post.

"Orin's a good man," he told her. "Don't let that Kentucky gentleman act fool you. He's the kind of pussycat who turns into a tiger when you need one."

Certainly he was polite enough, and mercifully unobtrusive. He'd been ordered to stay in the apartment on a round-the-clock basis while others stood guard outside on rotating shifts, but there was never any question about keeping his distance. Though he took his meals with her when they were sent in, he kept out of her way during the rest of the day. Most of the time he sat reading on the living room sofa where he spent the night. Since Kay discovered a well-filled bookshelf and a portable television set in the bedroom she had no need to join him. The knowledge of his presence was comforting enough.

Still, the fear stayed with her and could not be dispelled. It peered over her shoulder when she read, squatted beside her before the TV set. And it grinned at her directly every time she looked at a clock.

Ten P.M. What time would it be now in Guam? Had Mike arrived yet? Was he there now or had the sub already departed on its mission? How far was the run to the target area, and just exactly where was it located? The latitude and longitude mentioned by the tall man at the briefing meant nothing to her.

Here it was, thirty-six hours or more since Mike had left, and no word had reached her. But time passed somehow and Kay knew where it went to. The fear was feeding on it, gobbling up minute after minute, gorging and growing.

Words on the printed page no longer conveyed a meaning and images on the picture-tube blurred. On the second evening she found herself rummaging through the contents of the bookshelf and tossing its contents aside with mounting impatience.

The sound of her activity brought Orin Sanderson to the bedroom door.

"Anything wrong, ma'am?"

"I was just looking for an atlas or an almanac. Something with maps in it."

"Now don't you go fretting over that."

"Couldn't we send out for one?"

Sanderson shook his head. "Sorry." He consulted his watch.

"Maybe it would help if I told you they're almost at target area now. With any luck everything will be wrapped up in a few hours. If they stay on schedule they should be back at base again some time tomorrow morning."

"Will they call and let us know?"

"We'll get word when the time comes." Sanderson nodded gently. "Now just you simmer down. I fixed a pot of coffee—"

Kay managed a smile. "No, thanks. I'll be all right."

"Why don't you turn in? Best thing for you right now is a good night's rest."

So Kay went to bed, but not alone.

The fear crawled under the covers beside her, and in the dark she could feel it lying there cold and still, lying in wait to embrace her, drag her down into dreams and the deep. The deep, far below the surface of the sullen sea, where in his stone house at R'lyeh, dead Cthulhu waits.

She fought the fear but the dreams came and she found herself there in the depths, floating amidst the titanic towers of tumbled temples, weed-encrusted and foul with the stench of age-old ichor. Through eon-old emptiness and the silence of uncounted centuries she sought for a vanished presence but nothing remained except the miasma of an ancient dread. Then ahead there loomed the gigantic fissure in the sea-floor, and beyond it the immense jumble of jagged rock rising to pierce the surface far above.

Now she was rising too, moving upwards past the crazed configuration towards the point where a portion of the stone citadel reared unbroken, soaring beyond ink-black waves into an ice-gray sky. And its outlines kept melting and changing shape so that she could not define its semblance or size or perceive anything of its portals save that they were open.

Closer she came, nearing the enormous entry, peering into the yawning darkness, her fear mounting at the thought of what she was soon to see. Nothing could surpass that fear, or so she thought, even as she stared.

But she was wrong. The greatest fear was yet to be; it came upon her now as she gazed beyond the parted portals, gazed deep into the house of Cthulhu rising above the water, gazed into the abode of evil and found it—

"*Empty!*"

The scream burst from her lips as she awakened; awakened to the sudden blaze of lights in the bedroom and the sight of Orin Sanderson moving towards her through the doorway.

"Ma'am—?"

"I had a nightmare." Kay raised herself on one elbow, pulling the covers up in a self-conscious gesture as she strove to still the trembling. "Don't worry—I'm fine now."

"Good. I was going to wake you anyway. The call just came through."

"Call?"

Sanderson nodded. "It's all over. Mission accomplished."

"What happened?"

"No details. But Mike can tell you all about it when you see him."

Kay wasn't trembling now. She sat up quickly, unmindful of exposure. "How soon will that be?"

The security agent smiled. "My orders are to escort you back to Los Angeles. He'll be coming in some time tomorrow. I gather the chief of operations will be on hand to meet him there and get a firsthand report as soon as he arrives."

"Wouldn't you think he'd come here directly instead?"

Sanderson smiled. "I've been in this line of work twelve years now, ma'am. So far all I've learned are two things."

"What are they?"

"Don't think. And don't ask questions."

Kay did her best to follow Sanderson's example, but it wasn't easy. There was so much she wanted to know, so much she wanted to understand. Had her last dream been precognitive or symbolic of reality? The empty crypt beneath the awesome opening—did that mean Cthulhu had been destroyed? Obviously so, if Mike was returning. She remembered Lovecraft's story; how the ship had rammed the monstrous creature, ripping its slithering shape asunder, only to have its substance recombine. Still there were no nuclear weapons in Lovecraft's day; now even alien life-forms couldn't withstand atomic disintegration.

Don't think about it, don't ask questions. Besides, there isn't time.

Kay packed hastily as Sanderson busied himself on the phone.

Whatever had happened didn't affect security precautions, she noted. Sanderson's car was tailed by a second vehicle manned by other agents; it followed them all the way to Dulles International. There it halted as Sanderson drove through an inconspicuous service-gate at the far end, halting before an unmarked hangar staffed by men who wore uniforms without insignia. The Lear jet poised for departure waited, and it too was devoid of any identifying markings.

There was no direct communication with anyone in the ground crew; Sanderson merely nodded to them as he led Kay directly up the boarding ramp and into the plane.

The entry-way closed behind them immediately and the ramp was wheeled away; already the craft was throbbing as though impatient for takeoff. Up front behind the cabin door the pilot, copilot and navigator were completing their final checkout but the spacious passenger area was deserted.

From the looks of the elaborate setup—kitchen, portable bar, radio and television combination unit, conference table, even a bedroom compartment in the tail—Kay guessed the jet customarily carried top military brass or government officials, served by a full staff.

Confirmation came from Sanderson as they taxied down the runway. "Too bad we're not carrying the usual service crew," he said. "But the less people involved, the less risk."

"Don't apologize," Kay told him. "I'm happy just to be going home." She settled in a lounge chair as they took off and in moments the plane was smoothly airborne. "How soon will we get there?"

"Estimated flight time is approximately three hours." Sanderson stifled a yawn and she glanced up at him.

"Tired?"

"Just a smidge." He grinned. "That sofa in the apartment was a little on the lumpy side."

"There's a bedroom in back. Why don't you get some rest?"

"What about you?"

"I'll be perfectly comfortable here." She gestured toward the radio-television unit, then at the coffee-table before her. "Look—they've even supplied newspapers."

Sanderson blinked. "I'd be breaking orders."

Kay shook her head. "Not breaking—just bending them a little. Go ahead. I promise to wake you in plenty of time before we land."

"Thanks, ma'am." Sanderson turned and moved towards the compartment, this time making no effort to conceal his yawn.

Kay watched him as he went. No wonder the man was tired; he'd been on duty day and night and the strain showed.

Now that the danger was past she could feel it herself, but fatigue was counterbalanced by adrenalized anticipation. Mike was safe and in just a few hours now they'd be together. Now she must relax.

Reaching down to the coffee-table she picked up the latest editions of the *Post* and *Times*. Maybe there'd be some story or at least a bulletin, however censored or disguised, which would give some clue as to what had happened.

She found nothing. Apparently the security lid was still clamped on, or had been at the time the papers went to press.

Tossing the papers aside, Kay decided to investigate the radio-television unit. But when the fading musical program was interrupted by the crackling voice of an announcer, his message was addressed solely to hemorrhoid sufferers. And the flickering television screen offered nothing but the black-and-white images of the Bowery Boys.

Kay leaned back, closing her eyes, then opened them quickly as she felt herself surrendering to sleep. No sense taking chances.

No sense. What a change had been wrought in the meaning of that phrase! A week ago none of this would have made sense to her, and thanks to government security—censorship, really—it still wouldn't make sense to most of the world. People would go on as before, listening to hemorrhoid commercials and watching old B movies just as though nothing had happened. The Great Old Ones would never disturb their dreams.

Of course she had no proof that her dreams came from such a source, nor even a theory as to *how* they came. But the conviction remained. Somehow the dreams were a method of communica-

tion between the alien presences and mankind. Not all men were
capable of receiving and recalling their messages; only those
gifted—or cursed—with a certain form of creativity.

Wasn't that what Lovecraft had tried to convey in "The Call of
Cthulhu?" That sensitive artists, sculptors and painters in particular, responded to such dreams and reproduced their memories in
clay or on canvas?

And what about Lovecraft himself? Were such dreams the
source of his own knowledge? Was he hinting as much when he
wrote about the nightmares of his supposedly imaginary characters? If so, that might explain everything.

Kay stared into the dusk beyond the cabin windows and
nodded to herself.

In the light of what she herself had experienced it *could* make
sense. Even in the mundane world of skeptics and scoffers there
were records of many whose dreams were not like those of other
men—so-called "psychic sensitives" such as Edgar Cayce. Their
slumber-visions seemed somehow to link them to sources of
alien awareness.

Had Lovecraft been such a man? By his own account he'd
dreamed vividly throughout his entire lifetime. And he himself
admitted that dreams were frequently the direct source of his
stories.

Suppose that the psychological explanations of his work were
correct—but that cause and effect had been reversed? Scholars
suggested that an allergy to seafood may have led him to write
fantasies such as *The Shadow over Innsmouth*. But maybe it was the
other way around—what he wrote was the truth which came to
him in dreams, and it was his fear and hatred of the sea-creatures
which prompted his aversion to seafood in waking life.

Kay nodded to herself. If true, the pattern was all too clear.
Those same scholars tried to link his Antarctic tale with his physical reaction to low temperatures. But couldn't that reaction be
psychosomatic? Couldn't it be that frightening dream-glimpses
of Kadath in the Cold Waste resulted in a dread of cold extending
into his daily existence?

And his much-debated dislike of "mongrel" infiltrations from
Europe, Asia and Africa—how much of this stemmed from

dreams of hybrid presences spawned by the mingling of men and aliens? How much came from knowledge of those who secretly worshipped the entities he encountered beyond the wall of sleep?

Perhaps his "mongrels" were symbolic. And his preoccupation with ancient houses, ruins and graveyards, with the creatures of superstition emerging from such settings—suppose this was not based on a fear of death but on a fear of certain forms of *life*? Because the dreams told him that death is *not* the end—there are things which continue to exist in an ageless half-alive state, things which can be summoned forth again. *That is not dead which can eternal lie . . .*

Kay frowned. Was this how it had happened? Did Lovecraft dream true? Did he augment his knowledge by secret study and further research in waking hours? And were his stories actually disguised warnings? If so, such warnings had finally been heeded, just in time.

Time. Kay glanced again through the cabin windows at the darkened sky. Looking at her watch she was surprised to see that almost three hours had passed. She'd promised to wake him before they prepared to land.

Rising, she started up the aisle to the compartment. Physical movement was a reassuring reminder of reality—or what she accepted as such. How had Jung put it? *The Individual is the only reality*. Meaning that everything is a matter of subjective interpretation. Here she was, forty thousand feet in the air, travelling at a speed faster than sound. Would Lovecraft have accepted this as reality fifty years ago? Only with difficulty—and perhaps what she now found difficult to accept in his writing was also valid.

Kay opened the compartment door and peered into the cubicle where Sanderson sprawled face down upon the bunk-bed.

He was so still, so motionless, that for a moment her heart thudded in sudden dread. Then, to her relief, she heard the faint rasp of breathing.

She reached down and touched the agent's shoulder. "Wake up," she murmured.

He stirred and turned over, eyes blinking. "Sorry to disturb you," Kay said, "but it's almost time."

"Thanks."

Sanderson smiled and swung his legs over the side of the bunk. Rising, he moved to the doorway and followed her back into the main cabin.

Kay watched as he lowered himself into a seat. "We should be landing soon," she said.

"There's still time." Sanderson gestured across the coffee-table. "Sit down."

She nodded and complied. "You really must have been tired. Feel better now?"

"Much better. What were you doing while I slept?"

"Trying to get my head together. Thinking about Lovecraft and some of the things he wrote."

"Lovecraft?"

Kay nodded self-consciously. "Sorry. We haven't discussed him, have we? I don't suppose you know what I'm talking about."

Sanderson smiled. "What do you want to know about Lovecraft? He was telling the truth, of course. It's Nye who distorted it."

Kay leaned forward. "You know about him, too?"

"Enough to realize that what he preached to the Starry Wisdom people was revised to suit his own purpose. Actually mankind wasn't in existence when the Great Old Ones came to colonize the earth. Take a closer look at the story of creation in various religions. Almost all of them say the same thing in different ways. God, or in some versions, a group of gods, created man.

"And that's what really happened. The Great Old Ones were here first. The world they ruled must have been much different than the one we know today—and when it changed, in convulsions which crushed continents, they fled into other dimensions. But some remained, submerged beneath the sea or trapped under mountains of ice; physically powerless but psychically potent.

"It was then they created life as we know it, both animal and human."

Kay met Sanderson's stare. "But why?"

"For food."

"But that's—insane!"

"Insanity is merely man's reaction to a reality he cannot face. Now you know why Nye concealed this from his sect. If they guessed the real reason for their existence they wouldn't follow him or do the Old Ones' bidding. But it's true. Azazoth, Yog-Sothoth and the others, created lower life-forms and animals to devour each other, and all these became the food of man. And man, in turn, is here only to feed the Great Old Ones.

"Not physically, you understand. The Great Old Ones aren't nourished by flesh—they feed on human *emotion.*

"This is the source of their strength. And the most powerful, the most satisfying of these emotions is fear.

"Men were bred for fear, just as they themselves bred plants and animals selectively for their own most desirable qualities. From time to time new strains were added to what mankind in its vanity calls the human race. Matings were arranged with certain alien life-forms—the sea-creatures, the so-called spawn of Dagon, are an example. There have been other unions with the winged beings from the outer rim of the galaxy, and sometimes such experiments succeeded. The blending of blood resulted in hybrids with a heightened capacity for emotional response.

"Naturally, most men were unaware of all this—do you suppose their own animals know that they are used as food or even bred as pets for sheer amusement?

"But sometimes hints come to them in dreams. The legends of incubi and succubi emerge from nightmare glimpses of such matings. And the mutations which result live on, explaining the myths of vampires, werewolves, creatures half-beast and half-human. How many times have you remarked upon people whose faces bear a resemblance to some animal? This is not coincidence, nor is the appetite for cruelty and torture and mass-murder which we dismiss, wrongly, as 'animal' behavior.

"All such attributes increase fear, and throughout the ages the Great Old Ones have feasted upon it, gaining strength to stir, to break through the barriers, to rise again upon the earth and claim it as their own.

"And always a few men have guessed or discovered the truth. Those who learned little called their knowledge magic, sorcery, witchcraft. And those who knew all—through dreams and inspiration communicated to them by the Great Old Ones—have kept the faith. They worship and help speed the day when the Old Ones return.

"Never before has the world been as full of fear as it is now. Never have the worshippers been so powerful and purposeful. The waiting and planning is at an end, for the Great Old Ones are strong again and their time has come. The stars are right and the way is open at last."

Kay listened in growing bewilderment; once again she reminded herself about the inconsistency of speech, how people varied their vocabularies to fit the situation. Even so she'd never imagined the hardheaded but softspoken Sanderson could talk like this.

Her reaction must have been evident, for now Sanderson gestured quickly. "Please forgive me. I didn't mean to upset you, Mrs. Keith."

Mrs. Keith.

He'd never called her that before; it was always "ma'am." There was no reason for the change, unless he himself—

She rose involuntarily, unable to control her expression or her words. "You're not Orin Sanderson!"

His silent smile was answer enough. Kay took a step back, eyes widening.

"But how—?"

"The exchange was made while he slept." The smile never wavered. "Perhaps you may recall another Lovecraft story—"

"'The Thing on the Doorstep!'" Kay remembered it only too well. A witch, a woman whose blood bore the taint of the sea-creatures from Innsmouth, took over her husband's body in place of her own. "Then it's true, all those legends about demonic possession—"

The smile broadened. "Really, Mrs. Keith!"

"Who are you?"

"Merely one of the many who serve."

Kay turned and ran to the front of the cabin, tugging at the door. It didn't budge.

As she pounded on it, the figure of Orin Sanderson rose.

"You're wasting your time," he said. "I did not come alone."

She turned, eyes widening. "You mean the pilot and the crew are—?"

"It is not necessary to be asleep in order for the exchange to take place." He nodded. "Don't be alarmed. We are here to protect you on your journey."

"But why? We'll be landing in Los Angeles in a few minutes."

Still smiling, he glanced out of the cabin window to his right. Kay peered past him, gazing down—and it was there, far below, that she found the answer to her question.

They were flying over an endless expanse of open water.

Almost endless.

Kay must have fainted, for she was no longer aware of the passage of time as she rested on the lounge. At intervals she opened her eyes to find the familiar figure of Orin Sanderson seated beside her, then closed them again at the sound of the words and phrases issuing from his lips.

The whispered fragments filtered through.

"Nye's plan . . . you'd been Keith's wife and he had to make contact, find out how much you knew . . . totally ignorant, of course, but when you got involved with Miller it was too late to let you go.

"Followed you . . . that meeting in Washington . . . luckily we learned of the seek-and-destroy mission in time. But someone had to be chosen . . . you were ideal, he said . . . take over the plane . . . risk . . . not dealing with a Lavinia . . . he insisted . . . written in the stars . . . all precautions . . . even if something does go wrong, the essence will be preserved . . ."

When the needle-point of the syringe entered her arm Kay didn't feel it. She blacked out again, and her next recollection was of staring through a cabin window as the plane began its descent, circling the rocky land-mass thrusting up from the sea below.

Numbly she glanced at the figure beside her as he spoke, anticipating her question.

"Rano Raraku," he said. "The crater of an extinct volcano—you see it? Just behind the Poike promontory."

"But where are we?"

"Easter Island."

It was like something heard in a dream, and she seemed a part of that dream as she heard herself reply.

"The place of the statues—I remember seeing pictures—huge stone heads standing and staring out at the sea."

"I'm afraid they're not standing now. Most of them tumbled down when the quake hit last week, and the tidal wave did the rest. The village at the west end was levelled. Hundreds of people, thousands of sheep—all gone, washed away."

"But there's someone there now!" Kay felt herself coming awake again as she stared down. "I can see light—"

"Torches, guiding us in." He gripped her arm. "Better sit down. We may have a rough landing."

For a moment she was fully conscious, fully aware, and fully frightened.

"Why are we here? Tell me—"

He forced her down into a seat, held her as she fought him, fought the fear. The numbness returned; from far away she heard the sound of her own screams rising amidst the roar of reversed-thrust as she sensed the bumping, shuddering shock of the plane's touchdown.

As they lurched to a skidding, skittering halt she sank back, welcoming the numb sensation because it insulated her from the fear. Maybe it was a dream after all—it *had* to be a dream.

Kay was quite calm now as the Sanderson-shape guided her from the cabin and helped her down the rope-ladder dangling from the exit door in lieu of a landing ramp.

The three members of the plane's crew were already waiting there below and she was relieved to see their uniformed figures and quite ordinary faces. Perhaps Sanderson had lied to her—surely these young men didn't appear altered in any way.

The others assembled there, the group of men with torches, were obviously Polynesian and orientals. They were wearing nondescript seaman's garb and their speech was unintelligible, but nothing in their demeanor gave cause for alarm. Indeed, their voices hushed as she came into the circle of torchlight and they stared at her in a manner which suggested an exaggerated respect, almost a reverence.

"Come along now," said Sanderson—*it has to be Sanderson*, she told herself—"He is waiting."

And then he was guiding her away from the slippery open

stretch where the plane had landed, leading her past clusters of tumbled, dripping boulders and great open fissures in the stone surface which slanted upwards to the slopes beyond.

Following them came the others, carrying their torches. Their progress was silent, and as they wound their way along an avenue of rock the plane behind them disappeared from view.

Now there was nothing but the night; darkness and desolation and the faraway sound of wind and waves lashing against the stony shores below.

Suddenly another sound arose; the voices of those behind. Again she could not distinguish words or phrases, but the cadence was unmistakable. They were chanting. Chanting as they clambered upwards, torches flaming against the sable sky. An image came to her—the image of a religious procession. That's what it was; a pagan ritual, a journey to some secret shrine where a secret presence waited—

"Peace and wisdom to you!"

She recognized the voice even as he stepped out from the shelter of the rocks before her.

Reverend Nye gazed down at Kay from the slope ahead, his tall form flickering in the flaming torchlight. He was dressed in black and his face was black. Now, as he raised his hands in greeting, she saw that they were no longer gloved.

As he gestured upwards and outwards she saw what those gloves had always concealed.

The palms of his hands were black too. Not pink, but solid black.

Kay stared at them, stared at him.

The Black Man.

The Black Man of the witch-covens, the Black Man of the legends. Nyarlathotep, the Mighty Messenger.

It wasn't a dream. He was real, and she was here, and Mike—

Did she scream the words or had he read her thoughts?

"Miller is dead," he said.

Then she did scream, but he went on, giving no heed.

"All those who sought to destroy R'lyeh were themselves destroyed. No matter, for we came here to wait. Now you are here and the time is here to bring chaos out of order."

This wasn't street-talk, the language of a political assassin, or even the rhetoric of the flamboyant preacher-man—not when spoken here in this place of darkness, not when it issued from those black lips—

And his lips *were* black, Kay realized. She'd never noticed them before, never glimpsed the black tongue curling within the black cavern of his mouth.

"This is the hour!" the Black Man cried. "For now the stars are right!"

The black fingers rose, stabbing at the sky, and Kay stared upwards, her eyes fixed on the stars—the stars which were not fixed.

Not fixed, but whirling. Whirling and wheeling and moving and melting, so that the familiar patterns merged in new configurations of cold flame.

The Black Man's hand stretched forth to still the murmur that arose, and he glanced past Kay, nodding quickly. "Abbott," he said. "You and Sato will prepare and conduct her—"

Kay turned as the Sanderson-figure moved away. But now two others advanced on either side to grasp her shoulders tightly. One was tall and ruddy-faced; the other, squat and swarthy.

She struggled, but their grip was firm and their hands stripped away her clothing until she stood naked in the circle of torchlight.

The Black Man lifted his arms.

"Behold the bride!" he chanted.

And from behind her the voices rose in response. "Behold the bride!"

Then, somewhere in the darkness, a drum sounded. Sounded and boomed as the stars blazed down and Mike was dead and she was shivering with shame and cold but they held her fast as the Black Man beckoned, turning to lead the way.

Now they were forcing her forward, dragging her up the slope of Rano Roraku past rows of toppled statuary—the great stone heads with pegged bases, guardians of the crater above. Kay fought and twisted, but could not free herself. They half-carried her towards the rim as the carven faces loomed on every side— strange faces with upturned noses, scornful lips, and no eyes. *What was it that even stones were not meant to see?*

The drums thundered and the voices chanted, and past the crater ahead she could see the jagged outlines of the Poire promontory beyond, looming through a veil of mist.

Was it mist or miasma? Now the odor welled forth, nauseating and overpowering, a sea-stench swirling over her bare body, enveloping it in a reek of corruption which suffused her senses. Behind her the drums boomed, the torch-bearers echoed their endless litany.

"Behold the bride!"

Kay reeled and stumbled, dazed by the mingled waves of sound and stench. Frantically she closed her eyes, striving to shut out sight and sensation, but the echo of the chanting remained. *Behold the bride.*

And another echo now—the voice of the Sanderson-shape as it had whispered to her on the plane. *Someone had to be chosen . . . you were ideal, he said . . . risk . . . not dealing with Lavinia . . .*

Lavinia?

Suddenly she remembered the name and its source. Lovecraft's story, "The Dunwich Horror." The half-witted albino girl, Lavinia—who became the bride of Yog-Sothoth.

Kay opened her eyes, and as she did so, the foggy curtain ahead began to part.

Something moved in the mist.

It rose—huge, black, oozing and bubbling forth from the great volcanic crater where it had watched and waited—its squamous shape silhouetted against the stars as it wriggled up and out, flowing towards her.

A single glimpse caused her to scream so loudly that she did not hear the drums, the chanting, or even the sound of the approaching planes overhead.

They flung her forward.

Then the writhing appendages extended to embrace her, and she knew no more.

III

SOON

Mark Dixon was in the hotel lobby phone-booth talking to his city editor when the shooting started.

"Hold it," he said.

Turning, he glanced through the plexiglass door, then ducked involuntarily as another shot sounded.

Heller's face scowled out at him from the two-way. "What's going on?"

"The Mayor," Mark said. "He just arrived—." Raising his head cautiously, he peered through the glass as a fusillade erupted from the lobby beyond. "Someone's shooting at him—up on the balcony—security people moving in to cover—can't see—"

"Get down and let me look!" Heller shouted. "You're blocking the screen!"

Mark ducked again, leaving the two-way clear. Heller squinted through it just as the final round of shots echoed. Since the public phone-booth was only equipped with a standard transmitter he had neither depth-focus nor wide-angle, and all he saw was the crowd near the lobby entrance, milling and screaming. Somewhere in the center was the Mayor and his bodyguards.

But now, when the final shot burst from the group, everyone glanced up, screaming. Heller's range of vision didn't include the mezzanine above, but he did see the body toppling over the balcony railing and hurtling to the floor of the lobby below.

Then, as the crowd closed in and the tumult rose, Heller's voice rasped full-volume through the audio.

"Never mind taping, I'm sending a team for full coverage. Just get what you can and get over here—fast—"

"Will do," said Mark.

And he did.

In just short of half an hour he hurried into Heller's office atop the Times News-Center in downtown Los Angeles. The wiry little man behind the desk was already pressing buttons as Mark entered. Everything went off—the two-ways, the intercoms, the TV units, even the screen facing the desk where direct-wire reports snaked unceasingly from the computer read-outs.

Mark had never seen that screen blanked before. Not that he'd had much opportunity. As a junior researcher—"cub reporter," wasn't that what they used to be called in the old days?—he'd only entered this office twice during his year here. For that matter he scarcely ever spoke to Heller himself on the two-way; usually he reported to one of the senior researchers on an outer office desk-slot, and he doubted if Heller remembered him by name.

But all that was changed now.

"Sit down, Dixon," said the city editor. He pressed the recorder-button and nodded curtly. "From the top."

"I got to the hotel early," Mark said. "The banquet was scheduled for noon but at twelve-thirty the Mayor still hadn't showed, so they opened the doors anyway. That was in the Gold Room, on the second floor—the guests were in the foyer, having cocktails. Most of City Hall was there—drinks were free, I guess—I talked to Stanley, one of the press secretaries, and he said His Honor had been delayed—"

Heller gestured quickly. "Stuff it. You came down to the lobby phone and called me. Why?"

"I was coming to that. Stanley said the Mayor might not show. It seems there was another death-threat this morning."

"He told you that?" Heller frowned. "How come?"

"I guess he was unwound—he'd made a few trips to the bar. Nobody else had spoken to him and when I started pressing it just sort of slipped out. It sounded important enough to put in a call to you."

"Details?"

"The threat came at nine, when City Hall opened. Some secretary took the call—they asked for the Mayor, but he wasn't in yet."

"They?" Heller leaned forward. "Who were these people?"

"Only one. Somebody wearing a ski mask."

"Did he identify himself in any way?"

Mark shook his head. "He was monitored, of course, and they did a voice-scan on the filmstrip. It could be someone who'd called before, but they're not positive. Anyhow, the message was the same. Resign or die."

"But the Mayor showed for the banquet anyway." Heller frowned. "Reason?"

"I gather the threat wasn't specific as to time or place. And since it was a political thing, all the party bigwigs there to kick off the campaign, I suppose he thought he had to appear. It wouldn't do to look like a coward when he was going to announce his candidacy for re-election—"

"Stuff that, too." Heller jabbed a finger at Mark. "You go down to the lobby and phone me. You're in the booth—His Honor comes through the front entrance with his security—"

"Six of them, all plainclothes detail. Officer in charge, Lieutenant Eduardo J. Morales. I have the other names written down here."

Heller waved impatiently. "Later. Keep rolling."

"They're halfway across the lobby when the shooting starts. No warning. At first they don't know where it's coming from. Morales pulls the Mayor down and shields him with his own body. Another officer, Sergeant Perez, spots the man on the mezzanine balcony, and opens fire. Then the others see the target and join in. The assassin doesn't try to take cover—just gets off two more shots at the Mayor and Morales, missing them both. Then he's hit.

"He falls forward over the railing and lands on the lobby floor, minus his face. Perez was the man who got him—he was using spreader ammo. It's a miracle nobody in the lobby got hurt."

"Let's stay with the assassin."

"I ran out of the booth and shoved through the mob. Two security men took the Mayor out by a side exit and the rest were clearing the lobby. All I got was a fast look."

"Scan it through."

"White male, brown hair, height around six feet, little on the thin side, dressed in work clothes. He must have sneaked past security with a painting crew—there were paint-stains on his coveralls." Mark Dixon grimaced. "And a lot of blood. The whole front of his face, blown away—"

"Skip the local color," Heller said. "Let's get to the weapon."

"I couldn't. Somebody picked it up on the mezzanine and yelled down that it was an automatic."

"No I.D. on the assassin?"

"If there was, they hadn't found it yet. Like I said, all I got was a quick look before they shoved me out. Officer doing the shoving was a Philip Kaufman. He's the one who gave me the names of the other security people."

"What else did he give you?"

"Nothing. Except that he's positive the assassin was one of the Black Brotherhood."

Judson Moybridge switched off the television and the wall-screen faded as Mark entered.

"Just catching the evening news," Moybridge said. "Shocking business. Shocking. No wonder you sounded so upset." The portly attorney gestured towards the wet-bar. "Can I get you something?"

Mark shook his head. "All I want is information."

"In that case, let's go out to the patio. Shame to waste such a lovely evening."

And it was indeed that, Mark noted, as he followed Moybridge through the French doors onto the poolside terrace.

Here in the deepening twilight he settled himself on a lounger to gaze across the placid pool at the multicolored coruscation of lights blazing beyond and below. It was a magnificent view, and only a man of Moybridge's means could situate himself here above the city for such a nightly spectacle.

Not that Mark begrudged him that privilege. Whatever Judson Moybridge enjoyed was well-earned. It had taken him thirty years as a corporation attorney to elevate him to this hilltop eminence, and he had little else to show for his efforts—neither wife nor family. Unless Mark himself could be counted as family. After all, until he'd turned twenty-one, three years ago, the attorney had been his legal guardian.

Mark looked up at the sound of ice tinkling in a glass; his host had apparently helped himself to a drink from the portable cabinet beside his own lounger.

"Sure you won't join me?" Moybridge said.

"No, thanks."

"Suit yourself." The attorney lifted his glass and swallowed, then set it down on the patio deck. "Now, then. Information. What sort of information?"

"First, you can bring me up to date on that news report. My car radio's out and I haven't heard anything since I left the office. Did they find out who he was?"

"You're talking about the man who made the assassination attempt?" Moybridge shook his head. "Prelim examination indicates his hair was dyed, fingertip pads eradicated by acid, some laryngeal surgery performed recently to alter vocal scans. That, and the absence of clothing labels or anything else that would serve as a clue to his identification, seems to establish him as a professional."

"Was anything said about his weapon?"

"Yes, they mentioned some name, but I wasn't paying attention. I gather it was just an ordinary revolver." He hesitated, noting Mark's frown. "Something wrong?"

"Very."

Moybridge reached for his glass, staring at the younger man as he sat up and brushed thick dark hair back across a tanned forehead. Nice-looking boy. Could have been my own son. Hate to see him tensed up like this. Another sip, and then, "What's the problem?"

"Don't you see? Here's someone who's taken elaborate pains to conceal his identity—a real pro, you say. But when it comes to making his move he acts like an amateur. A professional assassin would take precautions to conceal himself. He'd use a high-powered rifle equipped with telescopic sights and a silencer, or get his hands on one of those new supersonics. But this man just climbs up on a balcony in full view of a hundred witnesses and blasts away with a noisy, old-fashioned handgun. It doesn't make sense. Unless—"

"Unless what?"

"Maybe that's what he intended. He wanted to be seen and heard, wanted to make sure that—whether his attempt failed or succeeded—it couldn't be ignored or hushed up."

"In other words, a psychotic seeking publicity."

"Publicity-seeker, yes. But not a psychotic; at least, not in the ordinary meaning of the term." Mark nodded. "I talked to one of the security officers. He agrees that this was the work of the Black Brotherhood."

Moybridge gulped the rest of his drink. "How often must I tell you—"

"That there is no such thing as the Black Brotherhood?" Mark shrugged. "I know the story—it's a practical joke, a hoax dreamed up by some imaginative trouble-maker, publicized until it became a media event, then a widespread popular delusion used to explain any unsolved crime of violence. You've explained it to me a dozen times. But now I want you to tell me the truth."

"But I've always told you the truth." The attorney rose stiffly, face and voice conveying cold anger. "You read my book. You were still living with me in the old house when I researched it."

Mark nodded. "Those trips you took—the calls to Washington, interviews with government people. I used to wonder what they told you."

Moybridge poured himself another drink. "It's all in the book," he said. "*The Fall of Cthulhu*—doesn't the title itself answer your questions? I proved my point, and since then a dozen others have confirmed the facts.

"You weren't even alive when it happened, all this nonsense about the earthquakes, what they meant and what they produced. It was sheer hysteria—just the old devil-theory, people looking for a scapegoat. But now we know the truth. Easter Island was accidentally destroyed during a thermonuclear weapon test—that's a matter of official record. As for this man Lovecraft, we both know the answer. In the five years since my book was published, other researchers came to the same conclusion. He was gifted, persuasive, and a classic example of the paranoid-schizophrenic."

Moybridge paused to drink and Mark eyed him through the gathering darkness. "I read what you wrote. But where's the evidence?"

"Right before your eyes," said the attorney. "A quarter of a century has passed since those quakes occurred. But in spite of the panic, in spite of all the crackpot prophecies of the crazy cults, nothing happened. The quakes stopped, didn't they? And no slimy monster ever emerged from the sea. We're still here, thank God, safe and sound as always. And now that Lovecraft's work is out of print—"

"That's another thing," Mark said. "With all the interest in this Cthulhu Mythos, you'd think publishers would take advantage of the market. But I can't even find his books in the second-hand stores. Do you suppose there's some kind of government censorship involved—buying up copies and destroying them?"

"I suppose nothing of the sort."

"What became of your copies, the ones I read when you started your book?"

"I got rid of them when I moved here." Moybridge sighed. "Look, there's no point in discussing this any further. I've done my best to answer your questions—"

"All but one."

"Which is?"

Mark stared at the attorney. "Why did you get involved in all this? Why did you neglect your own law practice just to write a book disproving the Mythos theory?"

"I told you, there's no point in discussing—"

"But there is. Because I trust you. I've always trusted you, more than anyone I know."

"Then trust me now." Moybridge moved to Mark; in the darkness his face was a blur except for the sombre eyes. "We used to be so close, until these last few years. I'm not complaining—you're a man now, it was right for you to leave and go on your own. But I've missed you, and I still think of you as my own. It's your welfare that concerns me, now and always.

"That's why I want you to quit this investigation. There is no Black Brotherhood, believe me. But there are political fanatics—dangerous, unprincipled men who exploit the present social unrest for their own ends. They've seized on this old superstition to rationalize their violence. You can't stop them, and there's no point in trying. If you stand in their way they'll destroy you."

Moybridge put his hand on Mark's arm. "Please—for both our sakes—"

Mark stepped back. "You still haven't answered my question. Why did you write that book? What do you know? Tell me why you're so frightened—"

"Frightened?" The attorney's voice was shrill. "I never said—"

"You don't have to. Look at your hand; it's shaking so hard you'll drop that glass. I tried calling you at your office earlier today—they said you haven't been in for weeks. Why are you hiding out up here? Don't you see? I want to help you, but there's no way unless you tell me the truth. Is the Brotherhood after you too?"

"Get out!"

"Please, listen to me. You're in some kind of trouble, I know it. If you're involved in this—"

"I'm not involved. And you're not going to involve me!" Moybridge's voice rose. "Just get out and stay out. Out of here, out of my life, out of this investigation!"

He stood silent then, watching Mark turn and go through the doorway, following his progress across the living room and listening to the sound of the front door closing behind him. Moybridge remained motionless until he heard Mark's car starting and moving off.

Only then did he summon sufficient strength to cross the patio and reach into the portable liquor-cabinet beside the lounger. The way his hands were trembling, he thought he'd never get the cork out of the bottle.

But he managed.

Mark managed too, but it wasn't easy. The headache was killing him, pounding and throbbing through his temples. And his neck hurt too; he had to loosen his collar in order to breathe.

What had happened back there? It wasn't just a quarrel, no sense pretending that. He'd never seen his former guardian frightened before, never seen anyone so disturbed over an abstract difference of opinion.

Only this wasn't just a matter of opinion. And in spite of what Judson Moybridge claimed, the facts were otherwise.

The Black Brotherhood was no invention of the media—it

definitely existed. And the current wave of assassinations and assassination-attempts was too widespread to be dismissed as the work of a few political subversives. There was nothing political about their threats or their predictions of calamities to come.

The arguments Moybridge advanced in his book and repeated in books by other skeptics just didn't hold up. Even with the sudden disappearance of Lovecraft's work and its curious un-availability in reference libraries, there seemed to be a general public awareness of its content; an awareness fostered by the Black Brotherhood's statements and by word-of-mouth revelations.

According to these sources, the official government reports were part of a deliberate cover-up. During the quake-cycle of a quarter-century ago, Cthulhu had actually risen from his slumbers when the sunken city of R'lyeh partially emerged from the sea. He then began a journey marked by the destruction trailing in its wake—ships and planes vanished, entire populations of isolated islands disappeared. Secret missions were mounted; a thermonuclear blast destroyed both Easter Island and the suicide-squadron sent against it.

The story had never been officially confirmed or denied, but it didn't end there.

According to stubborn rumor, Cthulhu had not died. No weapon could annihilate an alien life-form capable of reconstituting its atomic components. The immortal entity had once again found refuge in a secret lair beneath the sea.

And now the various cults which preached his coming had also submerged. In their place was the Black Brotherhood. Black as in magic, not race, Mark reminded himself. Naturally the group must have a normal proportion of non-caucasians—particularly in Los Angeles, where the population was presently twenty-two per cent black, seven per cent oriental and over thirty per cent Hispanic.

Yet no one really knew the cult's components—how many were white, how many black, how many were activist, or mere believers. Probably the actual membership was small, but its influence was expanding and every incident of terrorism added to the cult's strength.

No official denials, no scholarly efforts by men like Judson Moybridge, could stem the rising tide of tension surrounding the concept of Cthulhu's coming. And no action on the part of the law enforcement agencies had succeeded in locating, let alone breaking up the secret sect responsible for the spread of violence and disruption. Not just here but throughout the world, the pattern was evident—bombings, arson, sabotage; the murder or mysterious disappearance of prominent citizens both in and out of public office, preceded by open warnings, as in the case of today's attempt.

No doubt the authorities were staging widespread undercover investigations, but without results. What had once been a minor problem was rapidly becoming a major governmental headache.

Headache.

Mark blinked as the pain pulsed behind his eyes. He rolled down the window for air and the night-chill fanned his forehead. Fog was rolling in from the sea; to his left he saw mist shrouding the expanse of trees and shrubbery behind the walls of Parkland Cemetery.

He had no love of graveyards, but this was a welcome sight—it meant he was nearing his destination. A turn to the left brought him to the little house situated across the street, and he pulled over to the curb at the dead-end.

A moment later he was ringing the bell at 1112 Parkland Place.

Light flickered up behind the window flanking the entrance, and then a voice sounded from behind the door.

"Yes—who is it?"

"Mark."

The door opened and Laurel Colman peered out at him. She was wearing a robe and her hair was up; obviously she'd been preparing for bed, and her face still bore traces of cleansing-cream. But even without makeup the tiny brunette's fine-boned features and slightly slanted eyes with their sapphire glint exerted a strikingly exotic effect.

The eyes were troubled now. "What on earth are you doing here at this hour?"

"Let me in."

"Of course." Laurel stepped aside, permitting him to enter. "But tell me—"

"Later. Got any aspirin?"

"Sit down. I'll bring it."

She led him into the living room, then vanished; reappearing a moment later with two tablets in one hand and a glass of water in the other.

As Mark gulped and swallowed, the girl eyed him, frowning. "What's wrong?" she said.

"Nothing. Just another headache."

"Really, Mark, you've got to see a doctor. You promised, remember?"

"I know." He nodded. "There hasn't been time."

"You were going to call me tonight," Laurel murmured. "What happened?"

He told her and she listened intently, without interruption. "It's Moybridge I'm worried about," Mark said. "You know how close we've been. Ever since I was three, when he took me out of that orphanage—brought me up in his home just as though he was my real father—"

Laurel glanced up quickly. "Are you sure he isn't?"

"I used to wish he was, sometimes, but that's impossible. Once years ago, when I was fourteen or fifteen, I asked him outright. Took a lot of courage for me to do so, but it must have taken even more for him to answer."

"Gay?"

Mark shook his head. "Sterile. Some childhood disease—mumps, or scarlet fever. That's why he never married. And I suppose it was one of his motives for becoming my guardian. In the years right after the big quake a lot of youngsters were left without parents—just dumped on doorsteps in some cases. Orphanages were overcrowded and the authorities launched this foster-parent program. Moybridge was one of those who responded, and I'm lucky he chose me."

"Then you really don't know anything about your background?"

"Nary a hint. The last name—Dixon—was Moybridge's mother's maiden-name. He made it mine, legally, when he took me into custody. He had the old place on Las Feliz then and Mrs. Grimes, his housekeeper, looked after me. Those were the years when he was building up his law practice, but he always found time for me. Like I said, I was lucky.

"I remember how pleased he was when I took up journalism at UCLA. He had an in with somebody downtown and helped me get on the paper after I graduated. Then he bought the new house and I moved into my own apartment. But there were no hard feelings; he encouraged me to be on my own. We kept in touch, and whenever I had a problem he was ready to help. Until this thing about the Black Brotherhood—"

Laurel frowned. "I've never read his book, but from what you've told me he must have done a lot of work on it."

"That's right. He started researching while I was still in school. It took him years to finish the thing."

"I see." Laurel looked thoughtful. "But what got him into it in the first place? Did he have friends who were interested, someone who suggested he write it?"

"Not that I know of. But while he was working on it, he scarcely talked of anything else. By the time he did the final draft he hardly even bothered with his practice—junior partners at the office took over. Then, after the book was published, he seemed to lose interest. He got back to business, bought this new place, and settled in. I don't think either of us ever mentioned Lovecraft again until tonight." Mark twirled the empty glass between his fingers. "Now, suddenly, this outburst. Threats. Warnings. Why?"

"Did you stop to think it's only natural for him to be concerned with your welfare?" Laurel said. "Up to now you haven't had anything to do with this Black Brotherhood business. Now you're involved and he's worried."

"Then why does he deny that the Black Brotherhood even exists? Why is he lying about what's happening? Does he know something we don't?"

Laurel shrugged. "Everyone's edgy these days. It's not just the terrorist thing, either. Look at all those items about continental shifting, or whatever it is. I was reading something in a newsmagazine just the other day about nuclear waste polluting the atmosphere and changing the climate—what they call the 'greenhouse effect.' They say we may be due for another series of earthquakes like the ones twenty-five years ago or even worse."

She smiled. "Of course I don't believe all those predictions about the end of the world."

"Neither do I." Mark rose. "But perhaps Moybridge does. Maybe he knows a secret."

"You mustn't let it get to you, darling." Laurel stood up. "Look, it's really quite late—"

Mark put his glass down on the coffee-table, then moved to Laurel and took her in his arms. Her lips had the faint flavor of cleansing-cream, but that in no way decreased the sudden, surprising surge of pressure in his loins as he held her slight form close. His hands were already fumbling with the buttons of her robe.

"Mark—stop—anyone in the street can see us—"

"Not in the bedroom."

He led her there, and this time the robe came off.

The exotic face, mirroring the mix inherited from an Irish father and Japanese mother, stared up at him with a hint of teasing mockery.

"I thought you had a headache."

"Yes. But I'm counting on you to cure it."

"I'll do my best," Laurel murmured.

Pulling him down upon the bed, she kept her promise.

Darkness. First solid, then spreading to surround him—a cascade of cold, an icy wave combing a frozen sea to crest and crash upon the shore of night, blotting out sight and sound and sensation—

"Mark—wake up!"

He opened his eyes to stare at the swaying shadows on the bedroom ceiling as Laurel shook him into awareness.

No, it wasn't Laurel. The room itself was shaking. And from all around the rumbling echoed in a rising roar.

"Earthquake!"

He rose swiftly, pulling the girl to her feet as the floorboards throbbed and groaned.

"Outside—hurry—"

Laurel scooped up a robe and slippers from the chair beside

the bed as he grabbed his own shoes and crumpled clothing. Then they stumbled down the hall into the living room; from the bedroom behind came the sound of shattering glass. As they ran toward the door a lamp toppled and pictures spun from swaying walls to smash against the floor.

Now the entire house was shaking as though in the grip of a gigantic hand as Mark tugged against the front door, straining to force it ajar. The barrier gave way; he thrust Laurel through the opening and followed her into the fog-filled night beyond.

Behind them the invisible hand tightened and squeezed; there was a burst of implosion as a portion of the roof gave way.

They ran together across the heaving lawn, seeking the safety of the street.

"Look out!" Laurel screamed.

Glancing up, Mark saw the globe of the street-light spiralling down amidst a shower of sparks which vanished in the thick fog.

"Get to the car!" Mark shouted.

But his car was no longer at the curb. Peering to his right, he saw it lodged sideways against the concrete embankment at the dead end, its hood buckled beneath a fallen telephone-pole. A nimbus of light flickered around it, turning the fog green as the thrashing power-lines whipped crackling tentacles about the trapped vehicle.

Suddenly a warning hiss sounded against the background of distant rumbling and then the greenish glimmer turned red as the car exploded into flame.

Something hurtled overhead and Mark pushed Laurel down as they stared into the crimson mist. Trickles of gasoline had spread across lawn and pavement and they too were turning red as fire flared forth to consume them. Soon it would reach the house beyond, and then—

Mark rose, turning left towards the street entrance. Here a tree had fallen with power-line wires tangled in its branches. Now it too was beginning to burn, blazing up to bar their way.

The only avenue of escape lay straight ahead across the street, where the wall of Parkland Cemetery rose behind the thick veil of mingled fog and darkness.

Without a word Mark started forward, gripping Laurel's hand

in his own. At least they'd be safe there in the open, if he could manage to scale the stone surrounding the graveyard.

Moving to the far side of the street through the swirl of fog he saw that the problem had vanished, together with a portion of the wall itself. A wide breach yawned at their right where one section had collapsed and given way.

He nodded at the girl. "Come on—before the fire spreads—"

They clambered over the rubble beneath the opening, then stood, spent and silent, at the edge of the fogbound tract beyond.

"I think it's over," Laurel murmured. "Listen—"

Mark nodded. The rumbling noise was fading in the distance and the vibration beneath their feet had halted.

He took a deep breath, watching Laurel button her robe and tighten the sash around her waist. Suddenly he was conscious of the chill enveloping his own body, and of the bundled clothing clutched in his left hand. He dressed hastily, slipping his shoes over bare, bruised feet. Behind them sounded the telltale crackle of rising flame, but he didn't look back. Escape lay ahead, through the fog-filled trees. And now that the quake had died—

Died.

Laurel sensed it too, because her hand was shaking as she touched his shoulder.

"I don't like graveyards," she whispered. "Let's get out of here."

"Can't risk the street now," he said. "Not with those power-lines down. We'll just cut straight across here to the main gate on the boulevard side."

"Do we have to? I'm frightened—"

"Be thankful we got away in time," he told her. "At least we're safe here. Come on, take my hand."

Her trembling fingers closed about his own as they started forward, moving between the trees and down a fog-wreathed gravel path which wound its way between mounded graves and tilted headstones. The fog was thicker here; it hung over the silent cemetery in an all-encompassing shroud.

Suddenly Laurel gasped and tugged at Mark's wrist, pulling him back.

He glanced down quickly, staring into the open pit directly before him.

The invisible hand had been at work here too—uprooting markers and headstones, clawing at the graves beneath them. Great fissures slashed in all directions through the sandy soil, ripping deep into the earth.

Gazing down into the grave ahead, Mark saw the splintered casket, its oaken lid torn free. He stared at what lay within—and through the swirl of fog a grinning skull stared back, its empty eye-sockets phosphorescent in the night.

Laurel made a sound in her throat, then turned away, pulling at his hand. Swerving to avoid the opening, they started forward.

Now, as they quickened their pace, the furrows were all around them. Shards of shattered urns lay scattered amidst the toppled tombstones; they slowed again to circle other disembowelled graves, but neither paused to peer at what lay within.

They were off the gravel pathway now, moving through a maze of fog and pitfall. Mark peered at crushed cenotaphs and cracked monuments, then almost stumbled over the statue of an angel with broken wings.

They were reaching the heart of the cemetery, the century-old section where marble mausoleums rose and granite tombs still stood. But these were not entirely intact; in many instances the quake had wrenched the ornate wrought-iron grilles and gates from their doorways. And radiating from them, in all directions, were the deep furrows in the earth.

The yawning grave. For the first time Mark knew the meaning of the phrase; the meaning and the menace. Laurel panted beside him as they leaped to span the crevasses, moving past the openings which led to the domains of death. It was a shambles, and now he noted the acrid reek of decay arising from the furrows to mingle with the clammy fog.

But worst of all was the silence, the deadly silence of mounting, muting mist, of night and nightmare, broken only by Mark's labored gasps and those of his companion.

And by the *other* sound.

A dog was barking in the distance. Its bay rose faintly from somewhere behind them in the darkness. And then came the padding, scraping noise, echoing through the night as the barking deepened.

Mark halted, glancing back through the fog. He saw nothing, but the sound was louder now. Laurel heard it too and her cold hand tightened on his wrist.

"Something's coming!" she cried. And then, as she turned to stare into the mist behind, "Oh my God—"

Mark saw it then, or thought he did.

A dim shape rising out of the heaped-up earth at the edge of a furrow; a hint of head and shoulders silhouetted against the fog, twisting sideways so that the canine muzzle came clearly into view. A gigantic dog loomed up from fissure to peer—then disappear.

Or was it?

Dogs bark, but their bay does not dissolve into laughter.

And now the cackling rose, and something slithered forward along the fog-filled furrow.

Laurel screamed and suddenly her hand pulled free. Before Mark realized her intention she was running, racing blindly into the fog beyond.

"Stop!" Mark shouted. But the running figure vanished in the darkness, moving toward a cluster of tombs rising on a mound above the furrows radiating from it.

Not furrows. These were *burrows.*

The realization came with icy clarity. A quake might rend the earth, but it could not fashion what lay hidden below—the regular pattern of tunnels crisscrossing the cemetery six feet beneath its surface; hundreds of tunnels clawed through the clay in a century of effort, by things that moved from grave to grave in search of—

Sustenance.

Mark plunged forward through the fog, shouting. "Laurel—wait—come back!"

There was no response, and no way of glimpsing the girl through the mist-filled darkness swirling around the tomb-mouths ahead.

But now again he heard the cackling; it came from somewhere ahead, from the mound where the open fissures converged on the tombs. And for a single instant he caught a glimpse of the canine snout rising out of the earth, followed by a body that loped and bounded upright on two splayed legs, with grotesquely-elongated arms or forepaws avidly extended.

Then it was gone, swallowed by the dark, just as Laurel had been.

"Laurel!" he called, and as he did so, glanced down just in time to avoid dropping into one of the tunnel openings. Then he was racing up the mound where the tombs loomed in the fog-chilled night.

"Laurel—where are you?"

The answer came in a scream, rising from the mouth of a mausoleum to the left.

As he started towards it the scream halted abruptly, but now the cackling echo rose, followed by an indescribable sound; a mingled snarling and gurgling.

Mark ran across the slanting slope, eyes glued on the open doorway ahead so that he did not see the toppled headstone in his path.

He tripped and fell forward, striking his forehead against the granite with a force that stunned him. For a long moment sight and sound faded as he fought to retain consciousness. Then he lay gasping as his vision cleared again and he felt the sudden throbbing in his temples, the piercing pain in neck and shoulders. But he wasn't bleeding and he could see and hear clearly once more. He staggered to his feet, staring at the doorway of the tomb, forcing himself to focus attention on whatever sound might echo from within.

But all was silent now. Mark moved closer, then halted at the entrance as he strained to sense what lay beyond.

Silence and darkness.

Somehow he knew that whatever had found its way here had departed, vanishing while he had lain unseen on the slope where he had fallen.

"Laurel?" Softly he called her name, but there was no reply.

Mark took a deep breath.

Then, cautiously, step by step, he passed through that dark doorway, into the noisome blackness. His footsteps echoed hollowly on the stone floor of the mausoleum. Pressing his right hand against the cold marble of the wall to guide his way, he

STRANGE EONS   177

moved forward into an unseen realm of reeking stench and icy chill. Once again he whispered Laurel's name.

It was his feet that found her, pressing against the sprawl of her robe on the floor before him.

She lay unmoving and he did not breathe her name again. Instead he stooped quickly and gathered her limp form in his arms. She was so slight that he had no difficulty in carrying her back to the entrance, then out into the foggy night. It was there, as he stared down at her, that he realized why she seemed so light a burden.

Whatever had seized her in the darkness had not harmed her body; limbs and torso were mercifully intact.

But she no longer had a head.

How long had he been running?

His last clear recollection was the sight of the torn and twisted stump of the gushing neck. He dropped his grisly burden then, and what followed was a panting progress through realms of charnel horror.

Everything was fragmented into flashes, punctuated by pain stabbing at his skull. *A splitting headache*, wasn't that the old phrase? A headache that split the distinction between reality and hallucination.

There had been a girl named Laurel and she was dead, but how could he be certain of the rest? If there was no dog-thing, then why did he retain the memory of it with such hideous clarity—the glimpse of dripping snout, of scrabbling arms fringed with silvery fur? Could this be any less real than his vision of an army of such creatures tunneling through the graveyard to find and feed upon that which lay beneath?

Or was that merely an evocation of one of Lovecraft's stories, something he had read?

But Laurel's head was gone.

And he *had* run, *had* reached the boulevard gate on the other side of the burial-ground. Here the sepulchral silence gave way to strident sound—the wailing of sirens in the distance, wailing of voices in the nearby streets. Roar of flames in the night, shriek of tortured metal as cars collided in zigzag course, crash of falling brickwork, blare of bullhorns at a barricade as uniformed figures fought the looters invading a shattered shopping-center.

Laurel's head was gone.

He had to get downtown, get to Heller, tell him what happened back there in the cemetery. The quake was the big story, it must be as bad or worse than the one twenty-five years ago—but he had a story too, and it must be told.

No car. Then walk, it can't be much more than a mile. Dodge the huddled bodies, the burning brands.

Chinatown was on fire. An old man ran down the street, hair and beard haloed in flame. A gas-main exploded in the distance and the old man disappeared; concussion—shock-waves—a rain of debris—a fiery wall rising to bar the way.

Go around it. Cross under the freeway span, but hurry. The stretch ahead had already collapsed, scattering debris, tumbling cars like crushed tin toys and spewing forth their passenger-dolls. But dolls do not writhe and scream. The sound made his head throb.

Just be grateful you have a head. Laurel's head is gone. Must tell Heller—

Mark gasped and wheezed his way up Bunker Hill. Here smoke mingled with the fog, searing his lungs and making his eyes burn. But now he reached the summit, and downtown lay ahead.

Staring into the spiraling smoke, he saw the phrase monstrously embodied.

Indeed downtown lay ahead. Lay in the deed's aftermath, the deed of the quake which laid the high-rises low, smashed spires down from the skies, pounded the Pavilion and Music Center to the pavement, torn off the top of City Hall.

Laurel's head was gone.

And the Times News-Center was gone. In its once-proud place on the horizon there rose a pillar of fire.

So he couldn't tell Heller. He couldn't tell anyone. Except Judson Moybridge. That was it, he must get to Moybridge.

He must have lost all sense of time because now he was climbing again, not downtown but here, near the hills. Was it reality or imagination that evoked a dim memory of a man with a car, a young black man who stopped and beckoned to him?

"You wiped out, man—better ride with me—where you going? I figger on trying 101 if it ain't blocked. Okay, I take you far's the bottom of the canyon. Then I gotta split."

Splitting headache.

But it must have happened that way, he must have ridden. Now he was here, climbing the hillside road in the dark. Power-lines undamaged for the most part, but no light shone from the silent houses nestling against the slopes and few cars remained in their driveways. Everyone had panicked, run off. Gone—like Laurel's head.

"You see now? You were wrong, and Lovecraft told the truth. There are such things, because I saw one. God knows how many more were lurking there in those burrows—God knows what was released to swarm across the city. They'll have plenty to feast upon tonight, they'll gorge themselves—"

That's what he was telling Moybridge. Or was he talking to himself, mumbling in the darkness as he climbed? *Hallucination and reality.*

As he reached the summit the sky beyond was red. Red soaring, red roaring. Sound of flames and sirens, helicopters hovering overhead.

The ache in his head, pain in his neck and shoulders, matched now by sensation in lungs and loins and legs. Climbing, still climbing. *Got to get to Moybridge, tell him.*

The hilltop house was dark, but a car stood in the carport and there was another car parked on the street just beyond.

Mark found the gate unlatched; he entered and crossed to the front door. There was no response to his ring, nor to his knock; he rattled the knob but the door was locked.

Moving along the walk at the side of the house he found a shuttered window; it too was locked and he glanced around for a rock or stone to smash the glass.

As he did so he noted that the gate at the end of the walk was ajar. Pushing it open, he entered the rear patio. The fog was thicker here, swirling in from the sea to blanket the poolside area beyond.

But it wasn't the pool that concerned him; turning he saw the French door to the living room. It stood open, and from within came a faint humming sound and a flash of flickering light.

Mark peered inside. The humming and flickering came from the television wallscreen within. Its cracked face bore no image, merely a blur of clouded luminence.

He entered the room, found and pressed a wall switch. The lights stayed out, so there had been some damage after all. And if so, what happened to Judson Moybridge?

Mark called his name, then shouted, but there was no reply.

Again he felt the throbbing in skull and shoulders, and he wheezed as he crossed the room and started down the hall leading to the kitchen and bedrooms beyond.

There was no sign of disturbance, no sound except that of his own footsteps stumbling through the darkness. Then he remembered the lighter in his pocket and fumbled for it. The flame flared and held steady as he inspected the dining area and kitchen; both were empty and undamaged.

Slowly he made his way to the first bedroom, steeling himself to glance within. But here again the lighter-flame revealed no sign of occupancy, and the bath beyond yielded no clues.

Then he remembered Moybridge once mentioning that the second bedroom was used as a combination study and office.

Mark moved to the far end of the hall. The door here was closed, but not locked. He pushed it open, raised his lighter, moved inside.

The area beyond the doorway was a shambles. Books had been swept from built-in shelving to clutter the floor in random heaps. A desk-chair rested on its side amidst fallen file-cabinets, and their contents cascaded across the carpeting. The desk itself stood at an odd angle from the wall, its surface strewn with a jumble of papers and folders.

Mark stared, frowning. Only a freak of the quake could have produced such results. Or could it?

Earthquakes can open drawers, but not empty them. Earthquakes might hurl filing-cabinets to the floor but cannot force their locks or ransack their contents. Earthquakes can't open a wall-safe—

He crossed to the space behind the angled desk where the circular steel safe-door hung ajar.

The safe was empty.

Stooping, he surveyed the pile of papers at his feet. Some of them had come from the safe, no doubt of that; the leather port-folio of insurance policies, the long manila envelope inscribed with the name of a mortgage company, and the neatly-bundled sheafs of currency.

Mark picked one up and examined it. The scotch-taped stack was three inches thick, and the bills were all hundreds. A half-dozen more lay at his feet—a fortune in legal tender.

Obviously, whoever opened that safe wasn't after money.

He squatted, conscious of the pain which had spread to his chest now; his breathing was labored and he gulped for air. Some-thing was wrong with him, very wrong, but it would have to wait. Something was wrong here, and he had to know—

There were other discards from the safe here on the floor; receipts, stock certificates, legal documents. Near the bottom was an envelope he almost ignored until his fingers accidentally pressed against the hard object within. It wasn't another paper or letter, though whoever tossed it aside must have thought so. Mark ripped the flap open with his free hand and the contents of the envelope rolled into his palm.

It was only a tiny spool of microfilm, enclosed in a plastic pouch sealed with tape. Across the tape was a handwritten scrawl of identification.

"Excerpts—Necronomicon."

Again Mark's vision blurred and he felt a stab of pain shooting across his shoulders. *Hallucination and reality.*

The *Necronomicon* was hallucination; Judson Moybridge him-self said such a book existed only in Lovecraft's imagination. But the spool of microfilm was real, and it came from Moybridge's safe.

What else had that safe held—and who had come here to find it?

Mark rose, dropping the spool into his pocket. The lighter trembled in his grasp and the stabbing pains were stronger.

Hallucination and reality. Moybridge had sworn there was no such thing as the Black Brotherhood, but the Black Brotherhood preached the coming of the quake and it was real. Moybridge had devoted years of his life to prove Lovecraft's imaginings had no basis in fact, but tonight one of those stories came alive, and because of that, Laurel was dead.

If Moybridge knew the truth, why had he lied? *Laurel's head was gone. And where was Moybridge?*

Mark backed out of the room and edged his way along the hall, alert for signs or sounds that might betray a hidden presence. He saw nothing but shadows, heard only the humming from the cracked wallscreen in the living room. Beyond it on the patio the fog was dense to the very doorway.

He snapped his lighter off, then moved out into the shrouded night where water lapped and gurgled. The sound drew him to the side of the pool beyond and he looked down at its rippling surface where black bubbles boiled and burst.

Something was moving below.

Something was moving, writhing and rising upwards from the depths. And now, slowly, it surfaced.

Through coiling wisps of fog Mark stared at what floated in the center of the pool, stared and saw the bobbing body and bloated face of Judson Moybridge.

The glassy eyes bulged sightlessly and no sound issued from the twisted, gaping mouth, for the dead neither see nor speak. Moybridge was dead.

Stooping and leaning forward, Mark reached out towards the corpse.

And it was then, from the water's edge, that the hands rose swiftly to grip his ankles and plunged him down into the bubbling blackness below.

When you drown, your whole life passes in review.

So went the old wives' tale, but it was false.

Mark knew because he was drowning now, drowning in the pool beside the floating corpse of Judson Moybridge. Pain peaked in his head, throbbed through his neck and chest. He fought to free himself but the unseen hands held fast, dragging him down into the depths until his bursting lungs were filled with water.

That's when he must have died, but it was not the end. There was a dream . . .

In the dream he was still alive when they pulled him from the pool; wet and dripping, dazed and helpless, but alive.

He could see them now as they surrounded him, propelled him to his feet, half-carried him out to the car he'd noticed parked beside the curb just above the house.

There was something wrong with their clothing; it didn't fit. The garments had been tailored to follow normal human contours and his captors were not normal. A shambling gait attested to the malformation of their legs, humped backs and swollen necks expanded and contracted with the hoarse rhythm of their breathing; elongated wrists protruded from confining cuffs to terminate in webbed fingers that curled and clasped like claws. And what he glimpsed of their faces served to turn his dream into nightmare.

Great globular eyes that did not blink—splayed, flattened noses with flaring nostrils—wide, lipless mouths opening to display rows of tiny, serrated teeth—scaly skin stretched tautly over hairless heads—wattled necks with slitted sides that opened and closed in a perpetual pulsing—all this was part of the dream.

But it was their overpowering fishy odor which really repelled; their odor and their voices. The deep guttural sounds seemed only a semblance of speech, but he could recognize the laboriously-formed words only too well.

Two of the creatures sat or crouched beside him in the back seat of the car; two more occupied the front. The one who drove seemed to know the way, and it was he whose voice now droned through the dream.

"Not coast—high way gone—all wash away—must go back roads—through mountains—"

Then, mercifully, everything faded.

When awareness returned Mark realized that the night was cold, but he felt no chill. They had climbed above the fog, lurching and skidding; Mark opened his eyes to peer into the distant redness of the horizon behind and the sable darkness of the sky ahead where high peaks loomed.

As they swayed along the rising rutted roads cut into the steep slopes of the higher hills it seemed to him that the breathing of his companions became more labored; they gasped complaint but the driver kept shaking his bald and bulging head. Over and over he droned, "Only way—safe here—only way."

Safe they were from any human interference, for no other vehicles appeared on these perilous passes through the peaks. As a sullen crimson sun rose in the eastern sky a reddish radiance shone through gaps between the mountains at their left. Its source was the sun's reflection on water beyond and below, but Mark could not remember ever seeing the ocean so close to the mountain ranges here in the north. It was the jumbled geography encountered only during journeys into dreams.

Again he seemed to sink into a deeper slumber, rousing fitfully from time to time when the car halted to cool the boiling radiator. But always it started off once more, and the endless hours passed in undisturbed silence, for while his captors retained their grasp on his arms they made no effort to address him.

Dreams are timeless and he could not tell when it was that they skirted the valley where floodwaters covered houses to the very rooftops. Nor did he know the moment when they drove overlooking a muddy, rushing torrent in which bodies of men and cattle swirled amidst the red-flecked foam.

He roused himself to find that dusk had descended once again, and now the car was passing a leaning signpost—Los Gatos—30 mi.

They must be somewhere in the Santa Cruz mountains, or would be if such things actually existed in dreams. And it had to be a dream, he told himself; a dream of death. Reality had died somewhere back there in the city, just as he himself had died in the pool, drowning because he'd never learned to swim.

Better that it was so; better to be dead and dreaming than alive and actually in the clutches of these creatures, climbing once again into the tree-crowned twilight hills.

Occasional houses could be glimpsed now, scattered and silent, lightless and empty amidst the towering redwoods. He caught a glimpse of a street sign and its legend; Skyview Terrace. The car passed it, then angled off up a steep and narrow dirt road, scarcely more than a trail, leading up through a tangle of trees.

It was illusion, of course, for the dream was the only reality; this dream and these creatures. He knew what they were now, these fish-like hybrids; he knew from whence they came and where they must be going.

They were taking him to Innsmouth . . .

"Innsmouth?" said the voice. "Surely you know it doesn't exist. And never did—at least not by that name."

Mark opened his eyes.

The room was dark and the night-sky beyond the picture window was darker still. He seemed to be seated on a couch beside that window, a couch covered with a peculiarly coarse, rough cloth. Then he realized why it was so abrasive to his skin; he was naked.

The air was clammy and chill but this did not disturb him; pain and headache had faded so that he felt almost himself again. But how could that be, when he was dead and dreaming?

"Not dead, not dreaming," said the voice.

Mark peered around the room, seeking its source. Gradually his vision adjusted to the lack of light and now he could vaguely discern the outline of a shadowy form occupying the chair beside the far wall.

The substance of the figure was dim, but its erect posture, combined with the absence of the reeking odor and the precision of its speech, indicated to Mark that he was not in the presence of one of his abductors.

"Not abducted," said the voice. "You were conducted here."

Belatedly, Mark realized that he himself had not spoken aloud. And that meant—

"Reading your mind?" The voice held a hint of amusement. "Intuition. A parlor trick. If I could truly do so I would have known Moybridge was not to be trusted. As it was, I suspected such a possibility and ordered the search of his home. What was found there in the safe confirmed my suspicions."

"You had him murdered," Mark said.

"A harsh word. He would have died by this time in any case, when the waters rose."

"Waters—?"

"I forget, you don't know about the tidal waves in the wake of last night's temblors. The Los Angeles basin is no longer empty. The coastline from Baha California to San Francisco Bay has been inundated. Even here in the mountains we are only temporarily protected. See for yourself."

Mark glanced through the picture window at his left. He heard the murmuring sound before he saw its source; the unbroken expanse of water churning against the cliffside forty feet below.

"Still rising," said the voice. "It will reach us very soon now."

Involuntarily Mark started to rise, and his movement was greeted with a sardonic chuckle.

"Stay," said the voice. "There's nowhere left to go. What the quakes spared will be taken by the sea. Throughout the world the proud cities have fallen, and only the highest peaks remain. But new lands shall rise from the deep—old lands, really, for once they held domain over all the earth and now they emerge to rule again. Ancient ones and ancient ways shall be rightfully restored, and what remains of mankind will play a lesser role. Some as slaves, others as cattle to breed with those beneath the sea or feed those beneath the land."

"No!" Mark shook his head. "I don't believe—"

"Not even the evidence of your own eyes?" Again the chuckle sounded in darkness. "The breeding and the feeding have always endured, even when humanity thought itself supreme. Offspring of that breeding brought you here. As for the feeding—what men called their last resting-place was never truly that. Every cemetery is accessible from below, and all earth is riddled with gateways to the grave. What you saw last night is only a hint of what lurks there and in the caverns under mountain peaks."

Mark stared at the shadowy shape which was the voice's source. "Who are you?"

"My true name would mean nothing. But here on earth, in Egypt long ago, men called me Nyarlathotep."

The name echoed against the sound of rising waters. *Nyarlathotep. The Mighty Messenger of the Old Ones. Lovecraft's stories—*

"He knew, of course," the voice murmured. "A few have always known. Alhazred set down his knowledge in the *Necronomicon* so that men could communicate with their true masters. Still those spells and incantations held the possibility of harm if they fell into the wrong hands. It was necessary to seek out and destroy his work and brand him mad, even though he intended only to enlighten.

"But Lovecraft meant to warn, and this was the greater danger. Blind chance alone halted the coming of Cthulhu a little over a century ago; Lovecraft chronicled it all too clearly and foretold a time when Great Cthulhu would rise again. Widespread publication made it impossible to eliminate all copies in printed form, and inevitably some readers suspected the fact behind the fiction.

"It became important to discredit his tales, link them with so-called freak religious cults like the Starry Wisdom, a quarter of a century ago. To the initiates was entrusted the secret task of removing any tangible evidence which might confirm Lovecraft's revelations. Documents and letters serving as his sources were traced, the paintings of Richard Upton and their owners—men like Albert Keith—were destroyed.

"Then the prophecy of Great Cthulhu's coming was again fulfilled, or almost so. But somehow those in authority were alerted, and through a series of circumstances Keith's former wife became involved.

"A mission was sent against him, and I did what was necessary to thwart it. But to all intents and purposes it appeared that Cthulhu perished, and those in power felt safe once more.

"In that climate of complacency I resumed my task, creating the conditions which would disrupt man's rule. I devised the Black Brotherhood—using terrorism and assassination to distract mankind from the true nature of what was to come.

"This time there were no mistakes. And when the stars were rightly conjoined in the heavens, when the signs of earthly destruction neared again, all was prepared. Now it has come to pass."

"Why tell me this?" Mark stirred uneasily. "I don't see—"

"You shall."

There was a faint clicking, and suddenly light flared forth, flared with such blinding intensity that for a moment Mark's vision vanished. Then, slowly, his sight accommodated the intensity of the iridescence and he saw all too clearly.

Seated across from him was a black man wearing black clothing. There was something odd about the even intensity of his coloration, but this was not as disturbing as the source of light which revealed it.

The light issued from a box of tarnished golden metal resting in the black man's lap. Its sides bore designs of writing figures, all eyes and tentacles, which resembled no life-forms Mark could remember. The box itself was neither square nor rectangular; it seemed shaped in accordance with a geometry of its own.

But the light itself captured his attention now, streaming forth from a great crystal supported by metal bands affixed to its multifaceted sides and base. The crystal appeared to be black, flecked with reddish veins, but the radiance it sent forth was like green fire. Mark blinked. "What on earth—?"

"It was not always on earth," the black man murmured. "Though it is here now to fulfil its power and its purpose. The Shining Trapezohedron—"

Lovecraft's name for it, Mark remembered. "Wasn't there a story, 'The Haunter of the Dark?'"

The black man nodded. "The light summoned an entity which brought death to its discoverer. But it has other properties. It is a focal point, a gateway linking the stars, opening the way to dwellers from other dimensions. The light can heal as well as destroy, and most importantly, it can transform.

"It was through the agency of the Shining Trapezohedron that I first assumed the semblance of man, long ago in ancient Khem. And it is destined to serve a still higher role."

Mark blinked again. It seemed to him that the crystal was pouring forth heat as well as light—and yet the heat was cold. He remembered his dream of freezing flame in Laurel's house; was this too a part of that dream?

"No," said the black man, softly. "The time for dreams is past and the dreamers—Alhazred, Upton, Lovecraft—have perished. Albert Keith dared to seek the source of his dreams and he too is dead. And you—"

"What have I to do with these things?" Mark murmured.

"Can't you guess? Moybridge knew, of course, but he never spoke. We counted on that because we rewarded him, and when he wrote the book at our command we felt secure. He helped discredit Lovecraft and we had no reason to believe he'd ever reveal his secret allegiance to our cause. But he did know and he retained information we furnished him, things like that micro-

film you found. We promised he'd be spared in return for his aid,
but when the quake came he was bound to suspect otherwise.

"It was then too late for him to reach the authorities, but there
was still a chance he could use some of those spells and formulae
against us. And we knew that you'd seek him out. So it became
necessary to recover the material in his possession and eliminate
him."

The cold heat was everywhere; Mark felt a tingling in his head
and shoulders. "Why am I here?" he said.

The black man leaned forward. "I told you that Albert Keith's
former wife became involved in the attempt to destroy Cthulhu.
But before it succeeded, she was captured and taken to where the
Old One waited. That night the bombs fell on Easter Island and
even Great Cthulhu could not withstand the forces unleashed
against him."

"Then he is dead?"

"Only two escaped—the woman called Kay Keith and myself.
I brought her secretly and safely to a place which had been prepared and watched over her until her time came. She died during
the delivery, as was only to be expected. But the child lived."

Mark frowned. "What child—"

"The union was consummated before the bombers came."
The black man stared from behind the beam of icy, burning light.
"As for the rest—a man named Heisinger was in charge of the
Keith estate. He had a nephew and through him arrangements
were made to rear the child as an adopted orphan until the time
arrived. Thus the seed of Great Cthulhu survived. No one suspected, least of all the child himself."

The black man smiled at Mark. "And you never did suspect,"
he said.

Mark tried to rise then, but the box tilted forward so that he
was held helpless and paralyzed in a column of livid light. The
scream died in his throat and he could only stare; stare at the
beam bathing his body and burning into his brain.

The seed of Great Cthulhu survived. Genetic heritage—no
wonder he hadn't drowned there in the pool. And the pains, the
difficulty in breathing, were part of a mutation process, meta-
morphosis into a shape which could survive beneath the sea or

soar between the stars. That change was not yet completed. But *the light transforms—*

Staring, it seemed to him that the black crystal behind the beam was a mirror in which he saw himself reflected, bathed in a funnel of flame.

And now, somewhere within his cerebral cavity a pinpoint of light pierced the pons, penetrating the *locus coeruleus.*

His image blurred, wavered; limbs melting, then multiplying—sprouting and spreading from a faceless, expanding form in which mere mortality merged into a greater guise of gigantic godhood. No pain now, only a pulsing and a potency, a pride and a power.

That is not dead which can eternal lie, and the time of strange eons had arrived. The stars were right, the gates were open, the seas swarmed with immortal multitudes and the earth gave up its undead.

Soon the winged ones from Yuggoth would swoop down from the void and now the Old Ones would return—Azazoth and Yog-Sothoth, whose priest he was, would come to lightless Leng and old Kadath in the risen continents which were transformed as he was transformed.

He stirred, and the walls surrounding him splintered and fell forward.

He breathed, and Nyarlathotep vanished into nothingness, clutching the tiny toy which was the Trapezohedron.

He waved, and the waters below surged upwards, boiling and beckoning.

He rose, and mountains trembled, sinking into the sea.

Time stopped.

Death died.

And Great Cthulhu went forth into the world to begin his eternal reign.